CW00340994

Avishag

Yael Lotan

AVISHAG

The Toby Press

First Edition 2002

The Toby Press LLC
www.tobypress.com

ISBN 1 902881 55 9, *hardcover*
ISBN 1 902881 56 7, *paperback*

A CIP catalogue record for this title
is available from the British Library

Designed by Breton Jones, London

Cover illustration, Biblical Figure by Abel Pann
Reproduction courtesy of Itiel Pann & the Mayanot Gallery, Jerusalem

Typeset in Garamond by Jerusalem Typesetting

Printed and bound in the United States by
Thomson-Shore Inc., Michigan

For my daughter Ilana, who is nobody's shadow

Avishag

A note on the names

Most biblical names are familiar to the English reader in their Authorized Version form – Saul, Jonathan, Solomon, Jesse, Abishag, Joab, and so on. But these are distortions, arising from the early translation into Greek (the Septuagint) and thence into Latin. I retain these spellings in some cases, and introduce a modern transliteration from Hebrew in others. Thus our heroine is *Avishag*, not Abishag, Joab is *Yoav*, and Solomon is *Shlomo*.

Ben means son, or the son of —, and is often part of the name. In most cases it is followed by the father's name, as David is called Ben Yishai, i.e., the son of Jesse. But sometimes it is followed by the mother's name, suggesting that she was the greater personage – for example, the three sons of Zeruiah, or Shamgar ben Anath (Judges 3:31), who was, perhaps, the son of a priestess of the goddess Anath.

DRAMATIS PERSONAE

in order of appearance

(in brackets, as spelled in the King James Version)

Avishag (Abishag)
David ben Yishai (son of Jesse)
Naamah – a servant*
Ornan ben Baanah – Avishag's brother*
Ira – a Levite priest
Eviatar (Abiathar) – high priest
Adoniyah (Adonijah) – son of David

I

Bathsheva (Bathsheba) – David's wife, the Great Lady
Shlomo-Yedidiah (Solomon-Jedidiah) – David's son and future king
Yoav ben Zeruiah (Joab son of Zeruiah) – David's nephew and captain
Yonadav (Jonadab) – David's kinsman and counsellor
Nathan the prophet
Kilav (Chileab) – son of David
Ittai the Gittite – chief of the royal guard
Benaiah, the Lion-slayer – a captain
Amnon – son of David
Tamar – daughter of David
Ahimaaz ben Zadok – a Levite
Ephrat – sister of Yonadav*
Kimham (Chimham) – son of Barzillai

* denotes fictional characters

Now King David was old and stricken in years; and they covered him with clothes, but he gat no heat. Wherefore his servants said unto him, Let there be sought for my lord the King a young virgin: and let her stand before the King, and let her cherish him, and let her lie in thy bosom, that my lord the King may get heat. So they sought for a fair damsel throughout all the coasts of Israel, and found Avishag a Shunammite, and brought her to the King. And the damsel was very fair, and cherished the King, and ministered to him: but the King knew her not.

(1 Kings 1:1–4)

Then sat Solomon upon the throne of David his father; and his kingdom was established greatly. And Adonijah the son of Haggith came to Bathsheva the mother of Solomon. And she said, Comest thou peaceably? And he said, Peaceably. He said moreover, I have somewhat to say unto thee. And she said, Say on. And he said, Thou knowest that the Kingdom was mine, and that all Israel set their faces on me, that I should reign: howbeit the Kingdom is turned about, and is become my brother's: for it was his from the Lord. And now I ask one petition of thee, deny me not. And she said unto him, Say on.

And he said, Speak, I pray thee, unto Solomon the King, (for he will not say thee nay,) that he give me Avishag the Shunammite to wife. And Bathsheva said, Well; I will speak for thee unto the King. Bathsheva therefore went unto king Solomon, to speak unto him for Adonijah. And the King rose up to meet her, and bowed himself unto her, and sat down on his throne, and caused a seat to be set for the King's mother; and she sat on his right hand.

Then she said, I desire one small petition of thee; I pray thee, say me not nay. And the King said unto her, Ask on, my mother: for I will not say thee nay.

And she said, Let Avishag the Shunammite be given to Adonijah thy brother to wife.

And king Solomon answered and said unto his mother, And why dost thou ask Avishag the Shunammite for Adonijah? Ask for him the Kingdom also; for he is mine elder brother; even for him, and for Abiathar the priest, and for Joab the son of Zeruiah.

Then king Solomon sware by the Lord, saying, God do so to me, and more also, if Adonijah have not spoken this word against his own life. Now therefore, as the Lord liveth, which hath established me, and set me on the throne of David my father, and who hath made me an house, as he promised, Adonijah shall be put to death this day.

(1 Kings 2:12–24)

But we will certainly do whatsoever thing goeth forth out of our own mouth, to burn incense unto the queen of heaven, and to pour out drink offerings unto her, as we have done, we, and our fathers, our kings, and our princes, in the cities of Judah, and in the streets of Jerusalem: for then had we plenty of victuals, and were well, and saw no evil.

(Jeremiah 44:17)

Chapter one

It was bitter cold in that place and a curious smell hung in the air. Strange people went in and out of the big hall, and every time they drew aside the leather curtain which hung over the entrance, an icy draught blew in, causing the flaming torches to flutter and smoke wildly.

The smell came from the torches, which were made of some unfamiliar wood, and also from a brazier that stood in the middle of the hall, filled with smouldering embers. From time to time someone would stir the coals and sprinkle them with a powder that made them flare up and spread a strong sweetish scent. It made the girl's throat tingle, but it was not unpleasant, only strange.

Now and then, when the rumble of voices in the hall ceased for a moment, she heard the wind whistling and moaning through the wall slits. The walls were built of stone, with tall narrow openings at regular intervals. Wooden shutters hung over the slits, but some of them were propped up to let in the air. Making sure no-one was looking at her, she crept nearer the wall and peered out under a shutter. She saw a dark mass of cloud flying across a rosy evening sky and felt a little reassured. The sky, at least, was the same here as at home.

The thick woollen rug on which she crouched was striped red and black and had long fringes, but the floor was paved with large stone flags and their chill penetrated through the rug. The feet of the people who walked about the hall were clad in leather buskins up to their ankles, ending in criss-cross thongs, which disappeared under their gowns.

For a long time she remained crouched in her corner, huddled in the great woollen mantle her brother had given her in parting. She kept tucking her face into its folds and breathing in the good odours of home, of the goats and of her brother. It sheltered her from the chill, the incense and the strange voices, which went on talking and talking, incomprehensibly. Now and then tears welled up in her throat and threatened to stream from her eyes, but fear or shame stopped them every time. Then she would raise her head from the mantle and look about her.

Soon the light that showed under the shutters faded altogether as night fell. The hall was quieter. Four or five dark-cloaked men still moved about, talking together or occupied with other tasks on the far side of the hall. Only then did she perceive, in the flare of the clustered torches at that end, a dais piled with rugs, cushions and furs. On it lay a figure huddled, as she was, in a great cloak. It was this personage whom the men kept addressing, and now she could hear his voice, low pitched and deliberate – the voice of a leading elder, expecting obedience.

One by one, the men bowed low and went out of the hall. For a moment she was alone with the elder on the dais, and her heart began to pound. Then a woman entered, swathed in white, her back bowed, her head veiled. She bustled up in short fussy steps to the dais and addressed the elder in a high, quavering but self-assured voice. Then she turned and approached the crouching girl.

With her heart in her mouth, the girl did not understand the old woman, who repeated irritably: "Get up! Get up! What are you doing? Get up and come with me!"

Her language was familiar, but her missing teeth and the unexpected words sounded strange in the cavernous hall.

The heavy mantle clung to the girl's legs and impeded her movements. She gathered its folds with trembling hands and wrapped it around her. Shivering with cold and fear she followed the old woman across the floor, her bare soles touching rugs and stone, rugs and stone, up to the sumptuous dais and the bundled figure that lay on it...

When morning came she felt as if she had not slept at all, though she must have caught brief snatches of sleep while remaining alert to every sound and movement, as she used to do when guarding her father's vineyard.

The old man was asleep. He lay on his back, propped up on a bolster; his nose raised like a sword, while rhythmic croaks tapering into soft whistles issued from his beard. All night, among the vast shadows cast by the flame of a single oil-lamp, he had been unquiet, tossing and twitching, muttering to himself. Once he drew himself up and clapped his hands, and the sharp sound echoed in the vast chamber. A moment later the old woman, who must have been lying behind the wooden screen at the head of the dais, came around with a brass jug and a beaker. The old man took a sip or two and fell back on his pillows, sighing deeply. Soon after he made a sudden movement and seized the girl's shoulder, pulling her close and down towards his feet. His legs were thin and hard as sticks and his feet were icy cold. Her own warmth under the rugs could not thaw them.

He did not say a word to her all night. Except when he tried to warm his feet against her stomach he seemed unaware of her presence. She felt a pain in her lower belly, where all her fears had knotted at his touch. Now, with daylight seeping into the hall, she watched him closely and all at once her fears dissolved. The danger had not passed. He might still wish to handle her body or to mount her, and she would have to submit. But in the pale morning light he looked so fine, his upturned face was so remote and austere – like the village priest when he spoke with the oracle – that her terrors vanished.

Was he truly the King? Perhaps he was not the King but one of his ministers, testing her?

Surely he was the King. She had seen them all bowing down before him. He had to be the King. The hair on his head, though turning grey, still had coppery strands that gleamed in the light, and in his beard too there were some fiery hairs. His hands, which were folded on top of the fur coverlet, were adorned with rings. And through the opening of his gown, around his stringy neck, she saw a fine scarlet cord threaded with gold. He was the King.

Again she felt afraid, but it was a different kind of fear from that which had gripped her in the night. Now she grew dizzy at the thought that he would soon wake and perhaps be angry with her, order her to be beaten, or punished some other way. He was the King, he could do as he pleased, they would all rush to do his bidding, and she knew that many had paid with their lives for disobeying him or provoking his wrath. And now the tears, which had been dammed in her throat since the day before, welled up and poured out on her face. She wept silently, curled up under the rugs, her forehead against her knees, until the old woman came and without a word dragged her off the dais and behind the wooden partition. A young Edomite maid led her to the women's house. There she was given food and a pallet to lie on till she would be called again at night. She had no other duties.

Twice seven nights she lay at the King's feet and he never spoke to her. She lay close to him, pressing her belly to his thin legs, and sometimes she rubbed his icy feet with her hands. Once he reached out and patted her head, as one pats a dog, but he did not touch her in other ways.

She soon grew accustomed to sleeping beside him on the dais, and his movements and snores no longer disturbed her. In the morning the old woman would rouse her and send her to the women's house.

The women's house was not at all like the King's fort. All day long it swarmed with children and slaves, resounded with shouts and laughter, reeked of food and smoke. At first they all stopped and stared at her, felt her mantle and her hair, which hung loose on her shoulders, and asked her questions as if she were a small child. They laughed at her Jezreelite speech. Then they ignored her, only now and then calling on her to help when another pair of hands was needed to move screens, tie knots in a loom, or hold a crying infant whose mother was occupied.

At first she could not tell them apart. They all looked strange – their dress, faces, manners and speech were unlike any she had known before, in her father's house. But she soon came to know them. She saw that the female slaves went bareheaded, except the very old ones, and barefooted, even out of doors. Two of them – at first she thought they were one – were black as charcoal, wore nose-rings through the septum and many copper anklets. Their stiff short hair was dressed in rows of knots with coloured threads and beads. Their speech was almost incomprehensible. Kushites, they were, the personal maids of Titipah, the Egyptian lady wife of one of the King's sons, who kept to her chamber on the roof of the women's house and was hardly ever seen.

Behind the women's house stretched a large walled garden. In it were two sunken cisterns with stone rims, shaded with palm-frond canopies. There were trees and shrubs the like of which she had never seen before, and on a high place against the eastern wall stood a horned altar as big as the one that served her whole village. On special days pigeons and quail and even sheep were sacrificed there, but almost every day offerings of fine flour mixed with oil were burnt by the women, on behalf of a sickly child or a woman about to give birth. At the end of the garden, clinging to the far wall like wasps' nests, were the slaves' huts. Beyond the walls all she could see was the farther range, blue-green under the wintry sky. The King's city could not be seen – it spread down the southern flank of the mountain on the other side of the King's fort. Sometimes when she walked about the garden she thought that it was the end of the world. Then she would crouch under a tree, hug one of the dogs and dream about her father's house. Then tears would run down her cheeks, wetting the dog's fur, and the animal licked her hands and face, as if it understood.

Twice seven nights the King paid no more heed to her than to a dog. Then came a night of storm, thunder and lightning and raging winds.

The King was awake and so was she. Now she clung to him, tendering her bodily warmth in return for his protection. His body was not at all like the warm, rounded limbs of her young brothers and sister, but he was the King. Surely lightning would not strike his house. As the tempest howled, his ringed hand patted her head. Then he tugged lightly at her shoulder and she wriggled up and lay alongside him. The King stroked her shoulder and arm. Then he uttered a soft sigh and drew the fur coverlet over her. His touch was very light. Finally he lay back, resting his head on his free arm.

"Shunem," he said aloud. "Or Sunem, as you call it… Yohanan ben Zimrah was born there."

"Not he, but his mother," said Avishag quickly, and her heart missed a beat. Was she allowed to speak to the King?

The King turned and peered at her in the dim light of the floating oil wick. She slid down and hid her face under the coverlet. But the King, now wide awake, uncovered her head and raised her chin.

"You are truly a Shunammite, a Jezreelite," he said in a very different voice, lighter and faster than his usual speech. "Always ready with an argument, all of your tribe!" But there was laughter in his voice.

At that moment a tremendous thunder crashed and rolled directly overhead and they clutched each other. A distant wail rose from the women's house. Had something happened there, had the lightning struck, or did they cry out from fear? The old woman stirred behind the screen and could be heard padding away, muttering under her breath.

All night long the tempest howled around the King's fort, only passing on towards morning. But the King slept as he had not slept for many a night, cradling Avishag's head in the crook of his arm. Her curly tresses pressed softly against his neck, arousing ancient memories that seeped into his dreams.

In the morning, old Naamah, coming in to rouse the maid, saw her nestled against the King's shoulder, fast asleep. The King smiled, put a finger to his lips and gestured to the old woman to wait yet a while. Naamah frowned, then hid a grin in her veil. Women and children had always been David's weakness, and the wild young Jezreelite was both woman and child.

Armed with a new confidence, Avishag began to explore the place. One morning she climbed up to the roof of the women's house and peeped into the Egyptian lady's chamber. It was of a splendour unmatched even in the King's own hall. The walls were covered with the most lifelike paintings of gardens, cattle, hounds and hunting cats, ponds with water-fowl and fishes... Lost in admiration, she did not notice the lady herself, who was reclining on a couch nearby, idly toying with a string of polished beads. The Egyptian uttered a deliberate little cough, startling her, and she started to back out of the room. But the lady, raising a languid arm, motioned to her to return.

"Who are you?" she asked Avishag, who stood before her in a respectful attitude, her head lowered and her hands pressed together at her waist. The Egyptian's voice was as high as a child's and her speech sounded strange, but her question was plain enough.

Avishag's name meant nothing to the Egyptian. The gossip of the women's house had not reached her ears. She was curious about the girl's hair – it looked like one of her own elaborate wigs, which hung on painted plaster heads ranged on an inlaid chest beside the wall. She made the girl kneel before her and felt her tresses. This was no wig but living hair, glossy and springy to the touch. The girl was sunburnt like a peasant, yet she was not a maidservant – that much was clear from her dress and manner. A daughter of one of the King's captains, perhaps. They were all barbarians, of course. Even the Prince, her husband... She sighed and lay back, her jewelled arm across her face.

Avishag rose and moved about the room, examining its furniture, rugs and games. She thought that the wigged heads were images, and the numerous cosmetic vials, boxes and saucers that surrounded them were offerings. A sweet fragrance hung in the room, like an essence of flowers. The Egyptian lady herself resembled a rare blossom, with her smooth creamy skin, delicate robes and glistening finger- and toe-nails. Her native land, the Dual Kingdom of the Nile, must be like the Garden of Eden.

Just then one of Titipah's Kushite maids came in and stared in astonishment at the girl, who was sniffing delicately around the chamber like a cat. She said nothing, since her mistress evidently did not resent the intrusion, but stood and stared, until Avishag felt the blood rising in her cheeks and ran out of the room and down the stairs to the garden. As she went down she heard the maid and the mistress twittering together in their high voices.

She enjoyed visiting the cooking yard, where at all times there were goats, sheep and pigeons roasting on spits, messes of lentils and onions bubbling in pots, bread baking in earthen ovens, and numerous small boys guarding everything from the circling, yelping dogs. It was a familiar scene, if much larger than the cooking yard at home, where food was prepared for no more than two-dozen men, women and children. Here the numbers were much greater, though she had no idea how many. The King's own food was cooked separately, supervised by old Naamah, or by one of the old warriors who had been with the King since their youth.

It took Avishag a while to notice all this, and to discover the degrees of quality in the food and the standing of the servants who came to fetch it. The King's priest, for one, had his food cooked separately by his Levite disciple, a tall youth dressed in goatskins.

When there were special guests, such as emissaries from Tyre or from the Philistine lords, the cooking yard became frenzied. Not only the dogs, but maidservants and slaves were cuffed and kicked, and odours of fine bread baking, wine casks being broached, onions frying in oil, sizzling meat basted in honey and pomegranate juice, wafted on the cool mountain breeze and must have driven the people of the King's city mad with greed.

The King's health improved with the weather. When the almond trees blossomed, sweetening the air with their clean fragrance, the sun relented and began to warm the fort. During the day the shutters were left off the wall slits. But the nights were still cold, and Avishag snuggled against her master, eager to offer him her warmth and grateful for his occasional caress. Only her dreams carried her back to her father's house, to the sights and sounds of her native village. Most of all, she dreamed about Ornan, her brother, for whom her mother had found a wife just a few days before Avishag was taken away to Jerusalem. Was he married now, and had his wife made him forget the little sister whom the King's men had carried away?

Preparations began for the holy festival of spring. Since the Ark had been installed in Araunah's threshing-floor, beside the King's fort, the festivals were more splendid than ever before. The priests of all the tribes and the elders of all the clans would come up to Jerusalem, and for a whole week the King's city would be bursting at the seams with pilgrims, its air rent by the bellowing of the sacrificial beasts. It was Ira, the young Levite, who told Avishag about it. He befriended the strange girl, who was neither a servant nor a lady, and who, though still a maiden, shared the King's bed.

Old Naamah frowned when she heard that the two young people were seen talking together in the garden and courtyard. Though the Shunammite maiden was not intended to be a royal concubine, even if the King were to recover fully from his old man's ailment, Naamah meant to guard her virginity, for all that she was merely the King's bed warmer. But there was little she could do, as neither Avishag nor Eviatar's acolyte could be ordered about like slaves. And there was another pair of eyes that followed the two young people when they talked in the garden, and who noted the girl's free and easy movements.

The Great Lady's lofty apartments overlooked not only the garden, but also the King's city and the valley of Kidron. They were reached by a staircase that rose from a secluded side court, and also linked by a passage to the upper storey of the King's own quarters. It was altogether a separate household. Whereas the Egyptian wife of Prince Adoniyah had to share in the provisions of the women's house, and her serving maids mingled with the others, the Great Lady's Hittite servants were hardly ever seen in the lively and populous quarters of the King's house.

Not since the last autumn festival had Bathsheva seen the King. When he fell ill and moved his sleeping quarters from the upper storey down to the hall, he ordered his wives and concubines to stay away. Even his sons were rarely admitted to his presence. Old Naamah let in only the King's captains, Zadok the priest and Seraiah the scribe. Foreign emissaries were kept waiting, even the messengers from Tyre, while the King and the hall were prepared to receive them in state. All this the Great Lady understood and bore in peace, but not the appearance of the young Shunammite. Whose idea had it been to bring a nubile maiden to lie in the King's bed? The girl's clan was connected with that of Ahinoam, the King's second wife, and hence with the sad and disgraced son whose name was never mentioned in the King's house. Did that signify? Or was it some plot devised by Adoniyah and his counsellors to undermine her standing and that of her son?

Bathsheva turned the question round and round in her mind. She stood at her window lattice and watched the young Shunammite strolling about the garden and the women's courtyard. When she saw the girl resting languidly under a tree or against a wall, the Great Lady's face grew dark with suspicion. Had her night with the King tired the girl so? And when she saw her sniffing about, curiously examining her surroundings, talking with the children and serving maids, a chilly premonition made the Great Lady shiver. It was said that the girl was exceedingly beautiful, but from her window Bathsheva could not see her features. A curly black mane hung loose over her shoulders and partly hid her face. The heavy mantle in which she huddled against the cold concealed her figure. Only her feet, small, brown and nimble in the thonged sandals, moving lightly over the stony ground of the garden, revealed that she was still a child. And then Bathsheva saw her holding long conversations with the priest's acolyte. That, the Great Lady knew, could only be an ominous development.

When she had first moved into the King's fort, Bathsheva – or Bathshua, as she was then – thought it advisable to bring her Hittite household with her. She knew that she would not be safe surrounded by David's older wives and their sons. Since the death of the rebellious Prince Absalom, it was Adoniyah, the son of the priestess Haggith, who was the heir apparent. It was said that his ambitions exceeded even those of his dead brother. He would remain an obedient son just so long as he was assured of the succession, but the King's passion for the Hittite woman threatened the fragile peace of the royal house. Nor would the Benjamite camp, which remained stubbornly loyal to the fallen house of Saul, fail to take advantage of David's weakness. And so, to be safe, Bathshua kept on her Hittite slaves and maidservants, and access to her apartments was guarded by her retainers at all times.

But all these measures did not avail to save the life of the first child she had borne the King – the infant Merari, who escaped from his nurse to play with the other children of the King's house, and died a painful death. The second son, whom she named Shlomo, though the King called him Yedidiah, was more carefully guarded than even that precious Ark of theirs.

And now, when the King was old and failing, and his house was a wasps' nest of intrigue, the sudden appearance of the young Jezreelite maiden as a royal bed-warmer was a very disturbing move. Not for the first time, Bathsheva regretted her isolation from the rest of the house. Her own servants knew nothing. The King, whom she could still cajole when she was able to approach him, was inaccessible. She had to make another attempt to win the trust of that thorny old warrior, Yoav ben Zeruiah, much as she detested him, or of someone else from the King's own clan. Now that her son was thirteen years of age, the seer Nathan's ban had plainly worn off and dealings with Bathsheva would no longer be regarded as unsafe.

"And the Jezreelite maid, the one who was brought to warm the King's bed – whose child is she?" Bathsheva asked with apparent indifference and refilled her guest's beaker with honeyed wine.

It was a wearisome visit. Yonadav, the King's nephew – the son of his older brother Shimeah – was fat and wheezy, and inclined to doze off in the middle of the conversation. He was a year or two younger than the King, and having led a quiet and moderate life, was likely to outlive him. He was the wisest man of his clan, having learned the languages of the Hittites and of Egypt, and was therefore a useful counsellor whenever their emissaries appeared before the King. His knowledge was a well-kept secret, and the messengers were often careless in speaking among themselves, believing that no one in David's house could understand their speech. But Yonadav was also a great genealogist, and could reel off the ancestry of every house in every clan in the principal tribes. Moreover, he shared with his royal kinsman a partiality for beautiful women. But as he grew older he had become something of a windbag, and Bathsheva felt like shaking him.

"The Shunammite, you mean, my lady… Avishag is her name, the daughter of Baanah, son of Ahilud, a great man in Jezreel…"

Yonadav sipped the warmed wine that was so kind to his old bones. He had just returned from the oasis of Ein Gedi, down by the salt sea, where he liked to spend the winter months whenever the King's service permitted. He had come back for the spring festival, but the winds that blew over the mountains were still sharp.

Bathsheva waited. Was she supposed to draw him out? Was there nothing more to be said? The old man was content to recline among the cushions, sipping her wine and munching dates and figs.

His rheumy eyes gazed idly at the dust motes dancing in the shaft of sunlight from the window, then fell shut.

"Ahilud," the Great Lady said in a loud voice, to prompt him. Yonadav opened his eyes and a faint smile flickered around them and vanished in his grizzled beard. Bathsheva was gazing thoughtfully into her own wine cup. "Ahilud," she repeated. "Or did you say, Baanah?"

Yonadav licked his sticky fingers and pretended to concentrate on forgotten matters.

"Baanah the son of Ahilud," he said pleasantly. "Of the house of Geber. Jezreelites, of the tribe of Ephraim. In the days when the children of Benjamin would seize their brides from among the dancing maidens at Shiloh, the clans of Ephraim sent all their daughters there, dressed in their finest attire and ornaments. By these unions they forged the alliance which made them strong in Israel, strong enough to contend with Judah…"

He was well launched, and Bathsheva resigned herself to a long lecture on the genealogy and chronicles of the Judeans and Israelites, a subject with which they were all absurdly fascinated. She waited patiently until he stopped, whether to catch his breath or because he had come to the end of a tale she did not know. Then, in the soft, sweet voice which men found enchanting, she said:

"And the girl, what is her name, Avishag? – Was she one of the dancing maidens?"

Yonadav stared. She had not heard a word he said. He had wasted a choice speech on this fine-looking woman who cared for nothing except herself and her son. Not for the first time he thought that his kinsman David, for all his warrior's prowess and skills of kingship, was a fool where his manhood was concerned. Just because he had lusted after her one summer night, did he have to make her his queen? And at such a price!

But Yonadav was too wise to show his impatience. "Avishag is merely a child, my lady. It was the advice of the wise woman, Eglah the Edomite, that the King be kept warm at all times, to restore movement to his legs. Heated stones were used, but they had to be changed often and it disturbed the King's rest. It was thought that a dog would do, but Zadok the priest disallowed it. Then it was said that the kings of Aram had maidens sleeping at their feet... Avishag was chosen to honour her grandfather Ahilud, who had kept his clan out of the Benjamite rebellion. When the King recovers and no longer needs her, a suitable husband will be found for her."

Having said as much as he intended to say, Yonadav raised himself with difficulty from the cushions and, red-faced and wheezy, bowed low to the Great Lady. And she, not such a fool as to believe that this was the whole story, pleaded with him graciously to stay longer, to eat and drink and rest. An old Hittite slave accompanied him to his house in the King's city, bearing a jar of pure honey from Bathsheva's beehives in Shechem.

Alone in her inner chamber the Great Lady removed her headdress and jewellery and knelt before the image of Arinna, the lady goddess of the Hittites, and prayed that her husband the King would not recover from the illness which rendered him impotent.

The King had hoped to be able to walk to the shrine of the Ark and assist at the first sacrifice of the spring festival. He wanted the people to see him hale and hearty, surrounded by his captains, as he had always been. But though Naamah rubbed his legs daily with a mixture of goat's milk, oil and myrrh, and though he drank all the strengthening potions prepared for him by an Egyptian physician, he could still only walk a few steps while leaning on a strong shoulder. It would not do for the people to see him so enfeebled. In the end it was decided to enclose Araunah's threshing-floor, where the shrine of the Ark and its altar stood, encircling it with hangings, and draw them back only for the first part of the ceremony, when the high priests offered the first sacrifice and recited the litany. The King could thus be carried in a litter into the enclosure and out again, unseen by all but his household.

The night before the start of the festival the King could not sleep. He had not yet moved his sleeping quarters back to the upper storey, because he hated to be carried up and down the stairs like a child by his man-servants. The day had been hot and dry, parched by an easterly wind that blew from the desert as from an open furnace. The sky was livid and there were no shadows. Men and beasts sought shelter and water and shut their eyes tight against the flying dust. The night was not much better. Such easterly winds often blew at the time of the spring festival. After a few days, the cool weather would return and linger for a few weeks more before summer came.

Still in the great hall, the King lay under a thin coverlet with Avishag curled up beside him. She had thought that when the nights turned warmer she would be excused from her duty, but the King wanted her to remain. He would stroke her head and shoulder, his hand growing heavier and slower as he became drowsy, until it came to a rest. By then the girl, too, was usually fast asleep. Some nights he talked to her, or rather he asked questions and she answered. He asked after some men of her clan who had taken part in the Ammonite wars or in the tribal skirmishes. He wanted to hear about the fields of Shunem and its vineyards, about harvests and crops, flocks and wells. Tonight he was wide-awake, as though he had forgotten how to sleep.

"Sing to me," he said at last, not in his king's voice, but sounding like an affectionate father or older brother. "Sing me the songs of your village. It has been a long time since anyone has sung to me here."

For a moment her mind went blank. The songs of her village? She could not recall any, not in this dark cavernous hall, so far from home. The King waited patiently, and then he began to hum, trying to recall a forgotten song. Only a small part of the melody and a few words came back to him, something about a lion and a bear that snatched a lamb from the fold. He stopped and laughed.

"I was a good shepherd," he said wistfully. "I loved the flocks and the fields of Bethlehem. Sometimes I have wished that I had stayed there, among the sheepfolds and the olive groves…! My portion was small, as I was the youngest son, but Ofrah, my maternal cousin, who was intended for me, would have brought some land with her. I would now be sitting at the gate of Bethlehem with the other elders of our clan, the father of a large house, full of years and bearing a good name."

"Like my father's father, Ahilud," said Avishag. "He sits at the gate with the elders, judging the people. He says, 'A good name is better than a precious ointment.'"

As she spoke a song came into her mind, one that the women sang at this time of the year:

> *"Lo the winter is past, the rain is over and gone, the flowers appear on the earth... O my dove, that art in the clefts of the rock, let me see thy countenance, let me hear thy voice..."*

She sang very softly, aware of Naamah's presence behind the screen, but the King was delighted and asked her to sing it again. Presently he fell asleep with a strand of her hair between his fingers.

Nothing Ira had said prepared her for the festival itself. Together with all the women and children she went to Araunah's threshing-floor. The tabernacle which housed the Ark, stood close to the flank of the mountain, and before it a huge horned altar. The hard ground, the altar, the gutters that led from it to the precipice, had all been washed clean. Ira had explained everything to her – the sacrifice was to give thanks for the past winter's rains, to bring down blessings for the new year, and to remind the Israelites of their deliverance from the Egyptian bondage. The arm of El, which had humbled the pride of Egypt and rescued the Children of Israel, was represented by the foreleg of the sacrificial ram, of which the priests alone might partake. The rest of the animal was to be a burnt offering. After the ram, other animals would be sacrificed to Yah, and the Levite high priest, wielding a trident, would offer their parts to the King's house and to the elders of the clans, who would carry them away to their own makeshift hearths in the city and its environs. Then, as the sun went down, the Israelites would sing the triumphal Song of Miriam.

But as it was taking place, Avishag could not make out what

was happening. She saw the King's litter carried into the enclosure and set down before the tabernacle, and the King standing up, wearing over his gown a cloth *ephod* fringed with blue tassels. Then the hangings were drawn back and the people could see the threshing-floor and the grand assembly in it. A great cheer rose and masses of people began to push closer. Some stumbled and fell and a few rolled shrieking down the hillside, until stopped by a boulder or a helping hand. Children cried and women ululated. In the meantime, the sacrificial ram was placed on the altar, its legs trussed together, while an acolyte held on to its horns. The high priest, wearing a splendid *ephod* embroidered with gold and encrusted with precious stones, stepped forward and slit the animal's throat. The blood spurted out, gushed down the channel and into the gutters, hardly spattering the priest. Now Ira stepped forward and hacked off the foreleg, raising it high for all to see, while the priests and the King and many of the elders chanted aloud. Then the rest of the animal was set to burn. Despite the lavish use of incense and aromatic woods, the stench was almost unbearable, and many people coughed and choked. Soon the hangings were closed, and the King was carried out and back into his house. Then the festivities began in earnest. Young Levites danced and played the viols, flutes and cymbals; countless bonfires were lit on the surrounding hillsides, and a shouting throng jostled this way and that. The women and children of the King's house formed a ring around a large hearth which had been laid on the terrace, and were soon engaged in their usual activities of gossiping, eating and feeding, scolding their children and sniping at each other, but in tones more solemn than on ordinary days.

Avishag's head began to ache. She had never seen so many people together or heard so much noise. She had eaten some meat with a wafer of unleavened bread and quenched her thirst with wine-and-water, and now she would have liked to return to the fort, but it was too early. She moved to the edge of the terrace and sat down in a shadowy corner, away from the fire and smoke. Leaning back against the low stonewall, she watched the moon rising, full and brilliant and with a shimmering halo, portending another day of desert heat. Some of the women made horn signs against the moon, and a few veiled their children's heads to protect them from her light. But Avishag felt no fear – her people had no dealings with the moon, which let them alone, content with a simple prayer and a libation at the beginning of the month.

Presently a small girl, Naamah's favourite grandchild, came toddling over to Avishag. Her mother, who had recently given birth again and not yet purified herself, had remained at home. Tired of following her grandmother around, the tiny girl made for Avishag and climbed onto her lap. Soon she slept, her thumb in her mouth and her face half-hidden in the girl's bosom.

The Great Lady had come down, hand in hand with her son, for the duration of the first sacrifice, but then she returned to her quarters, the lad following dutifully behind her. This was the first time that Avishag saw them, and she was astonished by the conduct of the others. They made way for Bathsheva, even bowed to her, but their faces were stony. They did not speak to her or to the boy. There was an uncanny hush around them, though the prince's eyes kept sliding towards the other children. When they left everyone sighed with relief and a cheerful babble broke out.

Back in her apartment, Bathsheva, her son and her priest supped on their share of the King's own sacrificial meat and unleavened bread, together with festive dishes prepared by the Great Lady's cook. When the priest left and the boy had gone to bed, she stood at the east window and looked down at the terrace where the women were still feasting. She noticed Avishag, who was dressed in festive white, like the other maidens who were not the King's daughters, with a girdle of brass links at her waist and her hair dressed in intricate braids with ornaments. There was something about the girl that aroused Bathsheva's disquiet whenever she saw her. Even when the sun went down and only the light from the fire, and presently the full moon, illuminated the crowded terrace, it was easy to distinguish the Shunammite. It was plain to see that she did not yet belong entirely to the household, but she was no longer an outsider.

Sitting apart in a corner, she held her face up to the moon, as though bathing in her cool light. Foolhardy girl! The moon could be harsh to such bold spirits.

It was time, the Great Lady thought, to make the Shunammite's acquaintance.

Chapter two

On the third day of the festival the east wind dropped. For a little while the smoke from the pilgrims' fires, the bleating and braying of their beasts and the cries of the boys being circumcised in the Levites' tent, hung in the still air. Suddenly a strong gust blew from the west and quickly dispersed the dusty pall which had hung over the King's city. A mass of dark cloud came hurtling up from the faraway sea, and a moment later the windows of heaven opened and a great downpour fell on Jerusalem.

Despite the chaos caused by the wind and the rain, which washed away tents and drenched their contents, the change was greeted cheerfully. Such generous rains at the end of winter, followed by the bright warm days of spring, promised fat grapes and a plentiful grain harvest. The ancient stone Ashera which stood on the rocky summit above the King's city, facing both east and west, received heaped oblations of honey and wine and fat sheeps' tails. The festival had done the King good. He felt stronger and made determined efforts to walk. He still needed a shoulder to lean on, but more for balance than support.

"If I were still a shepherd," he said to Avishag that night, "I could lean on my staff. I would choose me a stout acacia branch, and trim and shape it to fit under my arm. But I am the King, and it would not do for me to be seen hobbling and halting like an old householder."

The rain kept falling, steady and soft. They could hear the water rushing along the eaves and gurgling into the stone gutter that led to the cisterns. To Avishag it seemed that time had come around and she was once more the girl she had been when she had first arrived at the King's fort. Now that most of the pilgrims had left the city and the rest would leave the next day, she thought the world would return to its old ways.

The King, feeling well and confident that he was on the mend, was taking a greater interest in the events around him. For too long he had been content to leave the affairs of the land to his ministers and captains, who came to him only for approval. The success of the festival, the perfect burning of the first sacrificial beast and the healthy condition of the others, showed that he had not slipped from divine favour, as he had feared since he had fallen ill. When his spirits were low he could not bear to think about his family. His fine wives, his beautiful children – what had they brought him but grief and pain?

But now, recalling the fine crowd of women and children who had watched him from the terrace as he took part in the rites before the Ark, he grew quite cheerful.

"Were you on the terrace with the others?" he asked – slyly, as he had seen her there.

"I was, my lord. And I saw the Great Lady and her son," she added, hoping that the King would explain the curious scene she had witnessed.

"Aye. She came down for a little while," he nodded. Then he asked, "And the boy, Yedidiah, was he pleased to be there, among his brothers?"

Avishag hesitated. Did the King not know that the boy was kept apart, or that the others looked askance at the Great Lady and her son?

"Speak, child!" he said, tapping her arm.

"If you please, my lord, the boy was with his mother. He looked at the children and would have liked to be with them, but the Great Lady held him by the hand."

The King sighed. Bathsheva's fears of his family had been justified – or she believed them to be justified – by the death of their first son. Thinking about Merari, the infant whose happy laughter and bright eyes gave him so much joy, and whose final agonies crushed his heart, which had not yet recovered from the death of Absalom, he felt again the awful guilt of the ban imposed upon him by the seer Nathan. Bathsheva did not understand his family. She thought that Adoniyah would seek to destroy her remaining son – though why should he plot against this boy who was not a threat to him?

It was time to bring Adoniyah back from Hebron and install him at his side for all to see.

When Avishag returned from her visit to the Great Lady all the women crowded around her, begging for details. Had Bathsheva been kind? Did she offer the girl food? What was it like? Were her chambers very grand? Had the boy supped with them? Would Avishag go there again? What did the Great Lady want?

Avishag was puzzled. She answered their questions as well as she could. Yes, the Great Lady had been kind, had offered her ripe pomegranates from Jericho and a drink of almond milk with honey. Yes, her chambers were grand, though not so beautifully appointed as the Egyptian lady's. The boy did not sup with them, but she could hear his voice in the adjoining chamber, speaking as though he were learning something by rote. But as to what the Great Lady wanted of her, Avishag knew no more than when the servant had come to invite her, early that morning.

Somewhat disappointed, the women soon dispersed. Only Naamah and her friend Temimah, an old woman who usually sat, cross-legged and silent, at a loom in a corner, remained with Avishag. Naamah, always garrulous, asked: "And did the Great Lady – " here she exchanged glances with her aged companion – "did the Great

Lady know who you are, and why you have been brought to the King's house?"

"Whether she knew or did not know, I cannot say," Avishag replied thoughtfully. "But she spoke of it as if it were a small matter. 'The nights are still chilly,' she said, 'and your duty keeps you at the King's feet. What will you do when the nights grow warm?' I replied that I did not know, and would obey the King's command."

The two crones nudged each other and their whiskery, toothless mouths gaped with laughter. "Warm nights!" Naamah squawked. "Oh, she knows all about warm nights, does Bathshua!"

Avishag stared at the two grandmothers who were doubled up, cackling and slapping each other's knees. But they soon ceased, remembering their dignity.

"You are a good child, my daughter," said Naamah composing herself and wiping her eyes. "You answered her well."

Temimah nodded, adding, in her broad Judean speech, "She will send for you again, as my soul lives. And again and again, and will try to make you her spy…"

The King thought otherwise. "Bathsheva is lonely," he said when Avishag told him about her visit to the Great Lady. "She has kept apart from the others for so long, that now she can befriend only a newcomer like you. Be kind to her, child. She has been greatly afflicted and she is afraid."

But his mind was not on Bathsheva and her solitary life in the upper storey. That day he had sent Yoav ben Zeruiah to Hebron, to bring Adoniyah back to Jerusalem. Yoav, whom age had shrivelled to the semblance of a gnarled olive tree, had listened impassively while the King dictated a lavishly fond letter to his son. Ever since David taken ill in the autumn, Adoniyah had been acting as his regent. His seat was in Hebron, David's first capital, but he moved about the country with all the panoply of a ruler, to show the people – and most of all, the House of Joseph, to wit, the Ephraimites and their allies of Benjamin – that they were not without a master. For he knew that, were he to falter, to show the slightest weakness, they would soon revert to their unruly ways, as in the days of the Judges, when there was no king in Israel and every man did what was right in his own eyes.

Avishag, whose mind was perplexed by the Great Lady and the old women's talk about her, was reassured by the King's response. He was in better spirits than she had ever seen him.

"You shall see Adoniyah," he said to her, as he composed himself for sleep. "He is the best of my sons…" Here he paused and pressed his fingers to his eyes, to erase that other image, that of the goodliest son of all, Absalom, Absalom… "The Lord Yah took pity on a stricken father and gave me Adoniyah's shoulder to lean on," he continued firmly. "He will not bring down my grey hairs with sorrow to the grave."

Tears pricked Avishag's eyes and she put her hand on the King's shoulder, very lightly, to comfort him. Her touch was warm and sweet as a child's and the King placed his own hand over hers and pressed it without a word. They slept.

Adoniyah's house stood in the dell known as the Valley of Rephaim, south of the King's city, beside the road leading to Hebron. It was surrounded by the great mulberry trees under which the Philistines had encamped long before, when the King was still fighting for mastery over the land. They had abandoned their Dagons when they retreated from that final battle, and one of these stood beside the gate of Adoniyah's estate, a fearsome fish-tailed image in black basalt, its head crowned with a chaplet of myrtle. But though the house priest did not begrudge it a few drops of wine and oil, and the women renewed its chaplet from time to time, it was made to face an altar to the victorious Yah, Lord of Hosts.

The King realized that Adoniyah had become too great in his own right to live under his father's roof, but he wished him to move into the city. The Tyrian craftsmen sent by King Hiram and their Israelite apprentices were hard at work enlarging the royal residence. The King planned to fill in the gully between his house and the summit on its north side, so as to form a large base for a great house in which his whole family would reside, as well as a worthy abode for the Ark. His Jebusite predecessors had made a start, pouring rubble into the gully, and a path of sorts linked the two stony peaks. But the work would take a long time, and meanwhile the King wished to have his heir close at hand.

Adoniyah stood before his father in a respectful attitude, and Avishag saw that the knuckles of his huge hands, pressed together in front of his iron-studded belt, were white with strain. But his face was stolid and when he looked up his expression held nothing but regard for his father.

The King was in far better health and spirits than he had been six months before, when his legs had suddenly given way under him and even his speech faltered. Now he spoke as clearly as ever, his arms were as strong as any man his age could expect, and he was able to walk almost unaided. Adoniyah expressed his great joy and gave thanks to Yah, who had restored his father to health. He thanked the King for honouring him with the regency, and said he had no greater wish than to serve him, or to retire to his estate, whichever he was commanded to do. The King's city, he said regretfully, was too crowded and closely built to accommodate his household, but he would, if the King so wished, leave his family in the care of his steward and come and live at his father's right hand.

This was the first time that Avishag was present in the hall while the King gave audience. The King had told her to remain by his side that morning, so as to see Adoniyah. She stood by the wall, almost hidden by the screen behind the dais. When Adoniyah approached, the King rose and took a few steps towards him and embraced him lovingly. Then, leaning on his son's arm, he turned and sat in his high-backed, lion-footed chair.

Although he was taken aback by Adoniyah's objections, the King wanted only to please him. "I need you by my side," he said, speaking not in his masterful, audience voice, but in a cajoling, fatherly tone. "Your brothers are with the captains, scattered far and wide between Dan and Beersheba, and I am here with the women and children. Yah is my witness, I am full of years and have fed on sorrow. Must I cast all my reliance upon the sons of Zeruiah?"

Avishag was looking at Adoniyah, but when the King mentioned the sons of Zeruiah she glanced at Yoav, who had come back with the King's son and was standing beside him in the hall. He was waiting to take his leave before returning to his men in Mount Ephraim. If he was offended by the King's words his face, scarred like the bark of a tree, did not betray it. The King's son, however, was flattered by his father's appeal and held his head up proudly. He was a fine-looking man of thirty-five, not tall but well-built, with coppery glints in his beard. He would have been handsome, but that his left eye had a strong cast in it.

Adoniyah spent all that day at the King's side, hearing the reports of the scribes and dictating to them the events of his sojourn in Hebron and elsewhere. He also made a burnt offering of a suckling lamb on the great altar before the tabernacle, with Eviatar, the Levite high priest, officiating at his side. If anyone had doubted that the King's chosen heir was back and stronger than ever, the day's events would have undeceived them.

Avishag returned to the women's house after Adoniyah's audience with his father. By now the women had grown accustomed to her coming and going, like Naamah, between the King's fort and their quarters, and were no longer piqued by her special standing.

"Did the King affirm that Adoniyah is to rule after him?" was the question they all asked, and she admitted that she did not know. The King wished his son to live nearby, she told them, but nothing was said about the succession, not while she was in the hall.

The women chattered eagerly about the returning prince and his future prospects, urged the Egyptian lady's Kushite handmaids to reveal what preparations their mistress was making for her lord's visit, and even helped them to provide a fine feast for the occasion. Avishag was puzzled by these signs of goodwill towards the haughty Egyptian, who was usually spoken of with envy and dislike. Then she noticed that the women were doing everything in full view of the upper windows, at which they kept directing sly glances, and she understood. They wished to spite the Great Lady, to ensure that she saw and heard – and smelled – the lavish welcome given to Adoni-yah. It was not a secret in the King's household that the Great Lady nursed hopes that her son would inherit the throne, though he was the youngest of the King's sons and had neither a Judean nor an Israelite clan behind him.

Avishag followed the women's noisy bustle with her eyes, but took no part in it. She sat down beside old Temimah, who was work-ing at her loom, lending a hand from time to time when a thread broke and needed to be tied neatly into the weave. The old woman scarcely uttered a word, but Avishag knew she was happy to have her company. Presently they were joined by Naamah, who brought some food for her old friend and sat down beside her, stretching out her tired, swollen legs.

While the crone chewed her food, Avishag unravelled knots in the woollen skeins, an easy task for her young fingers. Naamah glanced at her, as though in two minds whether to confide in her old companion in the girl's hearing. But the urge to speak about the day's events was greater than her discretion.

"The priestess's son is favoured today," she began conversation-ally. "How his mother would rejoice to see him exalted above all his brothers!"

The crone cackled unintelligibly, her mouth full of barley pot-tage. Naamah nodded and went on. "He sleeps here tonight, with his Egyptian lady, and may stay a while. The King wants him at his side, not down in the Valley of Rephaim, but he cannot keep him. The son of the priestess knows the power of an oath, and he will not put his neck under the yoke without it."

Avishag would have liked to ask what oath, what yoke, which priestess – but desisted. The old women tolerated her presence, per-haps even liked her, but she was not yet one of the household. Not as she was at home, where she had always been indulged, where she could listen to the women's talk at the cooking hearth as well as to that of the men and boys in the fields, and ask questions to her heart's content. Moments such as this made her wistful, and she walked away.

Adoniyah remained at the King's fort for three days and three nights. He spent the days at his father's side and the nights with his Egyptian wife, the highest of all the wives of the King's surviving sons. On the third night the King, leaning on the arm of an old Gittite soldier, climbed up to the Great Lady's apartment and remained there until daybreak. For the first time since she came to the King's city, Avishag slept alone. In the morning Adoniyah came into the hall, bowed low to his father and begged leave to return to his estate. He gave many reasons, and though the King tried to keep him longer, he remained firm. Before the sun was in mid-heaven he was gone.

Though the King himself was fit and almost youthful again, gloom descended on his household. He moved his sleeping quarters back to the upper storey, to an eyrie of a chamber, which was almost filled by a great couch with bolsters and coverlets. Its window gave upon the city that clung like swallows' nests to the hillside below, and beyond it to the hills and dales leading to Hebron. Avishag was ordered to move up there with the King, and Naamah laid her own pallet in the passage outside the door.

But though the nights were balmy, and Avishag knew she was as secure as a babe in arms, she sensed a hidden unease among the King's household. A dark cloud seemed to hang over the fort, and even the garrulous Naamah held her tongue, as though afraid to speak.

Now and then the King absented himself from the chamber and spent the night with Bathsheva. He would return at daybreak, his beard and gown scented with the Great Lady's unguents, pat the drowsy girl on her head and call for his bath. He washed himself in a copper tub, for which ewers of heated water were brought up from the cooking yard. Then Naamah would comb and oil his hair and beard and bring him clean garments. Avishag served him his early meal, and helped him to go down the steep stairs to the hall. But if life was flowing as smoothly as spring water in a stone runnel, and even the Benjamites were holding their peace, and the King offered weekly oblations to the Elohim for giving him rest on every side – why, Avishag asked herself, had the guard around the King's fort been redoubled? Why did Adoniyah excuse himself from attending the King when emissaries arrived from Aram with solemn offers of a truce? Why did the sons of Zeruiah, Yoav and Avishai, take turns staying in Jerusalem, and why was one or the other always present at the King's side, like a weather-beaten old image? And as for Yonadav, that wily old counsellor – was he really ailing and unable to leave his bed down in the city, or was he keeping out of the way of possible trouble?

Avishag heard these questions asked and discussed in low voices in the women's quarters and in soft mutters among the King's men, but no-one seemed to know the answers. The women often glanced slyly at the upper windows of the Great Lady, but she did not gratify their curiosity and never looked out. Nor did her son.

Summer was mild that year, the harvest ample. All over the land the people were busy threshing and winnowing their wheat and barley, pressing their grapes and filling casks with good wine, spreading dates and figs to dry. They slept out of doors in their orchards and fields, under canopies of palm-fronds to protect them from the moon.

On one such night Avishag lay awake in the King's bedchamber. The King had fallen asleep, breathing lightly. Though clad only in a shift and without a coverlet, she felt hot and pressed her limbs against the cool stone wall. Was it the smell of the summer night, or the distant sound of a shepherd's flute, which suddenly seized her heart and squeezed it? She thought about the fields of Shunem, the flimsy hut in which she and her brothers and sister spent the nights, guarding their father's vineyard and melon field from the depredations of men and beasts. In her mind she heard the grasshoppers' ceaseless chirp, the wailing of the jackals, the snorting of the cattle in the nearby pen and the sleepy twitter of a bird in an overhanging branch. She began to cry.

Afraid to disturb the King, who had all that day sat in judgement, she tried to suppress the sobs that broke from her chest. But the King was an old man and his sleep was light.

"What ails you, child?" he said suddenly. "Has anything happened?"

His voice startled her and arrested her sobs. Swallowing her tears, she begged the King's pardon for disturbing his sleep.

To her surprise, he insisted. "Your father's father entrusted you to me, my child. No harm must come to you under my roof. Tell me why you wept."

"If you please, my lord. I dreamt that I was in my father's vineyard, now that the harvest is upon us."

The King was thoughtful. Avishag already repented having told him her foolish dream, telling herself it was her duty to be a comfort to him, not to burden him with her trifling moods.

Then he spoke. "You are young and you miss your father and mother, and I have kept you here for many months without sight of them. Doubtless they long for you also. I would send you now to pass the harvest season in Shunem, but I fear it is a bad time for you to travel. Will you wait till the autumn festival? Perhaps then your father will come to Jerusalem and take you with him for a spell, before the winter's rains."

Not even her brother Ornan was as kind and generous as the King, she thought, seizing his hand and pressing it to her forehead. But then his words entered her mind where they joined the many signs she had seen of imminent trouble, and put an abrupt stop to her childish delight.

"Why, my lord? Forgive me; it is not that I ask to go now to my father's house. It is only what you said, about it being a bad time. There are so many guards about the fort now, and other signs too… Is my lord in danger?"

The King was silent for a long time, stroking his beard and gazing at the play of moonbeams on the ceiling.

"It is not I," he said at last in a low voice, for her ears alone, "not I, but the sons of Zeruiah, who fear evil doings in this house.

Adoniyah is the first of my sons now, and my throne should pass to him. It is only right, now that his brother... But no doubt you know about my son Absalom, and what befell him. But Adoniyah is wholly of the tribe of Judah, his mother being a priestess in the grove of Baalei Yehudah. The Israelites are still at odds with us, the Hebrews of Judah. The Benjamites remain loyal to the house of Saul, and would put any of them in my place, even that crook-leg-ged, hare-visaged Meribaal, Jonathan's son. Their priestess Rizpah has rallied them against me time and again, and that old scorpion, Shimei ben Gera, still lurks, awaiting another chance to strike at me..."

Avishag listened with all her heart. Never had she heard the King speak this way. With his counsellors and captains he spoke in his elder's voice, weighty and slow. With Adoniyah he was ingratiating, with visitors and litigants sharp and commanding, and with the women of his house light and playful. This was another voice, urgent and direct, and in her mind she called it the voice of David.

"But is not Kilav your eldest son, my lord?" she ventured. Kilav was a warrior, though not a notable one. He and his family lived with the King's charioteers in the valley of Ayalon.

"He is the eldest remaining, but his mother, Abigail, was the wife of Nabal the Carmelite before she became my wife. He is not, therefore, wholly my son, and cannot be my heir. Absalom, now, he was the firstborn of Maachah, my wife who was the daughter of Talmai, king of Geshur. His mother wore the scarlet thread and her house has been allied with the tribes of Israel since the days of the Forefathers. He should have been king after me... – Would that I had given him the throne when he wanted it! Ah, my son Absalom, Absalom my son, will I ever forget you?"

And to her great amazement and distress, the King pulled the coverlet over his head and wept.

Having once opened his heart to the girl, the King often talked to her in the night. Her devotion and quick wit were like a balm after a long day spent in the company of men who wanted things.

Some wanted a favourable judgement, others revenge against their enemies, some plotted for the pleasure of plotting, others attempted to deceive him as to their intentions, and he was too weary to try to uncover their real thoughts. If Yonadav could be persuaded to come up to the King's house and sit at his side, he would have been greatly valued at this time. A mind like his, subtle and cunning as a serpent, would have been of better service to the King now than a new pair of legs. There are people, the King told Avishag, who can see what men hide behind their faces, and can hear the thoughts that lie behind their words. Hushai the Archite had been such a man. He was a staunch friend through many reversals and had baffled the cunning Ahitophel himself at a time when the kingdom hung in the balance, but Hushai was gathered to his forefathers these three years, the King said. As for Yonadav, though he proclaimed aloud his devotion to the King, he was not a man to lean on in time of trouble. He used his wisdom like a store of precious oil, which is sold to favoured buyers or withheld at will.

Before long, as old Temimah had foretold, Avishag was again called to the Great Lady's apartment and received very cordially. When she bowed, the Great Lady made as if to stop her and gently embraced her shoulders. Leading her by the hand she seated the girl beside her on the dais, taking pains to make her comfortable with bolsters and pillows. She gave her chilled water sweetened with date syrup, small cakes of fine flour with almonds, and other good things. And all the while she talked to her as if she were a favoured kinswoman.

Avishag answered her questions readily but briefly, seeing that the Great Lady listened with an unvarying smile no matter what was said. She even nodded and smiled when Avishag told her that her older sister had died of a snakebite.

Unlike the previous occasion, this time Bathsheva knew all she cared to know about the Shunammite, having questioned the King during his recent night-time visits. She knew that the King had vowed to treat the girl like a daughter and did not touch her, though his manhood had returned since the spring. Nevertheless, she felt that the King was keeping something from her. There was something about the girl that she could not fathom.

After a while the Great Lady's son came in. He bowed to his mother and stood in a respectful attitude while she told him who their visitor was. Shlomo, as his mother called him – the King's name for him was Yedidiah – was fourteen years of age. He was a well-made lad with his mother's long eyes and ivory skin. The dark down on his upper lip made him look older than his years. But he was still a child, and his eyes were drawn to the sweetmeats on the brass platter between them.

While he ate, more daintily and gracefully than any child Avishag had ever seen, the Great Lady talked about their forthcoming journey to her estate in Shechem. Shlomo asked questions and his mother replied. To Avishag's ears their talk sounded as if it had been prepared in advance, like the cakes and the jug of sweetened water. But what Bathsheva had not prepared was the boy's interest in the maiden. Once he had eaten and drunk his fill, his eyes kept straying from his mother's face to the visitor. Avishag saw this and grew uneasy. The Great Lady did not seem to notice. After a little while Avishag begged leave to return to the women's house. She had promised, she said, to help Naamah put up the hangings in the newly built antechamber to the King's hall.

The Great Lady urged her politely to stay and rest herself, yet rose to see her to the door. Before they parted, she took a brooch from her gown and fastened it on the girl's. It was a fine ornament, made to look like a flower, with a curious honey-coloured stone in its centre.

"Come back again soon, my child," she said, smiling and patting the girl's cheek, "to please a solitary old woman who has no daughter of her own."

Shlomo bowed to her when she took her leave, and she felt his eyes like a grown man's eyes, examining her from head to foot.

"Tell me, mother," said Avishag to Temimah that evening, setting before her a dish of tender mutton, chopped very fine and mixed with barley and raisins. "Tell me what did happen to the Great Lady's firstborn that made her so fearful."

The old crone was fond of the girl, who was kind and attentive to her needs. Naamah had told her that Avishag had the King's ear and urged her to make the girl her advocate, but she desisted. She had accepted her fate and was resigned to it. It was not the King's heart she would have liked to touch, but that of her son, Yafia, who had not come to see her since... since that dreadful day. Avishag's sweet countenance and nimble hands made a brightness in her darkened life.

"The child who died was Merari," she said when she had swallowed her first mouthful. Then she took another one, and when she had swallowed that she said, "And he was not Bathshua's firstborn." She took some more food. Thus the story came out piecemeal, like beads on a string, with intervals for chewing.

"Some said that Bathshua had a son by her husband, Uriah the Hittite, a sickly babe, who was brought up by a wet nurse in Shechem until he died. But now he is never spoken of; it is as though he never existed. Uriah was one of the King's foremost captains, a fine man in his high feathered helmet." Temimah shook her head sadly, and chewed another mouthful. "Then the King ordered his captains to make their homes in his city, and Uriah, who was a great man among his people, built himself a fine house just below the fort. – It is now the abode of Adoram, the master of the King's tribute. – When Uriah was with Yoav, besieging Rabbah of the Ammonites, Bathshua was alone, with neither a child nor a man to occupy her. One summer evening she caused her maids to carry her bath to the roof, and there – " Temimah's hand paused with the food on its way to her mouth – "she bathed and dressed her hair, and did her nails and whatever else she did to adorn herself – all in full view of the King's roof, where he liked to walk about at sundown!"

This story was not entirely new to Avishag, who had heard some of it even before she came to the King's house, and more since. But Temimah had to tell the tale in her own way. When she finished eating she leaned back on her bolster and continued.

"The King has always been soft-hearted with beautiful women, and Bathshua was a fine one, white and plump as a suckling lamb ready for the spit. That night he sent for her in secret. None but his manservant and her handmaids knew that he had lain with her. But it was not for the King's gift that Bathshua did what she did. Soon she sent to tell him that she was with child, and the King…" The old woman stopped speaking. She pulled her veil down over her face and rocked from side to side. Avishag waited, and a few moments later Temimah continued in a dull voice. "Uriah the Hittite was sent to the fiercest battle and died a warrior's death. His wife mourned him for forty days, and on the forty-first she came to live in the King's house, in the apartment of his first wife, Michal, the daughter of Saul, who had died some years before. Then he built himself a chamber up there, to be near her…"

The old woman raised her head. A fierce light burned in her eyes, but it soon went out and she smiled at the attentive girl.

"Why do you ask about such evil doings, my child?"

Avishag was at a loss for an answer. She always wanted to know everything – the names of animals and plants, the stories of people's lives. As a child, her endless questions had earned her a few cuffs as well as amused nicknames. But both her grandfather and her brother Ornan praised her quick wit and said that she would grow up to be a wise woman; yet she did not wish to become a wise woman, only a friend to the King.

Temimah understood. "It is for the King's sake, is it not?" she said to the girl, who was deep in thought. "You are so much with him and he is kind to you. But do not be afraid for him. The King, even now, is not helpless. When aroused, he will come out roaring like a lion and devour his prey!"

"You have not told me about Merari, mother. How did he die?"

"Oh, he was a greedy one, little Merari!" The crone chuckled. "He loved to eat, and would taste everything. Though he was Bathshua's son, he was a sweet child and the women liked him. None of us would have touched a hair on his head. As soon as he could walk, he would escape from his nurse and come here to play with the other children. You could hear his voice from afar, and it made us all laugh. The King adored him – but then David did adore all his children… One day Merari came and played with the children – there many here then – and the day was hot. He found a jar with cold pome-granate water and drank from it. Bathshua cried that it was poisoned, but others had drunk from that jar and no-one else was harmed. By nightfall he was very ill. He was as hot as a coal and screamed that his head hurt him. How that child suffered! He suffered for three days, his little body writhing and twisting, as though a scorpion had stung him. The King withdrew to the chamber over the gate, tore his garments and fasted, lying on the floor, praying for the boy's life. He made us burn frankincense and precious ointment before all the images of the house. He cast ashes on his head and prostrated himself before Yah, the Lord of Judah. But it was all in vain. The child died. We feared to tell David. He had grieved so much when the child was yet alive, what would he do now? But when he heard that the boy was dead, he rose and bathed and broke his fast. 'I shall go to him,' he said. 'He shall not come back to me.'"

"And was no one's hand in the child's death?"

"No hand, daughter. But who is to say, no eye? Perhaps when Bathshua moved into the apartment of Michal, Shaul's barren daughter, the curse fell upon her. And the seer Nathan had chas-tised the King for taking the wife of Uriah the Hittite. Perhaps he had cursed the child who was born of that act. A seer's curse can blight a field or set fire to an oak, and a young child is soft and easily harmed… But Bathshua believes Merari was killed by the people of this house, and so the King allowed her to have her own household under his roof. The boy she calls Shlomo never sees another child, save when he goes to his mother's folk in Shechem. It is said that he is wise and cunning beyond his years, and can speak the languages of the Hittites and of Egypt… Bless you, my child. Go in peace now, for I am tired and wish to rest."

Temimah's story explained why the Great Lady kept apart from the rest of the household, and why she had only her own Hittite servants about her. But her son was no longer an infant, and surely did not need to be so secluded from the King's household. Moreover, if it was true that the Great Lady had high ambitions for her son, then keeping him away from the King's captains, scribes and counsellors was a strange way of going about it. Avishag shook her head, perplexed. Since coming to the King's house she had grown accustomed to the speech and manners of its people, most of them Judeans, but the Great Lady and her son were unlike anyone else she met. She heard what they were saying aloud, but felt as if there were other, unheard, words being spoken behind their voices, in a language she did not understand. She wanted to find out more, to ask questions till she received a satisfying answer, but this was not her village, her family and clan, and she was no longer the petted child whose curiosity was casually indulged.

Ira, the young Levite, was back in Jerusalem. He had gone with his master, the old high priest Eviatar, to Gilgal, Gibeon and Beth-El, and other high places, to offer sacrifices and to sanctify altars and places of refuge.

Hearing that Ira had returned, Avishag waited for him in the cooking yard, but he did not come. Since he had left, a younger lad of the Levites prepared the food for the high priests, and now Ira was free of this duty. When the sun was about to set and still he did not appear, Avishag wrapped herself in a veil and went out of the fort to the Levites' tent, down by Araunah's threshing-floor. On her way there she saw how closely the guards surrounded the King's house. Small bands stood every few arms-lengths, while others paced, javelin in hand, back and forth between the bands. Like all the King's guards, they were Philistines, men from Gath and Ekron, who wore the Philistine helmets. Sensing the unease in the air, Avishag asked one of the gate guards to accompany her to the Levites' tent.

When they reached Araunah's threshing floor, the soldier stopped. As a Philistine he feared to go near the Ark, which had afflicted his people in Ashdod with the plague. Avishag, too, was afraid. She stooped and took off her sandals, for this was sacred ground, and drew the veil across her face. But when a strange Levite came forward and called out to her, "Woman, begone! This is holy ground!" she answered him boldly, though her heart was in her mouth: "I come from the King's house! Let me speak to Ira the Levite!"

Ira, who was at table when he was called out, was amazed by Avishag. He had last seen a girl who wandered about the King's house like a half-tamed doe. Now, though she was wary of the old Levites, whose harshness to women was well known, she all but commanded him to return to the King's house with her. Amused and curious, he excused himself to his elders and accompanied her.

"Yes, it is true," he said when they were seated. "Adoniyah asked the King to swear an oath before Yah to pass the throne to him. My master had shown Adoniyah the horn of oil with which old Samuel had anointed the King, and told him that it was kept in readiness for him. But the King only pledged his word and refused to swear an oath before Yah till he was fully restored to health. Therefore Adoniyah returned to his house in the Valley of Rephaim to look after his own estate."

"And the Great Lady? Does she hope to place her son on the throne?"

Ira looked about him carefully. They were seated on a stone ledge within the fort, with the garden and the women's quarters to their right. The darkness was relieved by the gate-guards' campfire and by light from the women's house, whence came sounds of song and laughter. But for slaves and maidservants walking to and fro between the wings of the King's house, they were alone.

"You must not speak about that!" Ira warned her in a low voice. "We hear that the Great Lady is urging the King to declare Yedidiah – whom she calls Shlomo – his heir. But the King refuses. Adoniyah has done no wrong. To set him aside, to deny him his right and put in his place the son of the Hittite's widow, would enrage Judah without appeasing the Israelites..." He fell silent. A young maidservant had stopped to hear their talk.

Avishag rose. She thanked Ira for his visit and prayed El to grant him a wholesome sacrifice on the morrow. The young Levite smiled to himself and turned to go. Until this evening he had known only the gossip of the Levites' tent. But now he learned something of which the others were ignorant – Avishag's place as the King's secret counsellor. For he doubted not that she was acting on her lord's behalf. But should he tell his master, Eviatar the high priest, or keep his peace? He decided to say nothing. Yah, the god of Judah, had sent the girl to the old King, to stand him in good stead with her quick wit and warm heart.

Chapter three

"I was fleeing from Saul," the King said. "Hiding behind a boulder, I waited for Jonathan and his boy. But it was Uriah the Hittite who came forward, all drenched in blood." His voice shook. "He tried to embrace me. He said Jonathan had sent him to warn me. I felt his bloodied hands clutching at my arms…"

The King was troubled by the nightmare. He rubbed his arms where the dream man's hands had touched him. Avishag rose and fetched a beaker of water, and when he had sipped of it, she moistened a cloth and passed it gently over his face, hands and arms.

"Why did King Saul wish to harm my lord?" the girl asked, seeing that the King was still brooding on his dream. "Did he not give my lord his daughter Michal in marriage?"

The King lay back with his eyes shut. Then he sighed and turned to look at the girl at his side. Curious as a child and soft as a woman, she had good understanding and often saw farther than most people.

"King Saul was possessed by an evil spirit," he replied, "a demon who tormented him. When in the demon's power, he saw the shadow of mountains as mountains, and all men as his enemies. He would hurl his javelin at the wall, believing someone was hiding behind it, ready to fall on him. Twice he almost killed his favourite son Jonathan, whom he loved more than himself. I was but a lad of sixteen years when I came to his service, and at first he liked me well. When I played the viol before him his demon would leave him in peace. Then he would raise his eyes and look about him, saying, 'Are you all here, my friends? Whom, then, did I see, grimacing and threatening me?'... His children Jonathan and Michal, Avner ben Ner and all about the King were pleased, and hoped that the demon had departed from him once and for all. As for me, I had never seen men and women so fine as Shaul's children – so handsome and so tall! The King himself in his youth stood head and shoulders taller than any man in the land, until his demon broke his back. Jonathan, his firstborn, was like one of the mighty men that the daughters of men bore to the sons of the gods. All the people loved him, and I too loved him better than myself. It was he who prevailed upon his father to betroth Michal to me, though she had been promised to Paltiel ben Laish. And she..."

The King paused. He remained silent for so long that Avishag thought he had fallen asleep. Though curious to hear more, she kept very still, so as not to disturb his old man's rest. Suddenly he stirred.

"Michal never forgave me," he said abruptly. "She saved my life once, when her father's men came for me, by putting an image in my bed and making believe I was ill. But she never forgave me for loving Jonathan better... As the song says, *'Love is fierce as death; jealousy is harsh as Sheol.'* That jealousy made her barren, and it was her barren womb which killed her in the end."

He shivered and made a horn sign with his left hand. The girl rose and fetched a woollen coverlet and spread it over her lord. He fell asleep, but Avishag lay awake, listening to the sounds of the guards as they paced around the King's house.

The King wanted to send Avishai ben Zeruiah, Yoav's brother, to accompany the Great Lady and her son to Shechem, but Bathsheva asked for Ittai the Gittite. The old Philistine captain of the guard had been with the King since his early days in the service of Achish, king of Gath, and had proved his devotion through many reversals. Unlike the sons of Zeruiah, he never disputed an order and never reproached the King. He chose a score of tried and trusted warriors from the household guard, and early one morning a great caravan of laden mules and asses, servants and armed men, left the King's house and began to wend its way northwards through the mountains.

That evening the King held a feast in his hall, with the women and older children about him, as well as his counsellors and captains. Even Yonadav was sufficiently recovered to make his way up the hill to the King's house. There were dancers and singers to entertain them and much sweet wine and strong ale. Avishag had never seen such a gay and attractive throng. She stood near the King to serve him, and many eyes were upon her, making her heart pound with sweet terror and pride.

The King was in good spirits that evening. He enjoyed the singing and the dancing, and even tried to play the viol, though he had not done so for the past year. But his hands had not recovered their skill and he desisted, saying firmly, "If it be the will of Yah, I shall play again." Nothing irked him, except Adoniyah's absence. A runner had been dispatched to his house in the valley of Rephaim, but the runner came back to report that the King's son was away from home, buying rams in Moab beyond the Jordan.

Avishag did not know all the men, nor even all the women who were gathered in the hall that night. There was a rare visitor from the south, a man honoured and loved by the King – the great warrior Benaiah, known as the Lion-slayer. A tall dark man with a sparse beard, his left arm hung stiff and withered at his side, as he had lost the use of it in battle many years before. There were also the King's son Shefatiah and his mother Avital, who lived in Hebron. They had come to Jerusalem with Shefatiah's new wife and daughter, to offer a thanksgiving sacrifice before the Ark. The wise woman,

Eglah the Edomite, who lived beside the sacred spring of Siloam on the far hill, was there too. The King wished to reward her for her good advice when he was ill.

He gave her a mantle of badger skins and a cup of polished agate with fishes carved around its base. "Stay in my house," he said to her, speaking in the broadest Judean. "Make this maiden your disciple," he added, pointing to Avishag. "Teach her your skills, for she is wise beyond her years."

Eglah observed the girl carefully and they looked into each other's eyes. A shiver passed through the girl and for a moment she did not hear the din of the crowded hall, as though she and Eglah were alone.

"If it please my lord," said the Edomite woman, "let the girl come and stay with me under the tamarisk by the sacred well of Siloam. There I could teach her many things."

The King was taken aback. He looked at the two women who stood facing each other. The Edomite was not old, but her face was a weather-beaten crag under her bonnet of skins, and her hands were like a raven's claws. She reeked of rancid butter and asafoetida. Beside her, the girl looked like the dawn, fresh and clear.

'No,' said the King, 'the girl will remain at my side.'

"Are you ready to fall upon your sword?" Yoav roared, bursting into the antechamber where the King was conferring with Yonadav, Adoram and the scribe Seraiah. They had been talking about the tribute and about the payment to Tyre for the cedar wood, which King Hiram had sent for the King's house. Yoav's stormy entrance startled them all. But Yonadav was the first to recover.

"Are you mad, Yoav?!" he said severely. The King, Yonadav and Yoav were kin, and had played together as children in Bethlehem. But whereas Yonadav had long since assumed the manner of a royal counsellor, the sons of Zeruiah had never learned to address David as the King. Yet it is doubtful that he would have been the King but for their ruthless devotion to him.

Yoav lowered his eyes and made a cursory bow. Then he burst out again.

"The Hittite widow is in Shechem," he growled, "conspiring against you. She is trying to rally the tribes of Israel to her side, to declare her son king over all the people... And you, my lord, allowed her to take a company of mercenary guards to the very citadel of the Israelites! And not one man of Judah with them!"

The King frowned and his face darkened, but he said not a word.

"And how did you hear of their plotting, Yoav?" asked Yonadav smoothly. "Have you spies among those people who reveal to you what is said in their secret counsels?"

"What is it to you, Yonadav? If the King chooses to favour his enemies and scorn his friends, as he has done before, I shall not stand idly by. A new conspiracy is afoot, as thick as that of –"

"Enough!" roared the King. "Say no more, Yoav!" His face turned very pale, then flushed dark.

The old warrior bowed, but did not desist. "And will you flee again from your city, David, as you did then?" he taunted. "Twenty years have passed, my lord. The lad, perhaps, may not be old enough to..."

The King stood up and would have struck Yoav, but Adoram and the scribe interposed themselves. Yoav stood his ground, unmoved by David's rage. He knew that the deed which Absalom had done on the roof of the King's house offended his father more than the rebellion itself. But it was necessary to make mention of it now. Time and again it had fallen to the sons of Zeruiah to provoke the King's wrath, or all would have been lost.

The two men glared at each other, while Yonadav urged the King to resume his seat on the dais. The scribe, Seraiah, was trembling, fearing for Yoav's life, for he had never seen anyone stand up to the King as did this gnarled old warrior. But it was the King who lowered his eyes first. He turned and resumed his place on the dais, leaning on his bolster with a weary air.

Silence fell. Yoav saw that his report was not lost on the King. Wordlessly, he undid his buckler, propped it against the wall and sat down. Yonadav smiled faintly in his beard and motioned to the scribe to offer the great captain a beaker of chilled water.

They waited for the King to utter the first words, but these were long in coming. At last he said, plaintively: "Are the tribes of Israel so discontented with my rule, that they would put a beardless boy in my place? Even if Yedidiah were not the son of the Hittite widow – has not Adoniyah a greater claim to inherit my throne?"

But his kinsmen understood that he no longer doubted. Now he would listen to his counsellors and look for a way to stop the conspiracy.

Yoav related all he knew. The Great Lady's caravan, he said, had attracted all the malcontents of Israel, who were chafing under the rule of Judah. Wherever the caravan stopped, the boy was brought out in his finest raiment, displaying the scarlet thread at his throat, to speak with the elders and give them gifts of great value. His mother kept out of sight, conferring only with some wise women and priestesses of the goddess Arinna, upon whom she also lavished gifts. Once arrived in Shechem, the King's son was asked to sit in judgement in a case which had plainly been prepared for him, a quarrel between two brothers over a well. When he gave his answer the people cheered and kissed their fingers to him, though it was a small matter and easily settled. Now every morning there were plaintiffs clamouring for him outside his mother's house, and the officers of the city had to drive them away, telling them to plead before the elders at the city gate.

"You had better act now, David, to crush this conspiracy before it gathers strength," concluded Yoav. "Else by the year's end another rebellion will erupt in Mount Ephraim." And catching Yonadav's eye, he added, "my lord!"

They then conferred gravely for a long time.

Avishag heard about it before the day was done. Yonadav sought her out, to warn her that the King was in a rage that could bring on his ailment. He had found the girl attentive and quick, and eager to listen to all his stories and ramblings. He knew that she had relieved Naamah of some of her duties, yet the old woman liked her well. But it was when the King told Eglah to teach the girl her skills that Yonadav realized Avishag's importance in her master's eyes. They spoke together at length, sitting in the garden in the shade of a sycamore, while the King's household dozed after the midday meal, and bees hummed among the flowering shrubs. The girl asked many questions about the matters that puzzled her, which the women either did not know or did not wish to tell her about, and the old man replied with unusual frankness.

"No one may mention the name of Absalom in the King's hearing. He was David's favourite – especially after Amnon, the first-born son, had done a vile thing to Tamar, who was his half-sister and Absalom's womb-sister. But after avenging his sister's honour by killing Amnon, Absalom fled to his grandfather's court in Geshur, and did not return for two years, nor did the King agree to see him for a long time after his return. Finally all was forgiven – Absalom had Yoav to thank for that – and all the people, Israelites and Judeans alike, believed Absalom to be their next king. But he was too hasty; he could not wait for the King to be gathered unto his forefathers... You know that his rebellion swept the whole country, and would have succeeded in supplanting the King, but for what happened in the grove of tamarisks. Absalom was caught by his hair between heaven and earth, and Yoav killed him... The King has never forgiven Yoav for this act, though it secured the throne for him. As for what Absalom did with the concubines on the roof... The King has not set eyes on them since that day... But you must know them, for they are the living widows sequestered in this women's house. The sons of Zeruiah would have had them killed, too, but David is soft-hearted with women."

Then Yonadav spoke of the Great Lady and her son. He did not believe that the Israelites would flock to Shlomo, no matter how many gifts they were given. His doubtful parentage made him far less suitable than any of the King's other sons. A Hittite on the throne of Judah and Israel? Yonadav thought this was unlikely, even though the Israelites were discontented with the dominance of Judah.

"But she is a cunning woman, and she has been laying plans for a long time. Now that the King is well again and spends some of his nights with her" – it seemed that there was no piece of household gossip that did not reach the old counsellor's ears – "she may persuade him to renew the promise to put her son on the throne. And the outcome...? These are interesting times, my child, are they not?' he concluded, patting her knee and winking.

"Behold, thou art fair, my love, thou art fair," he hummed under his breath, his gaze lingering over her face and neck. *"Thou hast dove's eyes..."*

The old song might have been written for her. He envied David. Perhaps if the King died soon...

Avishag bowed and raised the old man's hand to her forehead, thanking him for his confidence. She had listened attentively and her eyes told him that she did not miss a word he said and had taken it all in. She watched him as he waddled away slowly, shielding his eyes from the glare of the sun. She was glad that he had sought her out, though she knew that he did so as much from curiosity as from love and concern for his kinsman the King. The King esteemed him as a man of knowledge and wisdom, but Avishag saw that Yonadav loved himself above all.

Now she understood old Temimah's reclusive ways – she was one of the women whom the King had left to keep the house when he fled from Absalom's rebels. When the prince entered Jerusalem he followed Ahitophel's evil counsel – a tent was pitched on the roof of the King's house, and there, before the eyes of the people, Absalom lay with his father's concubines...

But though the King could not bear to set eyes on the ravished women, two of whom killed themselves for shame, yet he mourned bitterly for his rebellious son, and still repented that he had not ceded the throne to him... What would he do now that two sons claimed the throne, and the people's heart was divided?

That evening the King was amazed to hear that Yonadav, the wily counsellor who trusted no one, had talked so freely to the girl. She repeated what he had said, omitting only the mention of Absalom. The King was troubled and grim.

"The tribes of Israel are as unstable as water," he growled. "A stone in their path will turn them aside, a fallen branch will divert their course. When their own son Saul ben Kish, a Benjamite, ruled over them, they called on the men of Judah to help them drive out the Philistines. And when I and my men of Judah crushed their enemies, the daughters of Israel sang my praises: 'Saul hath slain his thousands, and David his ten thousands,' so offending their king and turning him against me. And did not their elders come to me in Hebron, grovelling and pleading: 'Behold, we are your bone and your flesh! We beg you, come and rule over all Israel!'?"

In the flickering light of the oil lamp his face looked heavy and tired, with a dark hue about his features and neck, which boded ill. The girl tried to make him more comfortable, but he stopped her with a gesture. He wished he could sleep, to enjoy at least in slumber the peace he had hoped to secure for his old age; but now even sleep rebelled against him. Thinking about the burden of kingship on an old man's shoulders brought back memories of his carefree youth, when his highest dream was to join King Saul's men for one good battle, then return in glory to Bethlehem and marry his cousin... It was then that he told Avishag about the time that Samuel, that fearsome old seer, came to Bethlehem, having been sent by God to choose one of Jesse's sons to anoint, even though Saul was still very much alive and his rule seemed firm.

"My father did not care for the old man, but he feared him and did not dare refuse to do his bidding. One by one he sent for my brothers, from the eldest Eliav – a huge man to this day, though he's old now and stooped – and Avinadav, the second – he died of a snakebite not long after – till at last they sent for me, the youngest and smallest. I was behind the house with my big sister, Zeruiah, waiting for the seer to depart, because the household was besieged by the Bethlehemites, who were curious to see old Samuel. He was greatly feared in those days, not only for his prophecies, but also for his terrible rages..."

The King smiled, "He hated kings and kingship, he wanted the people to be ruled by the elders and priests, but God made him anoint first one king and then another. Had he lived long enough he would doubtless have tried to unseat me also, as he tried to unseat Saul... I was a boy of twelve, the youngest of seven sons, and though my mother's favourite, I was the least likely to be considered, being small of stature, unlike my great brothers... When the old man took me by the chin and studied my face at length, he nodded, took a horn of oil from his mule's saddlebag and poured some on my head. He said words I did not understand, in some speech I never heard before or since, and departed soon after. He would neither eat nor drink at our house... My brothers were angry, till they decided that the old man had gone mad, and pretended that his madness infected me too. Only Zeruiah stood up for me. She always did... Was he so very old, I wonder? I think now that he was not as old as I am today."

Avishag was entranced. She knew the story about the secret anointing of the young David while Saul was king, but had heard people say that this was a falsehood spread by the Judean enemies of King Saul. Many questions leapt into her mind, but she saw that the King was tired and needed to rest, and resolved to ask him at a more opportune moment.

The King was lying with his eyes shut and seemed to be falling asleep when suddenly he spoke. "Tomorrow I shall go to Shiloh," he announced, "to offer a sacrifice to El. Too long have I offered all my sacrifices here in my city, failing in my duties to the Lord of the tribes of Israel at his ancient high place. Perhaps the oracle will guide my steps."

Comforted by the thought of Shiloh, he fell into a light sleep, though deep rest eluded him. He sighed and moaned, turned from side to side, troubled by unwelcome dreams. The girl lay quietly, her slumber light as a feather. When the cool light of dawn entered the chamber and the King stirred, Avishag was up and ready to serve him. If he allowed her, she would accompany him to Shiloh.

A rams' horn was sounded when the King arrived in Shiloh, rallying the people of the surrounding country to their king. The elders of the clans of the House of Joseph hastened to the shrine, excited by his presence among them at El's ancient place of worship. From dawn to dusk they crowded around his tent, clamouring to feast their eyes upon their great defender from the Philistines, the slayer of ten thousand, the scion of the house of Boaz.

David was greatly cheered by the warm response of the Ephraimites, knowing only too well how sly and fickle the Israelites could be. Beside him old Nathan, clad in a mantle of pelts, received homage as the foremost seer in the land since their own Ephraimite Samuel. Moved by the spirit of the place, Nathan raised his arms and cried out in the great echoing voice of prophecy: "Thine house and thy kingdom shall be established for ever before thee: thy throne shall be established for ever!" And the people cheered.

But the oracle of Shiloh was not so forthcoming. Its ancient *hoshen* with the breastplate of sapphires, which had served the priests of Shiloh for divination since the days of the Forefathers, gave no clearer answer than the seer's broad promise. The King was disappointed and redoubled his devotions. A year-old red heifer was sacrificed, half its blood sprinkled upon the altar and the other half upon the congregation. Then its carcass was burnt to ashes, which were stirred with water for the purification of the suppliants. And still the oracle made no mention of Adoniyah, nor of any other successor to David upon the joint throne of Judah and Israel.

They remained at Shiloh for a week, and the King's tent was constantly thronged with people. The elders vied with one other for the honour of serving him, and the grove priestesses washed his hands and feet. Avishai ben Zeruiah – younger than Yoav, but even more taciturn and stiff-necked – remained at David's side day and night. Avishag made herself a nook in a corner of the tent, and contented herself with observing the people who came to see the King. She also saw the *bamah,* the high place, where the people had worshipped El since the days of the Forefathers, and was awed by its size. The stone enclosure around it was large enough to contain a whole village. No one ever entered it with shod feet, yet the ground within had been tamped down to the hardness of rock by generations of worshippers. The blackened altar was flanked by two great winged figures, the cherubim, the like of which she had never seen. Yet the people came and went about the enclosure, fearlessly, as though it were an everyday matter.

On the last night the King dismissed all his visitors and attendants, and called for Avishag. He was weary. The pilgrimage had not given him the assurance he had hoped for, though it confirmed the loyalty of the Israelites. The girl was glad to be recalled to her master's side. Since leaving Jerusalem she had not been alone with the King. Cheerfully she brought him chilled sweetened water and little cakes of ground almonds – for leavened bread was forbidden at Shiloh – and prepared his couch for the night.

"Three nights from this," said the King, "the new moon will be born. You may remain here and take part in the consecration. The grove priestesses will welcome you gladly."

"If my lord wishes, I will remain," she replied, crestfallen.

The King laughed. An invitation to take part in the consecration of the new moon at Shiloh, under the protection of its priestesses, was a rare honour. Yet the girl preferred to refuse the offer rather than leave his side. "No," he said, gratified. "It is for you to choose, my child."

"Then by your leave, my lord, I would rather return with you to the King's city."

The night was peaceful. In place of the clanking arms of the guards circling the fort, the only sounds here were the hoots of the owls flying out of the grove to hunt, and the distant barking of dogs in the village of Shiloh. The age-old sanctity of the place, the influence of God's great winged bearers, filled the place with a deep quietness, quite unlike the wild enthusiasm that the Ark inspired in its surroundings.

"Many years ago," began the King, and Avishag crept closer, for he spoke softly, "in the days of the Judges, this shrine served Judah as well as all the Israelite tribes. The Ark stood here then, in a great tabernacle that was called the House of Jacob. When the Israelites fought the Philistines at Afek, the Levites sent them the Ark to protect them, but they were defeated and the Ark was lost. The Philistines carried it to Ashdod and laid it as a trophy before Dagon in his temple. But then the Ark began to plague them grievously, so they took it to their other cities, first to Gath and then to Ekron... And still the Elohim afflicted them with a plague of mice and deadly buboes. At last the Philistines' priests and mages told them to send the Ark back to the land of Judah, and to propitiate it with golden images of mice and buboes – one for each of their cities. And so they did. They laid the Ark and a coffer with the golden offerings upon a newly-made cart, and harnessed to it two milch cows. They chained their calves behind, to test the divine will, but the cows took the straight way to Beth Shemesh, walking along the highway, lowing as they went, turning neither right nor left! The lords of the Philistines were amazed and followed them to the very border of Beth Shemesh... The people of Beth Shemesh were harvesting their wheat in the valley, when they lifted their eyes and lo! There was the Ark, coming back. They could hardly believe their eyes. They laid it upon their great stone, and offered sacrifices of thanksgiving to the Elohim. But soon the people of Beth Shemesh too were plagued and many of them died, because they had looked into the Ark when they moved it. They cried to God bitterly, and at last carried the Ark to Kiryat Yearim, where Samuel propitiated it."

"And what happened to Kiryat Yearim, my lord? Did the Ark plague the people there, too?"

"No. Kiryat Yearim neither suffered nor prospered," said David. "I knew that it was Samuel's custom to sacrifice to the Elohim at all the holy shrines – at Beth-El, Gilgal, Mitzpah and Shiloh – but only once in seven years before the Ark. Now the seer Gad told me to carry the Ark to the land of Judah, therefore I took it to Baalei Yehudah, where it remained for many years. When I became king of Israel as well as of Judah, I wished to bring the Ark to my new city, to seal the covenant between all our tribes and the god of Abraham, Isaac and Jacob. But fearing the power of the Ark, I sent it first to the house of a captain of my guard, a Gittite. Only when I saw that he prospered did I bring it to Jerusalem… Thirty thousand chosen men accompanied it with great jubilation. Then, as the Ark came into the city, Shaul's daughter Michal, the wife of my youth, looked down from her window, for by then she was ailing and could not leave her apartment. All the people were dancing and singing, playing upon instruments, and I also danced and leaped before the Ark, singing the praises of the Elohim. Shaul's daughter saw me and she despised me in her heart. Later she taunted me, saying, 'How glorious was the King of Israel today, leaping and dancing, exposing himself before the slaves and serving maids, as one of the vain fellows!'"

The King imitated Michal's jeering voice and smiled to see the girl's shocked face.

"But I answered Michal," he went on calmly, "I said, 'I will play before God, who chose me above your father and before all his house, to appoint me ruler over the people of Judah and Israel. And if it be vile, I will yet be more vile!' But then I ceased to reproach her, for she was ailing and soon after this she died."

When the King returned to his city, he found the Great Lady and her son back in their apartment in the upper storey of his house, as though they had never been away. Yoav ben Zeruiah spoke with the King privately, then he and his brother Avishai went to Mount Ephraim, to quell the embers of rebellion that Bathsheba had kindled. But the King knew that the sons of Zeruiah were heavy-handed, and he took counsel also with Yonadav and some old Levites, whose ways were more subtle.

Avishag was at the King's side when the Great Lady and her son came to sup with him. Yonadav, the King's counsellor, and Seraiah the scribe, were also in the hall. Knowing what had taken place since she had last seen her, Avishag wondered at the Great Lady's calm demeanour. As for Yedidiah-Shlomo, he made a deep obeisance to his father, and then seated himself on a low hassock beside his mother. The King asked Bathsheba about her journey and thanked her for the wine and oil she had brought from her estate.

He asked his son about the judgement he had given in Shechem, and the boy was not disconcerted but answered aptly and modestly.

Avishag served the King while Naamah and the slaves served the others. The King appeared to be drinking a great deal of wine, and only the girl knew that his wine had been diluted with pomegranate water. Yonadav, red in the face and short of breath, said – speaking as they usually did in Judean –

"My lord, did not the wise woman warn you against drinking much wine?"

"By your looks, Yonadav," joked the King, "'tis you not I whom wine has befuddled. Like our forefather Judah, your eyes are red with wine. But while his teeth were white as milk, your remaining stumps, brother, can scarcely grind bread soaked in milk!"

Yonadav laughed but darted a look of surprise at Avishag. It was not David's way to taunt his guests, not even his near kinsmen with whom he did not stand on ceremony. But Avishag understood that the King wished to appear as though he had drunk too much wine.

"The autumn festival shall soon be upon us," said the King, reclining upon the dais. "Time to pray for rain…" he added in a drowsy voice and closed his eyes. The Great Lady and her son gazed at him, intent and unmoving. Sitting side by side in their fine apparel, both ivory-skinned and dark-eyed, they were, thought Avishag, like a leopardess and her whelp, crouching before they leapt.

Without opening his eyes the King said: "I have sent my son Adoniyah to Gibeon, to carry the bones of the seven impaled men, the remnant of Shaul's house, for burial in the country of Benjamin."

Silence fell. The King appeared to have fallen into a doze, and his guests held their breath. Suddenly he opened his eyes and sat up.

"Yedidiah may come with me," he said to Bathsheva pleasantly, "when I go to meet my son Adoniyah at the sepulchre of Shaul's house, to lay these last bones with their fathers'. There we shall offer a sacrifice to the Elohim, to seal the peace between our tribes… That should please you, Yedidiah my son, seeing that you are both of Israel and Judah!"

The boy rose eagerly and pressed his father's hand to his forehead, thanking him for the honour. His mother's countenance remained smooth and untroubled and she too thanked the King cordially, for this would be the first time her son would appear before the people at his father's side. Old Yonadav looked from the King to the others and passed his hand over his face, as though to wash it.

"Well, my child?" said the King.

After his guests had left the King went up to the roof to cool his brow in the evening breeze before going to his bed. It had been a sultry day, and even after the sun had set, the dry heat of the desert baked the city as in a kiln. Avishag followed her lord to the roof and sat at his feet. The sounds of the King's house preparing for the night came up faintly – a crying child, a scolding mother, slaves squabbling around the garden cistern in the back.

The King stroked the girl's head and waited for her questions.

"Why, my lord?" she asked. "Why go now to the country of the Benjamites to bury old bones?" After all that had happened, she could not understand the King's willingness to go into the very citadel of his enemies.

"I am the captain of the people, but I am also their father," he replied in that gentle voice which only Avishag heard. "A father must sometimes chastise his children, but he must also listen to their cry, even if they disobey him. The sons of Zeruiah have gone to Mount Ephraim, and they will seize those who seek to destroy me and my house. But the discontent of the Benjamites and the pride of Ephraim cannot be quenched by force alone. They have not forgotten their King Saul and his son Jonathan. And though I had their bones brought from Jabesh-Gilead and laid to rest in their fathers' sepulchre – where my lament for them is carved upon a pillar for all time – still the Israelites chafe under my rule. By bringing the bones of the seven impaled men to the same sepulchre I hope to quiet their tumult. My son Adoniyah will also honour them. He will remain awhile in their midst and take a wife from one of their foremost clans."

A young moon girdled with haze rose and dimmed the stars. Now and then bats flitted silently across the roof. But the King and the girl sat securely under the canopy.

"Who were the seven impaled men, my lord?" asked the girl, whose curiosity remained unsatisfied. The King was surprised – he had thought all the world knew about them.

"Have they not told the story in Jezreel? Or perhaps you did not hear it, being a child…'

She saw that he was reluctant to cast his mind back to those events, but he took a deep breath and told her that dreadful story, which still sent chills down men's backs.

"Many years ago the people of Gibeon entered into league with the tribes of Israel, offering them Gibeon's high place in return for their protection against marauders. For the Gibeonites are a priestly tribe, like the Levites, and their shrine is ancient and holy. Some say that they won the treaty by deceit, pretending to have come from far away, for fear of Joshua and his host. But in truth, it is their custom to go about clothed in rough wool tunics and to live on alms and dried bread. Hence the Levites can offer sacrifices at Gibeon, but only the Gibeonites may draw the water and hew the wood for the high place, and so it has been since time immemorial.

"Now when Saul was King and was warring with the Philistines, he broke the covenant with the Gibeonites, believing that they were treating with the Philistines behind his back. He attacked Gibeon and seized seven of their elders and impaled them on the hill facing the shrine. Thereafter the oracle of Gibeon fell silent, and the Gibeonites withheld their services at the high place. No more sacrifices were held there while Saul lived. When I became King in Jerusalem, ruling over Judah and Israel, there was famine in the land for three years. Little rain fell and the harvests were poor. Then the seer Nathan revealed that atonement must be made for the crime of Saul against the Gibeonites. But the Gibeonites refused to take silver or gold or any such recompense, saying, 'Let seven men of Shaul's sons be delivered unto us, and we will impale them before our god upon the hill.'

"I spared Meribaal, the son of Jonathan, because of the oath I swore to his father…" The King paused and again drew a deep breath. The memory of Jonathan, like that of Absalom, always gave him pain. The girl waited. The King sighed deeply and rubbed his eyes. Then he went on.

"I took Shaul's two sons that were borne him by the priestess Rizpah and the five sons borne by Merav, Shaul's eldest daughter, to her husband Adriel, and delivered them into the hands of the Gibeonites, who impaled them on the hill at the beginning of the barley harvest. Rizpah, who was a priestess of Aiah, hung sackcloth over them and watched them day and night, to keep off the birds by day and the beasts of the field by night, until they had dried. Then the rains came, plentiful rains, and ended the famine. But the bones have remained on the hill to this day."

"Will Rizpah come to the burial of her sons' bones?"

"If the Benjamites so wish, they may send for her. But she is very old now, and lives in the grove of Aiah where no man is allowed to enter. Even if she is still alive, she may not hear of it in time… But I do not wish to see Rizpah, who has not ceased to stir her people against my house. Only the fear of that grove and its powers stopped the sons of Zeruiah from cleaving her in two like a log of wood."

While the King was away in the country of Benjamin his house and his city were closely guarded. The guards, under the command of Ittai the Gittite, circled the King's house day and night, but the defence of the city was entrusted to the warriors of Judah. By night their bonfires burned on the hillsides, and by day the warriors roamed the city, demanding provisions and eyeing the women.

Avishag moved her pallet to the chamber shared by Temimah and Naamah. She feared for the King and was ill at ease without him. The women of the house spoke in subdued voices and kept their children beside them. The Egyptian wife of Adoniyah, heavily pregnant, came down from her fine chamber, humbled by her fears, like any young woman about to give birth to her first child. The women, mothers and crones alike, were kind to her and tried to calm her fears. She listened to them avidly, but her terrors remained deep in her heart. She had heard that the Hebrews sacrificed their firstborn sons and the women's assurances did not set her mind at ease. While the King was in his house and her husband Adoniyah was nearby, she had felt secure, but now she wandered about the women's house and courtyards, her hair loosened, wringing her hands and crying, and would not let her maidservants come near her.

Avishag sought out the young priest Ira. He had all but taken over old Eviatar's duties, and before long would succeed him as high priest. Nevertheless, when Avishag sent for him he came at once to the fort and they talked at length. At her request, he agreed to speak to the Egyptian woman to assure her that her child would not be sacrificed.

"We hold no child sacrifices in David's city," he said. "Our firstborn are sacrosanct to God, but may be redeemed by the sacrifice of a firstborn lamb or calf. Elsewhere in the land a firstborn son is sometimes be sacrificed when a new house is built, and then buried under its cornerstone. But it has not always been the custom of Judah, nor does the King wish it in his city."

"But the kiln!" Titipah wailed. "Did not the King put the Ammonite children at Rabbah in a kiln? Will he not order to burn my child, an Egyptian child, likewise?"

When they understood her – for her speech was strange – Ira explained that the Ammonites' children were sacrificed when they were defeated, in keeping with the custom of their country and the worship of Moloch. The Egyptian listened and grew calmer. Later old Temimah took her by the hand and made her rest, and thereafter remained at her side until she came to term.

"And you too, my sister," said Ira to Avishag when they parted at the gate, "you need not fear for the King or for yourself. The King will return in triumph, and his son will be accepted by all the people. For the oracle has said that the House of David shall rule in Jerusalem for evermore."

Chapter four

The King's city was in a frenzy of preparations for the autumn festival. Thousands of pilgrims from far and wide would soon pour in and overflow to the surrounding hills. The officers of the city ordered stores of water and firewood to be made ready, and trenches dug for the waste. Some of the inhabitants received regular visitors, with whom they had family ties, while others hired out their roofs and courtyards in exchange for food or other provender. The King's house was preparing for numerous visitors, members of the House of David and of the many families with which it was allied by marriage. This time there was more room to accommodate them, for a new wing overlooking the valley of Hinnom had lately been built. The Levites laboured to cleanse the sacred precinct of Araunah's threshing-floor, with its tabernacle and the great altar. They spread fresh willow and myrtle boughs on the ground and planted cedar poles around it, to support a canopy of palm fronds. If the prayers for rain were answered, the first showers of the season would fall upon the canopy while it was yet green.

The King had returned from the country of Benjamin more

sanguine than when he had set out. Either the Israelites were not so mutinous as Yoav ben Zeruiah had claimed, or the King's appearance among them was enough to quiet their tumult, as he had hoped it would. After burying the bones of the seven impaled men, he stayed to join Adoniyah's hand with that of a Benjamite maiden and to bless their union on the first day of the marriage feast. Adoniyah remained in the land of Benjamin with his new bride and would return in time for the autumn rites.

Avishag helped the women with their preparations. Fresh hangings and beddings for their chambers, new gowns and sandals, gold and silver ornaments taken from little caskets hidden in crannies, kept them all preoccupied. Only the old women looked after the children, having little cause to adorn themselves for the occasion. The virgins of the King's house and two or three young widows took the greatest pains with their hair and raiment. The King's hall would be full of guests for three days and three nights, and many marriages were arranged at such events.

Avishag was engaged in weaving glass beads into the braids of Naomi, one of the King's granddaughters, when she was called to the forecourt. Coming out into the bright sunlight, she was dazzled for a moment and could not believe her eyes: her father, her big brother Ornan and her little brother Nadav stood before her, with Ornan's young wife peering shyly over his shoulder.

When the first greetings were over she led her family to the garden and herself drew water to wash their feet. She struggled to contain her tears. Her visitors were awed by their surroundings, never having visited David's city before.

"These mountains," said Baanah ben Ahilud with a sweep of his arm, "these mountains are not like our mountains. They are higher and stonier... 'Tis a harsh country, the patrimony of Judah. But you, my daughter," he added, taking her face by the chin and raising it, "you are flourishing here like a tree that grows beside a stream."

Presently they were joined by their old steward, Amos, who fetched their saddlebags, which were filled with the fruits of Jezreel, the like of which were not seen in Jerusalem. There were gifts for the King – a handsome painted cask full of fig nectar, and a snowy white coverlet made from the fleece of a rare kind of goat which they of the north were beginning to breed. For Avishag there was a new woollen mantle, woven for her by her mother. At the sight of it the girl could no longer contain her tears, but broke down and wept on Ornan's breast.

They told her that the King himself had bid the family from Shunem to come for the autumn festival as his guests. Moreover, the girl would be allowed to go home with them for a month.

Avishag had almost forgotten how close she and Ornan had been before she came to Jerusalem. Now she rejoiced to find that his wife Sarai – a sweet-faced brown maid from the Gilboa, the grand-daughter of an old companion of her grandfather Ahilud – had not caused him to forget his sister. As for little Nadav, he had grown since she had last seen him. Though only twelve, he was now nearly as tall as Avishag, and was comely like all the offspring of Ahilud. Watching him, she wondered if she might bring him to the Great Lady's apartment, to meet the boy Yedidiah-Shlomo... Together, she thought, they would be like the sun and the moon – Nadav dark and brilliant, Shlomo pale and cool. If the King allowed it, she would call upon the Great Lady in the morning.

But Nadav had a painful prospect in store for him, which made him less playful and talkative than usual. Before leaving Jerusalem he would be circumcised by the Levites, and the thought of it made him pout and hold back his tears.

Ornan assured his little brother that the ordeal was not as painful as his older friends boasted. "They wish to appear braver than they are," he said.

But Avishag, who had heard the screams of the boys from the Levites' tent during the spring festival, was less confident.

"I shall give you wine flavoured with myrrh, to make you

drowsy," she promised the boy, hugging him to her breast. "In the King's house the boys are circumcised when they are small, but wine flavoured with myrrh eases their pain."

That evening the King could hardly speak for weariness. Avishag kissed his hands, and making no attempt to hide her tears, she thanked him for bringing her family to the city. Then she asked if she might take her younger brother to the Great Lady's apartment. The King nodded and patted her head, then fell into a heavy slumber. His face and neck were no longer mottled and dark as they had been before his recent journey, and his hands were cool, but the girl feared that he was not well. Though a year had passed since he had fallen, Eglah the Edomite had warned that he would be weakest when the seasons changed. Tired as she was, Avishag tried to watch over him, but before the house had fully quieted down she was fast asleep.

The Great Lady was graciously pleased to have Nadav visit her son. She invited the lad to lodge in her apartments and offered to tend him after the circumcision. So it came about that the two boys, accompanied by Avishag and an old Hittite steward, witnessed the casting of the lots upon the two he-goats, one of which would be consecrated to El Shaddai and the other to Azazel.

All the sacrificial cattle were penned together down in the valley of Kidron, in a pleasant willow grove near the brook. The ram for the burnt offering and the bull for the sin offering had had their horns gilded and they stood apart, as though they knew their own importance. There were also year-old calves and heifers, goats and their kids and many sheep, making a powerful din together. A Levite boy was piling fresh hay before them, and when he saw the young prince and his companions he ran out and offered to show them the twin he-goats. Kept apart behind some staves, they were fine-looking beasts with unblemished horns and hooves and long white pelts. They stood side by side, their heads lowered as though to butt, their yellow eyes fixed upon the visitors.

"Bide here a while, masters," the young Levite said ingratiatingly, "while I tell the priests that you wish to see the casting of the lots."

Avishag was uncertain, but Shlomo was eager to see the rite and Nadav imitated his host in everything. While they waited in the shade of the willows the Hittite steward fetched water from the spring in a brass jar. A bird sang overhead and the incessant chirp of the grasshoppers in the glaring sunlight made them all drowsy. Suddenly Avishag heard someone call her name. It was Ira, though she did not know him at once. He was dressed in the holy-day garb of a high priest – a striped coat with linen breeches and a high cloth turban on his head – and he walked sedately down the path to meet them.

"Ira! Are you a high priest now?" she asked, surprised.

"Not yet," he replied, "but Eviatar is ailing, and Zadok is at the threshing-floor, seeing to its purification. I shall cast the lots," he added proudly. He took a cloth pouch from the breast of his coat and shook from it upon his palm some knucklebones marked with curious symbols. He held them up and asked the King's son to pick two. The boy grew tense. He stared at the bones as though reading their signs – and perhaps he did, as he was very learned. At length he chose two, and Ira replaced the others in the pouch.

"Might I also choose the he-goat?" Shlomo asked the priest.

"Nay, my lord," replied Ira, smiling. "That is why we cast lots – El and Azazel will choose their own."

The Levite boy separated the he-goats. They had been standing still, only their tails twitching, but they bleated sharply when he tethered them far apart. Ira approached one and held the knucklebones over its head, intoning a prayer to El to choose his own. Avishag saw Shlomo clasping his hands together tightly until the fingers turned dark red. He stepped aside, so that he stood equally far from either beast. His lips moved, as though he too were praying. And suddenly Avishag knew that he was pleading for the he-goat to his right to be chosen by El.

Ira shook the dice between his cupped hands. Then he opened

his palms and read the signs. He repeated the rite over the other he-goat. Their fate was sealed and he pronounced it solemnly. Shlomo flushed and tossed his head high, fingering the scarlet thread at his throat. El had given him a favourable omen.

Now the he-goats had to be kept apart. The one chosen by El had a brass bell tied around its neck, and the one dedicated to Azazel had a bone amulet to mark it. Though twins, their fate would be very different: the first would be sacrificed joyously on the great altar before the Ark, while the second, burdened with all the sins of the multitude, would be driven out into the wilderness under a hail of stones and curses... Shlomo, once more calm and smiling, took gracious leave of Ira and the young acolyte and led the way up the path to the King's house. Avishag looked back and saw Ira standing between the he-goats, gazing after the four of them as they walked up the hill. Did he know what the King's son had done? And did the he-goat dedicated to Azazel really have a cast in one eye, or did she imagine it?

Avishag had thought that once under her father's roof she would again be a child, her mother's only surviving and cherished daughter, her grandfather's favourite. But the intervening year had changed her – or so the others thought. Like an honoured guest, a visitor from the King's house, she was not allowed to help in the cooking yard or in the fields.

Some light rain had already fallen on the parched fields and breathed freshness into the woods. The fig trees and the vines were shedding their leaves and the first storks arrived, to rest a while on their journey from the far north to the Land of the Nile. Avishag spent the first few days under her father's roof clinging to her mother and to Ornan and his wife. She took pleasure in the chores that they allowed her to do, and especially enjoyed sitting at the old loom beside her mother. The evenings were cool enough for a twig fire to be lit upon the hearth, and she relished its familiar scent.

At the end of a week she rode, accompanied by the steward Amos, to her grandfather's house on the other side of the valley. She was bringing him greetings from the King and an invitation to come to Jerusalem and bide there as his guest.

"Tell Ahilud that I am old and wish to pay my debts before I am gathered unto my fathers," the King had said. "I am doubly in his debt – firstly, for not joining the Benjamite rebellion, and secondly, for sending you, my child, to gladden my remaining days." She had promised to repeat those very words to her grandfather.

Ahilud was the first elder of his clan, a great man in Jezreel. He had been a renowned captain in the wars with the Philistines and the Aramaeans, and now in his old age his judgement was sought in matters that confounded lesser men. He received his granddaughter with joy and pride, and made her sit at his side, as though she were a wise woman of twice her years. That evening, sitting among Ahilud's fellow elders, Avishag heard what the people of Israel said about the King and his sons.

"The King is old," they all said. "He has not many years left. It is time he chose his heir, so that the Children of Israel may know…"

But none of them said what they expected, or wished, the King to say.

"What do they wish to know, Grandfather?" Avishag asked later, aware that the elders had been careful not to speak too openly in her presence.

Ahilud peered at the girl thoughtfully. One of his eyes was completely covered by a white scale and the other one, too, was dimmed. But the girl's face was known and dear to him, and he would have been able to see it even if he had gone quite blind. Her voice revealed her disquiet, not like that of a fearful child, but rather like an elder or a wise woman who sees beyond the present and is troubled by the prospect.

"There are some in the house of Israel," the old man said, "who will always cry, 'We have no part in David, nor any inheritance in Judah. Every man to his tents, O Israel!' This cry has been heard before. If the rains fail and the harvest is poor, the King is blamed. Or if the tribute gatherers lay a heavy hand on the people, or are corrupt, as the sons of Eli the high priest were corrupt in past times – the King is blamed. And some of our people still regret the ending of Sheva ben Bichri's revolt… Yet it is plain that the son of Jesse is favoured by the Elohim, and has emerged stronger from all his adversities. Nor have we forgotten that he defeated the enemies of Israel. Therefore, while David rules, Judah rules, and there will be no more rebellions. Now that he has placated the Benjamites by burying the bones of the impaled men, no one will raise a hand against his grey head. But he is old and it is said that he is frail – who will come after him? Do you know, my child? Has he said whom he favours to succeed him?"

"He has not sworn an oath, Grandfather, but he has said that it must be Adoniyah ben Haggith."

The old man was silent for a long time. His dimmed gaze was drawn to the flickering embers on the hearth and Avishag knew that his thoughts dwelt on past battles, defeats and triumphs. He had known the King when they were both young men, and the elders of his day remembered the days of the Judges, before there were kings in Israel or Judah.

As though he heard her thoughts, Ahilud said: "My father was a young lad when the seer Samuel warned against the King. Not this King, nor Saul ben Kish, but any king. For our fathers were ruled by judges, some of whom were good and some bad, but not all were warriors. That is why the people clamoured for a king, to judge us and lead us in battle. Then old Samuel told them the manner of the King that shall reign over us, how he would take a tenth of all our harvests and take our sons and daughters and our cattle and put them to his work. 'Beware,' said Samuel, 'for in that day ye shall cry out because of the King that ye shall have chosen you.'"

Avishag was shocked. "Grandfather! Do you repent sending me to the King?"

The old man collected himself. "Nay, child!" He put his hand on her head. "I do not repent it. You have brought honour to my house and solace to the King. These are but an old man's wanderings… Our people were right to demand a king, for without one we were like chaff, scattered by all the winds that blow upon the earth. And David ben Yishai has been a mighty captain and a righteous judge… But Adoniyah ben Haggith, the son of a priestess of Yah? He is wholeheartedly a man of Judah, and the sons of Zeruiah are his arms and legs. He has been heard to say that if David chastised Israel with whips, he will chastise us with scorpions."

Silence fell. A great sadness came over Avishag.

"Whom then would you have, Grandfather?" she asked at last.

The old man frowned. "Not a year has passed since you went to the King's house, and already you say, 'Whom would you have?' Are you not an Israelite yourself…?" The girl waited, unabashed, and he went on. "My child, I am not a seer, nor have I an *ephod* to foretell the future. But the Children of Israel have no faith in Adoniyah ben Haggith, and you may say this to the King."

Ahilud's wife, Yocheved, kept to her chamber in the upper storey of the house. She had lost the use of her legs when she gave birth to her last child. A huge baby, like those borne by the giantess, he died as soon as he drew breath, but his mother never walked again. Women from all over the valley and farther afield came to seek her advice in matters of family and women-lore.

When Avishag came to see her, Yocheved dismissed her handmaids and sent away her visitors. Holding the girl's face between her hands she gazed into her eyes. Not a word was said, but a moment later a broad smile spread over her furrowed brown face and she embraced and kissed her granddaughter. She had sent a virgin into a man's bed, not to please a king – she cared little for such things – nor to gain a strong alliance for her clan by an astute marriage. A great devotee of the goddess, her purpose was deeper and farther than that of the men, and although barely a year had passed, she saw what she had hoped to see in her granddaughter's face, and felt that her purpose would prosper.

They talked at length and sang together, undisturbed, for

Ahilud never climbed to the upper storey unless Yocheved sent for him. He had lived long and knew better than to provoke the goddess Anath, whose image dominated his wife's chamber

Early on the third day, before the sun rose, Avishag left her grandfather's house to return to Shunem. She cried when she parted from Ahilud and Yocheved, for she knew she might never see them again. In her saddlebags were two precious gifts. One was for the King – an agate seal, minutely engraved, which when rolled over wet clay impressed it with a raised figure of the sun god rending a lion with his bare hands. It was the work of a Danite craftsman who lived thereabouts. The other gift she would deliver on her way back to Jerusalem.

At the end of the month she had to leave Shunem once again to go to the King's city. No more a frightened village maiden, but a denizen of the King's house, she begged them all to come to Jerusalem for the spring festival. By then Ornan's wife would have given birth, and if the child lived, a sacrifice for a firstborn might be offered upon the great altar.

Accompanied by a maidservant and the two men sent by the King to guard her, she rode first to Deborah's Palm in Mount Ephraim, to deliver Yocheved's gift to the priestess Dinah.

Dinah, who dwelt under Deborah's giant palm tree, claimed descent from that prophetess and was a great woman among the Israelites. Unlike her ancestress, who had led the tribes in the war against Hazor, Dinah cared little for captains and kings. She served the powerful oracle Nehushtan, the brazen serpent fashioned by Moses to heal the Israelites in the wilderness. Until the death of old Samuel it had been kept in Ramah, the seer's high place, but thereafter was given a sanctuary of its own at Deborah's Palm. A cloud of incense smoke hung perpetually over the sanctuary, for no other offering was allowed there – beasts were not sacrificed, meat was not eaten nor was wine consumed within the precinct.

The tabernacle under the palm tree was small and dark and filled with smoke and sharp odours. Avishag paused, her eyes stinging, and waited for a sign. Then she saw in the far wall a low doorway beyond which twinkled firelight. Nehushtan dwelt in a cavern to which the tabernacle was the porch. Deep inside, lit only by the flames of a brazier, it reared up on its staff, glistening and fearsome. The priestess Dinah came forward to greet the girl and accept the gift of sweet frankincense sent by Yocheved.

Dinah was neither young nor old. Her tangled locks were grey, but her face, which had the pallor of the cavern upon it, was unlined. She was taller than Avishag and almost fleshless, but vigorous and good-humoured. She soon put her young visitor at ease, and obtained answers to all her questions. In her turn, she replied graciously to all the questions the girl put to her; yet after a while she became grave and her mien forbidding.

"The men of Judah are stiff-necked and overweening," she said, holding the girl's hands between her hot, dry palms. Her voice resounded like iron in the cavern. "Yah, their chosen god, is likewise jealous of the other gods and cares only for his own honour. He has seized possession of the shrines of many Baalim in Judah, and would do the same for El Elyon, the god of Jerusalem, only the Levites are afraid. But most of all he is jealous of the goddess, and would drive her out of the land if he could…"

She closed her eyes and remained silent for a long time. Her face turned even paler and her hands grew cold. Avishag tried to withdraw her hands from Dinah's grasp but could not. Not daring to move, she was also afraid to remain where she was. The cavern was quiet. Lit by the dancing flames of the brazier, the serpent's fanged mouth seemed to stir.

Suddenly Dinah shook herself, opened her eyes and smiled at the girl. Her teeth were long and yellow, like the teeth of a mule.

"There is an ancient Ashera in Jerusalem," she said pleasantly. "Let not the King forget her. She was there before El Elyon of the Jebusites, and some say she was his mother. Who fails to honour the goddess will live to rue the day he was born…"

She let go Avishag's hands and patted her cheek. Gone was the clangour of her voice. She might have been speaking of family matters, of cattle or food. She told Avishag to sprinkle a little of Yocheved's frankincense on the brazier before Nehushtan, then she gave her a bronze amulet fashioned like a coiled serpent. No man, the priestess assured Avishag, could force a virgin who wore it between her breasts. After this, Avishag left her and rode back to the King's city, stopping nowhere except to eat and rest.

The days were now shorter and the nights cooler. Light showers fell on the parched mountains and clothed them in a fresh green coat. The harvest had been ample, the granaries were full. Now for the next winter's rains. The people heaped the altars with offerings of plump pigeons and cakes of fine flour mixed with oil, and hung blue-stained fleeces on treetops to attract the rain-bearing clouds.

As he regained his strength, the King's confidence grew. He heard the words the elder Ahilud had put in the girl's mouth and he nodded, but made no overt move. Adoniyah came often to the King's house and helped to judge the people at his father's side. He also went to the country of Benjamin, to bring home his new wife Hannah. She had remained a while under her father's roof, to assure the Benjamites of the King's good intentions, and when she came she brought a message of good will from the elders of her tribe.

Since the autumn festival the Great Lady and her son were seen more often about the King's house and in the city. They were gracious and generous and to all, and even the sons of Zeruiah found themselves thanking the Hittite widow and her son for favours and kindnesses they had not looked for. And the King saw everything but did nothing either to encourage or to restrain his contending sons.

Eviatar the High Priest, who had long been ailing, died, and his place was taken by Ira. The young Levite now served before the Ark beside Zadok. Wearing his late master's garments and turban, Ira was often addressed as Eviatar by people who had known the old high priest all their lives. The young man, who a year before had stood, dressed in goatskins, over the spit in the cooking yard to prepare his master's meat, now wore linen garments and walked and spoke sedately. His meagre frame filled out and his voice deepened.

Avishag rejoiced to see her friend grow so great. Whenever they met, Ira spoke to her kindly and was always willing to explain and advise. Thinking that he might be more favourable to the goddess than the older Levites, she told him of her grandmother's devotion to Dinah and the shrine at Deborah's Palm, but made no mention of her own visit there. Ira frowned and looked away.

"Nehushtan is held captive by the goddess," he said sharply. "Yah has no need of priestesses! Though they do not fail to pay him homage in their groves and shrines, yet their loyalty is to the goddess."

Avishag was taken aback. Both her grandmother and the priestess Dinah had said that the Levites were inimical to the goddess, but she had never heard any man speak so carelessly of her who was the mother of all living and the consort of the highest god. Thereafter she often looked to see if the Ashera on the north summit of the mount was receiving offerings as she had done since the world began. Rarely did a Levite appear there, and then only to pour a libation and mutter a brief prayer, but the worship continued in a seemly manner, led by other priests and priestesses.

In the month of Bul, when the winter's chill gripped Jerusalem and the rains were drenching the soil and filling the gullies, the King moved his sleeping quarters to a newly completed wing on the eastern side of the fort. It was a pleasant habitation, secure from the harsh western winds. A cunning vent high in the wall let out the smoke of the brazier without letting in the cold draughts. But now the King had farther to go when he wished to spend the night with the Great Lady.

It was Yonadav who proposed that the King and his family pass the coldest days in the oasis of Ein Gedi. "But," he added in Judean, looking into David's eyes, "take care not to leave either of your sons behind you in the city!"

The King thanked Yonadav for his counsel, but Avishag knew that he planned to send Adoniyah to Gath and to keep the Great Lady and her son with him at all times. Avishai ben Zeruiah would remain in Jerusalem with his men.

"Who would have thought," the King said to Avishag the night before the journey, "that the son of the Hittite widow – as my men call her to this day – would set his sights so high? A mere boy, whose beard has yet to cover his milky lips… And here is Adoniyah – a warrior, a judge and a great man in the land, yet they of Israel shy away from him as though he were of the seed of Amalek!"

The journey from Jerusalem to Ein Gedi was unlike any Avishag had ever known. It seemed as though the bottom of the world lay just east of Jerusalem and to it they had to descend. Down, down the precipice they went, the asses and mules treading delicately on the path that, though it wound sideways like a snake, was terrifyingly steep. The mountains fell away, the air changed from the sharp chill of the uplands to a dry warmth, and still the road led down, down, down… Beyond the vast chasm to which they were heading, on the far horizon, there rose mountains the colour of cyclamen. "Moab," said the King, who was riding a tall white mule at the head of the procession, pointing at the distant range. It was not a strange land to him – his clan was related to the Moabites, which was another matter that now and then incensed the Israelites.

At last, when the sun was about to sink behind them and the shadows lengthened in front of them, they reached the plain and the shore of the great salt sea. It flashed in the twilight like burnished silver and columns of glistening salt stood around its shallow rim. The caravan turned right and made for an inn that stood at the crossroads. There, in the spacious courtyard, tents were pitched for the King's family and supper was prepared for the entire weary host.

Later that evening, when the King and the Great Lady had retired, Yedidiah-Shlomo took Avishag by the hand and led her out of the compound towards the sea. He had been very attentive to her, in a manner both gracious and respectful, as though she were an older sister. Neither the King nor Bathsheva demurred. Perhaps they did not see the flicker of lust in their son's eyes, or else they found no fault with it.

They walked along the lake, which glimmered in the moonlight. Wavelets lapped the pebbly shore, making almost no sound. A little behind them walked a Hittite retainer and one of the King's guards, bearing torches.

"Not far from here," said Shlomo in his most beguiling voice, which had of late grown deep and manlike, "on the southern shore of this sea, the cities of the plain, Sodom and Gomorrah, perished in a rain of brimstone and fire. Our Forefather Abraham the Hebrew saved his brother's son Lot from the destruction, but as they fled Lot's wife looked back and saw the smoke rising from the plain and the sight turned her into a pillar of salt."

Avishag glanced fearfully at the standing columns of salt, seeking one that looked like a woman. What a strange place it was – without trees or shrubs, nor any sign of life, only the livid oily lake and the surrounding wilderness. This was truly a fitting abode for Azazel.

"Tomorrow," continued the young prince, "we shall reach the oasis of Ein Gedi and the rocks of the wild goats, where my father the King had his stronghold when he was pursued by Saul ben Kish. There are springs there and trees, and the rare Zori herb, from which our precious balm is made. It is never cold down here, and Yonadav says that bathing in the salt sea cures most ailments."

They stood awhile together, looking at the sea. From the nearby pen came the snorting of asses and camels and the tinkling of their bells. Avishag was weary and wished to withdraw, but the boy held her hand in a firm grip. He was tireless and eager to continue his discourse.

"When I am king, I shall build me a winter house in Ein Gedi," he said, "and a garden with all manner of trees, and a pond of fresh water to attract the birds. I shall spend all my winters here, with my wives and my companions."

"Will you leave the King's city for such a long time, my lord?"

The boy halted and looked at her. Her face was very dark in the dimness, and he could not see the look in her eyes.

"My mother says that you are a wise woman, Avishag, though you are not much older than I… Yes, Avishag, I shall leave the

King's city in the winter and enjoy myself here. My kingdom shall be secure, for my people shall prosper and no man shall rise against me, whether I sit on my throne in Jerusalem or go forth."

"Was that the omen you sought, my lord, from the lots that were cast for the twin he-goats?"

"So I did, O wise woman!" he chuckled softly. "And from the oracles, too." Suddenly he laughed aloud and let go her hand. "Fear not, Avishag, my dove. You shall always be safe with me, although I cannot say the same for all the others."

They stood face to face, for they were of the same height. It was too dark for them to see each other plainly, but something passed between them. A shiver went over Avishag's skin and she touched the amulet between her breasts, to remind the goddess of her promise, but at the same time she knew that she would never be helpless before this prince. He would not be governed by his lust, like his disgraced brother Amnon, nor would he risk everything in a headlong rush for power, like his other dead brother Absalom. But she also knew that, unlike his father David, Shlomo would never risk anything from weakness or from kindness.

Yonadav had built himself a handsome house in Ein Gedi, and was proud to offer it to the King and his family. Built of cut stones, it stood on a promontory not far from a spring whose water fell amid rich greenery into a broad pool surrounded by trees and grasses. Numerous birds nested in the boughs and mountain goats abounded on the sheer rocks above; together with the hyraxes and porcupines in the oasis, they provided rich feasts for men and for the leopards that haunted the place.

After a few days the King, accompanied only by Avishag and Ittai the Gittite, rode to the stronghold where he had hidden when he fled before Saul. They soon reached the place, but found that little remained of the hold – passing shepherds, Moabite salt-merchants and desperate men had made use of it through the years. The outer walls were crumbling, while the inner chambers, deep in the mountainside, had become too foul to use. Ittai pitched a tent for his master under a spiky acacia tree and built a small fire, and soon the three of them sat around it, eating the food and drinking the spring water they had brought with them from Yonadav's house. When night fell, Ittai buried the remains of the meal beside the fire and swept the ground around the tent with a bunch of tamarisk twigs.

"The leopard will not trouble us, nor the hyena nor the jackal," explained the King. "A child may fall prey to them, but not a full-grown man or woman. But they must be warned away."

Ittai was nearly as old as David, but strong and limber like a much younger man. Having retired to a corner of the tent, he soon fell asleep and his snores must have been heard far and wide through the desert.

The King, who had been light-hearted while they ate their supper, grew grave as night fell. Ittai's snores made him laugh momentarily, but he soon ceased to hear them.

It was then that he told Avishag about Jonathan.

"I never knew why Saul hated me so," David began.

"It was said that he envied me, for I had driven back the Philistines from the country of Benjamin and the women sang my praises. But I was his captain and had laid my spoils before him… Old Samuel foretold that his kingdom would not endure, nor did the oracles give him comfort. Perhaps he knew that I would rule after him. But he had given me his daughter and I had sworn an oath to him. Whenever I was with him he would embrace me like a son and swear that he loved and trusted me. Did someone poison his mind against me? I sometimes wonder if it was not old Samuel himself, whose mind was tortuous and beyond the comprehension of mere men. But for many years, though he hounded me, I would have given my life for Saul and for his house. Yet he hated me beyond all reason, and drove me out of my own country.

"From serving the King and living under his roof, I fled with my kinsmen to this wilderness, to haunt it like a pack of wolves. One night as we lay here, deep inside the cavern, the King with Avner ben Ner and their men came in to shelter from a dust storm. They did not see us, and built a little fire and soon went fell asleep. Then my men urged me to kill the King and thereby set us all free, but I would not raise my hand to him. I crept up to him and cut off a piece of his robe while he slept. In the morning, when they rose and left the cave, I went out and cried after Saul – I stood over there on the ledge; I shall show you the place when the sun rises, Avishag.

"'My lord king!' I cried. 'See, my father – the hem of your robe is in my hand! I cut it off but I did not kill you! I have not sinned against you, yet you hunt my soul to take it! After whom has the King of Israel come out? After a dead dog, after a flea! May the gods of the Forefathers judge between me and you!'"

Avishag shivered. She could see the scene as clearly as if she had been there, beside the young David. She saw Saul, the king whom Samuel had brought from behind the plough, a towering man, a proud man possessed by an evil spirit. Beside him stood the fabled hero, Avner ben Ner, himself like one of the fair giants of ancient times.

David sighed and resumed his story. "Then Saul lifted up his voice and wept: 'You are more righteous than I, for you have rewarded me good, my son, whereas I have rewarded you evil.'

He swore he would hunt me down no more, he begged me to swear that I would not cut off his seed after him, nor destroy the name of his father's house. I swore. It was not the first time, I had given him my oath on this before, and he went his way… but before long he pursued me again, trying to kill me wherever I went. And Jonathan was stricken and despairing, for he loved me as much as I loved him, and was torn between me and his father."

"Was this not the reason, perhaps, my lord? Could it be that the love between you and Jonathan kindled Shaul's anger?"

Had they not been alone in the wilderness Avishag would never had presumed to ask this question. Even now she feared that the King would take offence. He moved uneasily on his pallet and sighed again.

At last he spoke. "So says the proverb of the ancients: The

truth shall issue from the mouths of babes and sucklings… Yes, my daughter. Truly it was Jonathan's love for me that maddened Saul. For the Benjamites abominate such love. Perhaps because of the War of the Concubine in Gibeah, of which you have no doubt heard, and which all but destroyed their tribe. I do not know. They do stone to death a man who puts away his wife for love of another man. Indeed, even the rest of Israel, as also Judah and the Levites, scorn such men. Yet it is an open custom among the Philistines."

"And did Jonathan ben Saul put away his wives, my lord?"

"No. He had but one wife, Milcah, the mother of Meribaal, whom he cherished. But she died giving birth to their second son, and ill omens came thick upon him: Meribaal's legs were broken when his nurse let him fall, so that he grew up lame, and there was Shaul's madness… 'I saw you and my eyes have been enlightened!' he said to me when we met in secret, for his life had been growing darker year by year."

David's voice broke. He could not continue, and Avishag crept nearer, took his hand and placed it on her head.

Out in the wilderness jackals wailed at the young moon. It was an unquiet night and she slept ill, while the two old men tossed and snored.

Chapter five

"Have you ever seen the sea, Avishag?" said Adoniyah. "No, not this salt sea, which is but a basin – though there are storms here too, when the wind blows hard from the east. I speak of the great sea, which girds the earth. Its waves rise high as houses and it roars like thunder. Its waters teem with fish, from swarms of little ones, no bigger than locusts, to great sea-bulls that can swallow a man."

Returning from the country of the Philistines, Adoniyah had gone first to Jerusalem, where he conferred with the sons of Zeruiah and the scribes. He remained there a while with his Egyptian wife, who had just given birth to a sturdy girl-child, and then descended to the oasis of Ein Gedi. He brought word from Achish, King of Gath – not him whom David had served in his youth, but his son – and had much to tell. From the moment that Adoniyah's runners arrived, the Great Lady and her son disappeared. Their servants said that they had gone hunting for partridge.

Adoniyah was in an expansive mood. He had been received with great honour by the Gittites, and had also visited also the lords of Ashkelon and Ashdod. No longer did the Hebrews depend upon the Sea People's forges for their scythes and ploughs, as they had done in the days of the Judges. Now Dagon's people were eager to share their iron wares and skills with David's kingdom, which helped them fend off the grasping Pharaoh and to drive back the wild marauders from Edom.

Now, having bathed and supped, Adoniyah told his father, Yonadav and the rest of the assembly about his sojourn among the Philistines.

"Achish has built himself a court of polished alabaster, brought all the way from the Land of the Nile. Around it stand high pillars, plastered and painted in the likeness of bundled reeds, with lotus buds above. Hundreds of Gittites, of the King's family and of the elders of the city, fill the galleries around the court, to see the play of boy wrestlers, or the dancing of maidens. The boys are naked and the maidens bare their breasts, though they are of the highest families in the land. The officers of the city stand in the four corners of the court. They wear special armour, scaly like the skin of a fish, and they hold tall staves in their right hands, and a bronze bell hangs from their girdles. It is their duty to keep the order, for a thick crowd pushing against the pillars could bring the roof down."

The King listened to his son's report with great contentment. It was his proudest boast that he had brought about peace between the Israelites and the Philistines, who had fought numerous wars for several generations.

"Even when I was a lad," he recalled, "the house of Achish was a wondrous place. I had fled to Gath from King Saul, alone but for the three sons of Zeruiah and our armour bearers. Achish took me into his house, for he thought I would be of service to him, to set a trap for Saul. We were forbidden to walk about the city of Gath, but were confined to the house and served by the King's slaves. When Achish learned that I would not help him entrap the King of Israel he grew exceedingly angry. I feared for my life and the lives of my captains, and saw that we were caught in a snare of our own making. As the proverb says: 'A man did flee from a lion and met a bear.'"

"A Kenite servant warned us that the elders of Gath were urging Achish to kill us. 'Is this not David,' they said, 'of whom the Hebrew maidens sing, Saul hath slain his thousands and David his ten thousands?' The sons of Zeruiah said, 'Let us break through the King's guard and escape to the land of Judah,' but I did not seek a quarrel with the King of Gath. Then I thought of a ruse, such as Ahitophel himself might have devised. I took to acting like Saul when the evil spirit seized him, grimacing and speaking to unseen beings. At first they paid no heed. Then I made as if to put secret marks upon the gate and let the spittle run down upon my beard, and crowed and growled like a beast... The whole household gathered around to look on!"

He laughed as he recalled those antics, and Avishag saw him in her mind's eye – young and lithe, his hair like burnished copper and his green eyes flashing, as he capered and cavorted in the Philistine court, and she too laughed.

"At length Achish wearied of me and my men, for they feigned alarm at my behaviour. He said to his servants, 'You see the man is mad – why then have you brought him to me? Have I not a sufficiency of madmen, that you have brought this fellow to my house?!' And so the gate was opened and we were free – no, not quite free, but forced to return to our country... Thereafter I met Saul twice, and twice I spared his life, and twice he swore that he would cease to pursue me – and still he did not desist, until I despaired of my life. Therefore I went once more to Gath, but this time with a host of my own, all warriors tried and true, who had been with me in the Carmel and in the wilderness of Judah and Amalek. Our wives were with us too. Then I served Achish as the Gittites and other Philistines serve me now. I became his right hand, as Ittai the Gittite is my right hand, guarding the King's house and his city.

"We accompanied Achish to Gaza, Ashdod, Ashkelon and Ekron, when he called on the four other lords of the Philistines. These cities lie on the very shore of the great sea, and it is truly as Adoniyah says, my child. It is like a huge restless beast, though some have learned to ride it. They of Tyre are great seafarers, and some

Israelites also go down to the sea in ships. The Philistines are called the Sea People, for they came across the sea from Kaphtor, and indeed one of their forefathers' ships is kept in Dagon's palace in Ashkelon... But many who venture out are lost amid the waves, and Tiamath drags them into her lair and swallows them whole."

Adoniyah swaggered about the oasis, proud that the King had praised his endeavour and that the Hittite woman had taken her son and fled at his approach. Seeing his father's great trust in Avishag, and the beautiful maiden's quiet yet assured demeanour, he showed her more attention than he had done hitherto; her support for his cause might be of great value in the days to come.

On the third day Bathsheva and her son returned to Ein Gedi with their saddlebags full of partridges and three gazelles slung from their servants' staffs. Seeing Adoniyah in the forecourt, the Great Lady greeted him serenely and Shlomo bowed. Adoniyah stared after them, his good eye blazing and the other one looking bloodshot. Avishag, who was sitting under a carob tree beside the path, threading carob seeds for a necklace, saw it all.

The almond trees were in blossom when they returned to Jerusalem. Though the air was still sharp and at night people huddled around their braziers, there were many signs of spring. Scarlet anemones and pale cyclamens sprang up amid the rocks. Vast flocks of storks and geese flew over the mountains on their way north, and their cries resounded among the peaks.

Avishag spent her nights on a pallet in the King's sleeping chamber. He himself was comfortable and warm on his couch, bundled in his fleeces and robes, but he wanted her near him at all times. Old Naamah was free to pass her days in the women's house, where she wielded great authority.

The construction of the King's house continued apace, and his city also was growing. But the worship of the Elohim continued in Araunah's threshing-floor. The Levites were displeased. It was unseemly, they murmured, that the King lived in a house of stone and cedar wood, while the Ark was lodged in a tabernacle that was growing shabbier with every passing year. The priests themselves lodged pell-mell in huts on a nearby terrace, and were obliged to walk through mud and rain to reach the great altar.

Their grievance was made known to the King by Nathan the Seer, when he came, as was his custom, from his dwelling in Kiryat Yearim to kindle the fire for the sacrifices. The gaunt and taciturn seer had little love for the sleek, chattering Levites, but he dreamed of a great shrine to Yah on the summit of the Lord of the Heights, El Elyon. As in former years, when the spirit of Yah had moved him to chastise the King in the matter of Uriah the Hittite and other transgressions, now he came to reproach him for neglecting the place of worship.

Avishag feared no man as she feared Nathan. In Shiloh he had taken his place beside the King as one who was mightier and greater. His eyes were always raised above people's heads, or lowered to the ground. Never did they light on a person's face. When he walked, all men moved out of his way. A word, even a look, from such a powerful seer could blight a life.

"What then must I do?" said David plaintively. "When I wished to build a house for the Lord Yah in Jerusalem, you brought me word that it was for my son to build after me."

"And so it must be, for such was the word of Yah. But it is shameful that the tabernacle moulders and the priests who serve in the shrine walk through mud in winter and dust in summer. Your son shall build a great house here for the Lord Yah, but you must lay the floor for it. A stone floor, with paved paths leading to it from all sides. Also a carved alcove for the tabernacle of the Ark. Then you may bring the Cherubim from Shiloh, that the Lord may bless your remaining years."

He did not bestow a glance on any of the persons assembled in the King's hall, and only briefly on the King himself. When he finished speaking, he turned and walked out, the soles of his bare feet rasping on the reed mats on the floor.

"It is strange," the King said that evening. He was reclining upon a heap of bolsters, sipping warmed wine and water. The chamber was well lighted by three oil lamps, and they were alone. This was the hour of the day that Avishag loved best.

"It is a strange thing, and not known among the nations, that as well as priests there are seers and prophets who have no need of oracle or *ephod* to hear the words of God. Such a one was Moses, who brought the Children of Israel out of the desert. Such was Deborah, who gave the word to Barak ben Avinoam, and such was old Samuel, to whom God spoke as I speak to you."

"It is said, my lord, that King Saul was one of a company of prophets. How could he have been one?"

"Doubtless you heard it in Jezreel. The people of the House of Joseph, the Ephraimites and Benjamites, said this when it became known that their king was mad… But who can say if a man is mad or a prophet when he tears off his garments and writhes naked on the ground, mouthing strange words. Bands of prophets infest our land, begging alms and frightening people – are they all messengers of the Elohim, or are they feigning, as I did before Achish, for purposes of their own? Perhaps some are of one kind and some of the other. But the people fear them all, for they are fierce and raucous, and villages curse the day when such a company appears in its fields."

"How then can we know a true prophet or seer from a mad-man, my lord?"

"By their words, by their deeds, by the future… When old Samuel said to Saul, 'Return to your father's house, for the she-asses you have been seeking are found,' and lo, they were found – why then he was a seer! Likewise, he foretold that Saul's kingdom would not endure – and so it came to pass… And did not Nathan warn me that Merari would die, for I had done wrong to take Uriah's wife…? Yet even before it came to pass, I knew that Yah had spoken from Nathan's mouth, and I trembled."

The King resolved to bring the Cherubim to his city before the spring festival. He set his builders at once to pave Araunah's thresh-ing-floor with smooth stones, and to carve a deep alcove in the side of the mountain for the tabernacle of the Ark. Their task was made harder by the rains, which were plentiful that year, but the King was adamant and often went out to oversee the work.

"Adoniyah shall come with me," he declared, "to bring the Cherubim from Shiloh. We shall ride there in chariots and follow the carts with the Cherubim all the way."

One evening, when the King was closeted with Yonadav and the scribes, Bathsheva asked Avishag to come and sup with her. She treated the maiden as a dear and honoured friend.

"Is it wise," said the Great Lady to Avishag, after they had eaten and drunk, "for the King to ride so far and so long in a chariot, in which he must remain standing while it moves? Would he not be better advised to ride in a covered wagon, so that he may recline?"

Avishag, who had never seen a chariot and never ridden in a covered wagon, could not but agree.

"And will you say this to the King, Avishag? He listens to you, for he knows you to be wise and true."

Shlomo sat with them but said little. His eyes gleamed as they moved over Avishag's face and figure. Plainly, he and his mother feared that David would take Adoniyah alone with him to Shiloh, but knew of no way to make him change his mind. Avishag understood that the Great Lady wished her to repeat her kindly advice in the King's ear, to remind him of her love and devotion. It being sound advice, Avishag did as she wished.

Adoniyah rode ahead with his men to the valley of Ayalon, where the charioteers were encamped. His brother Kilav, the son of Abigail the Carmelite, dwelt there, being captain of the King's chariots and a great horseman. A high priest, the scribes, Avishai ben Zeruiah and Ittai the Gittite were to go with the King. They were all in readiness, awaiting the messenger from Adoniyah, when Avishag begged the King to let her accompany them.

"Why, my child?" asked the King. "It is a harsh journey, and women do not ride in chariots."

"If you please, my lord, I could ride on an ass beside your chariot…"

Her eyes beseeched him and he was puzzled. Ira spoke up: "No, Avishag. It is unseemly for a woman to ride among a company of men on such an errand. You had better stay here and see that the women of the King's house and of the Levites make ready for the arrival of the Cherubim."

"*My lord*?!"

Only once before had the King seen Avishag looking so downcast in Shiloh, when he proposed that she stay and celebrate the new moon in the grove. He could not bear to see her so distressed.

"Very well. You shall come with me," he said, and quelled Ira with a glance. "The grove priestesses at Shiloh will welcome you."

Adoniyah and Kilav met the King's party at a place called the Valley Gate, where the narrow defile that wound down from the mountains and through the foothills opened onto the great plain of Ayalon. Avishag was elated. The wide open land reminded her of her home in Jezreel, and the chariots with their prancing horses amazed her. Now she recalled seeing such a sight from afar when she was a small child. Who was it, she wondered, who had driven through Jezreel in a chariot twelve years before?

Adoniyah and Kilav were dressed in Philistine garb – short gowns with leather breastplates and feathered helmets that were tied under their beards. Such was the apparel of all the charioteers, and Avishag wanted to laugh but did not dare. The sun shone through a light haze and the valley was aglow with yellow bloom – sprays of fragrant mimosa, fields of mustard and here and there a spiky broom. But the smell of the horses overpowered all else.

They rested at an inn by the parting of the ways. The innkeeper, a large Danite woman with breasts as big as oil-jars, was overwhelmed with the honour of serving the King, and would willingly have killed all her cattle to feed him one choice morsel. She drove her slaves into a frenzy, sending them hither and thither, until Ittai the Gittite came forward and quieted the brawl. He gave the necessary orders and after they had rested awhile, the King's company gathered under the awning to eat and drink their fill.

Kilav sat at his father's side, since on that day he was the proud host of the King's party. He resembled his father more than any of the King's sons that Avishag had seen – slender of build, with copper hair and green eyes. Even in his voice and the tilt of his head he favoured his father, and Avishag gazed at him raptly, as though he were the young David. Though a year older than Adoniyah, he appeared youthful and full of light.

"Kilav does not seek to be King," said a voice in her ear. Ira had seated himself beside her, holding a fat roasted pigeon in one hand and a beaker of wine in the other.

"He married the daughter of a Kenite chief, and has built himself a great forge on the other side of this valley. The Philistines of Ekron and Timnah come to him to mend their ploughs as well as their chariots and swords, and he is a great man in this country. He has no wish to rule over Judah or Israel, but is proud to be the son of a king."

Having said this, Ira bit into the pigeon, which was dripping on the ground between his knees, and sipped from his beaker. He seemed to have forgotten that he had objected to Avishag's presence on this journey.

Nathan the Seer met them at Shiloh. He stood at the gate, looking, as he always did, grim and fearsome in his coat of pelts. But once inside the precinct, standing before the altar, he too was dwarfed by the Cherubim. Side by side they stood, taller than a man, blackened by the smoke of numberless sacrifices, their great wings almost touching and their lion paws outstretched. They were creatures of another world, and their features could not be recalled in the mind.

Avishag stood with the grove priestesses, watching the sacrifices. These were the last oblations that the Cherubim would receive before the long journey to Jerusalem. The Levite priests made a burnt offering of a year-old ram and entreated the Lord Yah to ride the Cherubim to Jerusalem and make its high place the greatest shrine in the land. Hearing these words, the priestesses stirred uneasily and murmured, but did not speak aloud. Then Nathan addressed a long speech to the Elohim, the ancestral gods of Judah and Israel. Avishag did not understand a word of it, but it seemed to placate the priestesses.

All that day, while the offerings were made and the smoke rose up to heaven, the King sat in the shadow of the Cherubim, solemn and unmoving, wearing a blue-fringed *ephod*. Avishag kept her eyes upon him, knowing that he disliked remaining seated for long. He had ridden a part of the way in the handsome painted chariot Kilav had brought for him, but made most of the journey from the Valley Gate to Shiloh in a comfortable bullock cart. He had also rested for a day and a night before the beginning of the sacrifices. But Avishag remembered the Great Lady's words and watched her master for any sign that he might feel unwell.

She herself had enjoyed the chariot ride at Kilav's side. The swift motion of its great wheels, drawn by two glossy brown horses, made her feel at one with the wind that blew across the valley. No wonder the chariot and horses were the mark of a King! And though Jerusalem, the mountain city, could allow little use of it, she thought that the royal chariot ought to be kept there, not in the valley so far from the King's house.

When night fell the priestesses led Avishag to their house, where a lavish supper awaited them. They served her eagerly and asked many questions about the King's city and the shrine of the Ark. The old crones especially were uneasy about the removal of the Cherubim.

"The Levites are hard men, and inimical to the goddess," they said, echoing her grandmother and the prophetess Dinah. "Now they speak as though the Cherubim were the servants of Yah – but they have been the bearers of the goddess herself since the world was made!"

"It was not the Levites who wished to bring the Cherubim to Jerusalem," said Avishag, "but the seer Nathan. He told the King that it was the will of Yah... Yet today he entreated the ancestral gods of Judah and Israel."

"And what of the oracle?" asked one of the venerable crones.

"Is the oracle to be served by Levites, or by any other men? That would be sacrilege!"

Silence fell. All eyes were upon Avishag, but she did not know the answer. It occurred to her that no one had mentioned the oracle of Shiloh, which had always been served by the priestesses. Were the Cherubim to be bereaved? In the morning they would be placed on two bullock carts, which had been prepared in advance, and begin their slow journey up to the King's city. She must speak to the King before they set out, for once they were on their way without the oracle it would be too late.

Before retiring, Avishag promised the priestesses that she would go to the King at break of day and beseech him not to separate the Cherubim from the oracle and its maidservants.

And so it came about that when the Cherubim were carried to the King's city, accompanied by a high priest and Nathan the Seer, the oracle too was taken there by six priestesses – two crones, two virgins and two matrons. If the Levites were displeased they did not show it. As for the seer – he cared only for the greater glory of the shrine in Jerusalem, and he knew that the oracle with its priestesses would make it all the more powerful.

That year, when the spring festival began, the Cherubim stood on either side of the alcove of the tabernacle of the Ark. As for the oracle, its shrine was placed on the northern peak, facing the ancient Ashera. The King made it known that it was Avishag who had prompted him to bring it with the Cherubim, and she shared in the homage rendered by the pilgrims at the shrine.

As soon as the festival was over, Ira the Levite – whom the people had taken to calling Eviatar, as though the old high priest had shed his ancient skin and become a young man again – Ira the high priest, who two years before had befriended the Shunammite maiden, when they were both of little importance in the King's house – that same Ira bowed before King David and asked for the hand of Avishag, the daughter of Baanah ben Ahilud the Jezreelite.

Naked and alone in the flimsy hut in the fig grove, lying on the bare planks of the floor, Avishag spent the night praying to the goddess. With her eyes wide open in the utter darkness, she saw her plainly – sometimes in the likeness of her grandmother Yocheved, or of Dinah the prophetess, and sometimes like a young matron at Shiloh, whom she had seen smiling sweetly at her suckling babe. In her presence the hut became as grand as the King's fort and as mighty as the tower of Lebanon.

Avishag's keen ears and eyes were this night sharper than ever, so that she saw through the darkness as though it were day, and could hear the spiders walking about their webs. Perhaps the priestesses had put something in the fig nectar that they had given her to drink before they left her, or it might have been her restless seeking spirit, which opened the night to her. Certainly the presence of the Great Goddess herself made Avishag feel as though a part of her was roaming far and wide in the world.

She had come to the grove to ask the goddess what answer to give Ira, but from the moment she entered the hut she never thought of him at all. The picture she had tried to paint in her mind, of herself as the Levite's wife, dissolved like a summer mist. Other pictures came in its place, in some of which she had no part. She saw Jerusalem as it had been before King David made it his capital, before even the pious pilgrimage of the Forefather Abraham, during the countless years in which the goddess, in the form of the Ashera on the north peak, and her son El Elyon, the Lord of the Highest Place, who dwelt on the south peak, savoured sacrifices upon these very rocks under the host of heaven.

She saw the King's city as the very navel of the world. Around its mountain were ranged lands and seas, forests and wildernesses, teeming with people and beasts. She saw a great temple rising on its summit, with vast courtyards, shrines and altars, attended by priests and priestesses, filled with throngs of worshippers from as far as Aram in the north and Edom in the south. Great choirs sang the praises of the Elohim, their voices rising with the smoke of the sacrifices and the sweet incense. And there was no more talk of Judah and Israel, for Jerusalem belonged to all, and its king was lord over all...

The sun was already climbing high in the sky when two young women came to fetch her. They found Avishag lying asleep in the middle of the hut; limbs outspread as though she were resting on the softest couch, a smile on her face and the serpent amulet nestling in the hollow of her throat.

"My lord – no!"

David looked at the girl, who was standing before him in a respectful attitude, as though she were not his constant and cherished companion but a common supplicant. He was glad that her eyes were lowered and she could not see the pleased smile on his face. How painful it would have been to lose her, if she had consented to become the Levite's wife… True, he had been gratified by Ira's request, which was a sign to all the world that he had kept his vow and the girl was still a virgin, for the priest would not take a wife who had known another man. Yet how dismaying the thought that Avishag might be lured away by the young man and disappear into the Levites' quarters! Ahilud, he believed, would have been content to have his granddaughter marry a Levite high priest in Jerusalem, for it was a place of honour. But David felt that another destiny awaited the Shunammite, from which she must not be turned aside. What it was he knew not, nor perhaps did the girl herself.

"I shall give your answer to the Levite, my child," he said gently. "Rest easy in your mind… Only do not stand so before me, Avishag. You are dearer to me than a daughter, and I am glad that you are to remain yet a while by my side."

His eyes filled with tears, for he had not meant to speak these words aloud. His heart overflowed. Absalom, Amnon and Tamar, the infant Merari, Yonatan ben Saul and his sister Michal, Asahel ben Zeruiah, Ahinoam and Maacah – where were they all? Gone. Only this singular girl, who knelt before him and pressed his hand to her forehead, remained to solace his grey head.

"I lost three of my children in one dire day," he told the girl that night when they retired. "Amnon was my eldest son, the first-born of Ahinoam. I have told you that my first wife Michal was barren. Neither with me nor with Paltiel ben Laish, to whom she was married when I fled from Saul, was her womb ever quickened. But Ahinoam – who was a Jezreelite maiden like you, Avishag – conceived Amnon as soon as I had lain with her. He was a fine, sturdy boy and no father was so proud as I was with him upon my knee. But no sooner was he weaned than his mother died, giving birth to a baby which did not live. We were in Ziklag then, and I was far from home, putting down those scorpions of Amalekites who still infested the Aravah. After she died everyone, men and women alike, cosseted the little orphan, never denying him anything. He was always at my side, and refused to remain with his nurses. Before he was ten years of age he was a skilled bowman, with his own little bow made for him by Asahel, who was the youngest and the best of the sons of Zeruiah, and was killed by Avner... – But I shall tell you about Asahel another time.

"And so for some years Amnon was the favourite of my house and of my captains, and no one ever rebuked him, though he was reckless and wild. Doubtless when the other children were born and he saw them in their mothers' arms he felt his loss. When Absalom was born to Maacah, the daughter of Talmai, king of Geshur, there was great rejoicing under my roof. Maacah was the Great Lady then, and Absalom was her firstborn, and moreover the handsomest child of all. Then Amnon fell into a rage, and would not come near me, but roamed in the wilderness, hunting and skirmishing with the Ishmaelites. At length, old Naamah – who was young then, and had been his mother's handmaiden – coaxed him back, and the sons of Zeruiah made much of him, until his good cheer returned. But he never again came to me as before, to speak his mind and to cajole me. I hoped that he would, for it vexed my heart to see him turn away from me. But I was King of Judah in Hebron, and there were battles to be fought and weapons to be got, spies and conspiracies and much coming and going... I saw little of Amnon while he grew to manhood. When I became King over Israel as well as Judah, and made Jerusalem my city, Amnon took a company of bowmen to Mount Ephraim, and stayed away from my house.

"Tamar was the second child born to Maacah. Like her brother Absalom, she was very beautiful to look at. When people saw the two, they would kiss their fingertips and exclaim aloud. Lad and maid, they favoured their mother's clan – tall, with thick hair the colour of honey, and not a blemish on them. A time came when my house was full of sons and daughters, and my heart grew proud. I forgot what befell the house of Saul, and rejoiced in the blessings of Yah... Then, one spring festival, in the twelfth year of my rule in Jerusalem, Amnon arrived. He came to lay before me a chaplet of gold, which he had taken from an Aramaean prince whom he defeated in battle. He was proud in his bearing and scarcely glanced at his brothers and sisters... Until he saw Tamar."

Avishag watched her master closely. She loved nothing so much as hearing him tell the stories of his life, though she feared that the pain that some of them awakened might make him ill. But he was resting easily upon the bolsters, his eyes fixed on a star that twinkled through the window lattice.

"I can see them now. Tamar stood among the women like a palm tree in a vineyard. Hiram of Tyre wished to marry her to his son, but I wavered, for she was young and I did not wish to part from her so soon. Amnon had not seen her since she was a little child, but she was so like her mother and brother, that he knew at once who she was. In those days he had two wives in Mount Ephraim, with children by them and by numerous concubines from Dan to Beersheba – but he forgot them all when his eyes lit on Tamar.

"Now, instead of returning to the north, Amnon stayed on in Jerusalem, lying at the house of my kinsman Yonadav. One day he sent to tell me that he was ailing, and I went to him. He lay on the bed, moaning that he was sickening unto death. As he spoke to me he grew stronger, and before long I thought he was his usual self. Then he said, 'Will my father allow my brother and sister, the children of Maacah, to come to see me? Being in their company will make me better, and I shall surely be well again soon.' Doubtless he knew that Absalom had gone to his estate in Baal-Hazor, and so Tamar alone went to see him that very day. She brought him some cakes she had made for him, for she was a kindly child and wished him well. Yonadav left them alone… He swore later that he had not known what was in Amnon's mind – and who could gainsay him?

"The girl wept and pleaded with Amnon, 'Do not force me, my brother! Where shall I carry my shame? And you will be as one of the vilest men in the land!'… But he was like a rampant bull. He took her by force and lay with her where he was. Then he fell into a rage, hating her more than he had loved her before, and he called his servant and told him to drive her out of the house… Oh Tamar, Tamar!… Broken with shame, she fled to the arms of her nurse, and tore her gown and threw ashes upon her hair, and mourned for her life. I knew none of it, for I had gone to Shechem that morning, and did not return to my city for twelve days. But Absalom came back from Baal-Hazor and found his sister sheltering in his house, desolate and crushed, and he swore revenge."

"Why did he not ask you, my lord, to punish Amnon for his crime?"

"He did come to me, as soon as I returned, and I was very angry, but could not bear to pass sentence on Amnon. I implored Absalom to spare his brother, saying that Amnon was orphaned of his mother as soon as he was weaned, and was later supplanted by his younger brothers and sisters… I beseeched Absalom to be content with the banishment that I imposed on Amnon, and he fell silent. Tamar hid herself in his house. Time and again I went to her and begged her to return to my house, but she would not even lift her veil in my presence. None but Absalom and her nurse ever saw her sweet face again. My palm-tree, my Tamar, was crushed… And Absalom kept his own counsel, and said nothing to me or to Yonadav, or to any man or woman of my house.

"I did not see Amnon again. Banished to Mount Ephraim, he remained with his bowmen, his wives and children, and consorted with his mother's clan. His name was not mentioned before me, and Tamar lived in her brother's house, desolate as a living widow. So two full years passed. One day, when it came time for sheep shearing,

Absalom asked all his brothers to come to the shearing feast at his estate in Baal-Hazor. He asked me also, and begged me come with my men, but I feared we would be too heavy a charge upon him, and blessed him and sent him on his way. He asked if he might bid Amnon come to the feast, and I was pleased, thinking that he wished to make his peace with his eldest brother.

"They sat in the field near the shearing pen, feasting merrily and drinking much wine. Amnon suspected nothing and sent his men to feast with the shearers. When he became drowsy Absalom's servants fell on him and killed him where he sat. The others, seeing what had passed, leapt on their mules and rode away in terror. Then a runner came to me here, crying, 'The King's sons are dead! Absalom has killed all the King's sons and there is not one of them left!'

"I thought that my house had fallen and prayed to God to kill me too. I tore my clothes and lay on the ground, and all my servants tore their clothes and wailed. Then Yonadav arrived, covered with dust and choking – for he had ridden hard to try and reach me before the others – and he cried aloud, 'No, my lord, it is an evil rumour that you heard! Amnon alone is dead, for Absalom resolved to kill him from the day that he forced his sister Tamar!'

Soon the others came back and told me what had happened... There was a great weeping in my house that day. Absalom, fearing my fury, fled to his grandfather Talmai, the King of Geshur, and I did not see him for three years."

The bright star had moved on its heavenly path and was no longer seen through the lattice. The King lay back with his eyes shut. Avishag took the empty beaker from his hands and extinguished two of the three oil lamps. A large moth flew up to the ceiling and was snapped up by a gecko.

"And what befell Tamar, my lord?" she ventured to ask, very softly.

The King did not open his eyes, whose worn lids were no thicker than a moth's wing. "Tamar died soon after. When Absalom did not return, and vengeance had been wreaked upon Amnon, she hanged herself… I caused that house to be destroyed, and the beam from which she hung to be burned. And so I lost three children in one blow."

"But Absalom came back, did he not, my lord?"

"So he did, but not to me… Yoav ben Zeruiah wanted to comfort me, knowing that I was remorseful and longed to see Absalom. He sent me a wise woman of Tekoa, who said, 'All that are born of woman must die, my lord King. We are as water spilt upon the ground that cannot be gathered up again. But the living you may still see under the sun.' So I sent Yoav to bring Absalom back to Jerusalem. By and by I sent for him to come to me. But when I saw him, my comely son, who was born to be king, though we kissed and made our peace, I knew I had lost him. He never forgave me my failure to punish Amnon as he deserved, and my harshness to himself, for even after he returned from Geshur, I could not bring myself to see him for two years. He had a little daughter then, a fair little maid who was born in Geshur, whom he named Tamar."

Chapter six

When twin sons were born to Hannah, Adoniyah's Benjamite wife, he invited all the House of David to a feast at his estate in the valley of Rephaim.

Though the moon of Bul had waxed full, little rain had yet fallen and the sun still baked the earth day after day. All eyes turned to the west, longing to see the rain clouds coming up from the distant sea, but the dome of heaven remained clear and burnished. The priestesses in their groves carried out their secret rites, the priests poured libations and sacrificed yearlings and the treetops everywhere were hung with blue-stained fleeces – and still the rains did not come.

The birth of twin boys at the house of Adoniyah was therefore a welcome augury. A company of prophets arrived at the gate and prophesied that both boys would reign in Jerusalem, turn and turn about. Having fed well and filled their water-skins, they went on their way. Then came a solitary prophet, naked and shaggy as a bear, who proclaimed in a dreadful voice that unless the twins were passed through fire before the month was out, the House of David would fall and El would anoint another to reign over Israel. Hannah, weeping bitterly, would have submitted her babies to the kiln, but Adoniyah took a cudgel and drove the shaggy prophet from his gate. Like all of the House of David, he disliked the rite and would submit no child of his to the kiln.

So confident was Adoniyah in his father's favour, that he invited the Great Lady and her son come to the feast.

"Let them see with their own eyes," he said to his companions, "the foremost Benjamite and Ephraimite elders sitting under my Judean roof, eating my bread and drinking my wine." To show his good will towards the Israelites, he asked Hannah's grandmother to name the twin boys.

"Hanniel and Gaddiel," said the crone: the grace of El and the fortune of El. And the King, hearing this, smiled and nodded, saying privately to Avishag, "Adoniyah has grown wise – he has learned that more is won by giving than by taking!"

The King made his way down to the valley of Rephaim and sat in state while the Levites offered sacrifices on behalf of Hanniel and Gaddiel. He held the babies on his lap and blessed them, and remained for the first evening of the feast. But in the morning, before the sun was up, he called for his mule to return to Jerusalem.

"No, my child," he said to Avishag, who had come out of the house in the cool dawn, intending to ride back with him. "You must remain here for the rest of the feast. Bathsheva and Yedidiah will doubtless leave today, but you must stay and return with the others."

He looked very earnest as he said this and Avishag bowed without a word. She watched him ride away with his Philistine spearmen, and saw him turn around and wave and nod to her before they disappeared among the great mulberry trees. She understood his meaning and was proud of his trust in her.

The Great Lady and Shlomo departed later that morning. Avishag stood with the young prince near the gate and waited while the mules were readied and Bathsheva made her farewells.

"Look – Dagon has been forgotten," said Shlomo in a low voice to Avishag. The great fishtailed image was indeed a sorry sight. It had not been washed or oiled for a long time. Its myrtle chaplet was withered and nothing remained of the offerings it had once received.

"This is unseemly," continued Shlomo, displeased. "It were better to return it to Ekron than to treat it impiously here, at the gate."

Avishag was struck by his words. "Indeed, my lord," she said, "the King's guards, being Philistines, must have been offended by the sight."

Shlomo looked at her and again she felt something passing between them, as it had done before, on the shore of the salt sea. As though he heard her thoughts, he said, "We understand each other well, my sister. We shall speak again when the feast has ended and you return to Jerusalem."

Only one Levite remained for the last day of the feast, Ahimaaz, the son of Zadok the High Priest. His father had gone to offer sacrifices at the great high places in the land, to entreat the Elohim to avert a drought, and Ira had returned to Jerusalem, for the King had decreed that a high priest must always be present at the shrine of the Ark.

Ahimaaz puzzled Avishag. Without his *ephod* and the linen turban, nothing about him suggested a priest. He was tall and spare, and was known as a fast runner. Yoav once said of him that were he not a born Levite, he would have become one of the King's captains.

"And so he might well be!" quipped Yonadav when he heard this. "Ahimaaz is a he-goat, rushing headlong to butt whatever stands in his path... A high priest has need of better wits than these."

On the third and last day of the feast Ahimaaz drank a great deal and urged everyone to do likewise. His high voice could be heard over the din, laughing and talking incessantly.

"They of the House of Joseph are unused to strong ale," he

shouted. "Wine and water is what they drink and the good ale of Bethlehem addles their wits." And indeed the remaining Benjamite guests were beginning to doze at the table before the sun had set.

Avishag, seated among the women of the house, watched and listened. The King would wish to know what was said after both he and the Great Lady had left. But while the Benjamites remained in the hall, the Judeans of Adoniyah's party reined in their tongues.

Naamah, who had spent most of her time with the young mother, now came and sat beside Avishag. She took the maid's hand and patted it fondly. "I give thanks to Yah," she said, sighing contentedly, "that I have lived to see these fine babes, the grandsons of Haggith."

"Why did Haggith not come to the feast, mother?"

Naamah squirmed in her seat, tugging at her dress and veil as she always did when she was both eager and reluctant to speak. At last she said, "Haggith has long ago retired to the grove at Baalei Yehudah. She came here once, to bless this house when the roof-beam was raised."

She lowered her voice further and was forced to speak into Avishag's ear, for there was a din in the hall. "She wished to come and bless the twins and to name them Pharez and Zerah, after the two who were borne to the Forefather Judah by his widowed daughter-in-law Tamar. For these are the names we are accustomed to give twin boys. But Adoniyah chose to honour his wife's clan…" And the crone nodded gravely and wiped her mouth with her hand, signifying silence.

When all the guests who were not of Judah had staggered sleepily from the hall and most of the women had withdrawn, Adoniyah bade the remaining assembly draw nearer to the dais and called for a brazier. Yonadav and the sons of Zeruiah were the oldest men present, and they must have drunk little, for they were clearer-headed than the other men. With them sat Ephrat, Yonadav's sister, a great woman in Hebron, who in her youth had been the wife of the King of Moab. While the men reclined on their bolsters, she sat upright, her yellow hawk's eyes watching the others intently. But a benign smile hovered about her lips, softening her countenance.

"Come, my sister! Come, Shunammite!" Adoniyah shouted, drawing the girl out of her quiet corner. "Sit beside me, Avishag. It is not often that we see you apart from the King, whose very shadow you are."

Avishag could not tell from his mien if he meant to sting or to flatter. She made her way across the hall, stepping carefully to avoid cushions and trenchers and spilt food and drink. She had on fine deerskin shoes, a gift from the Great Lady, and did not wish to soil them. The eyes of the gathering were upon her.

She took her seat beside Adoniyah on the dais and accepted a cup of ale from his hand. "Will you bless my sons, Shunammite?" he asked, his good eye staring at her intently. Avishag felt uneasy under his gaze, and did not know what blessing he wished for. The others watched her curiously.

"May the Queen of Heaven and all the host of heaven bless Hanniel and Gaddiel," she whispered at last, reciting her grandmother's formula, and tossed a few drops of ale. The others murmured a response and the feasting resumed. Servants came in bearing loaded platters and foaming jugs. Fresh torches were fixed in the wall brackets, brightening all corners of the hall, and all at once three Moabite dancers entered, shaking tambours and cymbals and ululating. Their round hips and full breasts swayed and tiny bells on their ankles tinkled as they snaked their way among the guests.

The men became absorbed in the sight, their reddened eyes following the dancers' movements, their hands clapping to the rhythm. The lady Ephrat and Avishag exchanged glances, the smile on the old woman's face broadening, as at the sight of childish play. For a moment Avishag considered begging leave to withdraw, but her eye caught a different exchange of glances, grave and intent, between Yoav and Adoniyah, and she stayed on.

The plentiful ale, the song and dance, the warmth of the brazier, all combined to befuddle those of the guests who succumbed to them. Before long they too staggered from the hall to seek their pallets. The lady Ephrat stopped the dancers with a gesture and sent them out of the hall. An old armour-bearer of the sons of Zeruiah brought in a bowl of cold water and a cloth, and the remaining guests washed their hands and faces.

Avishag rose and bowed to Ephrat and to Adoniyah. "By your leave… " she began, but the prince took her hand and drew her down again.

"Remain with us, Avishag. 'Tis true that we are all of Judah who are present here now, but you have the trust of my father the King." The others murmured assent. She resumed her seat, though with a heavy heart. It was doubtless for this that the King had ordered her to stay on, but she felt ill at ease, just as she had done when the elders of Jezreel conferred at her grandfather's house. Had they been talking together heedlessly, she would have listened to their every word. But she had not expected to take part in their deliberation.

"…and not merely of Judah," Yonadav was saying. "We are all of the clan of Caleb, whom some call Ephratites, whether from Bethlehem or Hebron."

"No, not all of us!" quipped Kilav ben Abigail, with a friendly smile at Avishag. He had arrived earlier that day, having ridden in his chariot all the way up from the valley of Ayalon. The sight of the chariot and its pair of horses had caused great excitement among the household and guests, and drawn curious onlookers from all over the valley. But although his mother Abigail was Nabal's widow, Kilav was also David's son, and was counted as one of them. He came but rarely to Jerusalem, being content with his life in the plain. His forge, his horses and chariots, made him a valuable ally to Adoniyah, as was his good standing with the Philistines.

Then the lady Ephrat spoke. Her voice was deep, almost a man's voice, and her speech was strongly marked by her years in Moab. "We ask you to remain, O Shunammite," she said to the girl, "for you have the King's ear, and we do not wish him to wonder about our councils. The King has made it known that Adoniyah ben Haggith is to rule after him, and we wish only to affirm our faith in his choice."

Avishag inclined her head and thanked the old lady for the confidence. Clearly, they knew she would report to the King and saw no harm in it. But, she wondered, if they were sure of the King's approval, why were they so wary of the Israelite guests? As though she heard her thoughts, Ephrat said: "We know that the Hittite woman and her kinsmen in Ephraim would rather put her son upon David's throne – now that they have used up the last of the blind and the lame of the house of Saul!"

The others laughed and slapped their thighs with pleasure at the old lady's wit.

"Why should we stir up that hornets' nest?" she continued. "Once Adoniyah is king over Judah and Israel, they will bide with us in peace, just as tonight – thanks be to Yah and El Shaddai – the Benjamite elders sleep secure and content under our roof, proud to have named David's grandsons."

"And no thanks to their warriors!" growled Avishai ben Zeruiah. His voice, harsh as a raven's, startled the gathering. But they understood his gist.

"So it is," said Yonadav. "If today the Israelites live in peace and plenty, is it not thanks to the arm of the King, to the host of tried and true warriors that he and his captains led for a generation? Was it not the young lion of Judah that curbed the ravening wolves of Philistia, Aram and Ammon, till they no longer dare to snap at his heels? The tribes of Israel live in peace behind our King's shield, each man under his vine and his fig-tree."

The wily old counsellor's words pleased them all greatly. Then Kilav spoke about the care of the chariot and the horses, for he was leaving them in Adoniyah's possession. The lady Ephrat spoke again, to advise strengthening the ties with the Hittite lords in the north. She wished to remind the men present that the north remained cold to the rule of Judah and the House of David. But Yonadav smilingly reminded his sister of the firm friendship of Tyre, David's unfailing ally in the land of the cedars. Nonetheless, he admitted that closer ties with the Hittites would not be amiss.

"Should I now marry a Hittite maiden?" asked Adoniyah, laughing. "Soon my house will overflow with women of all the nations of the earth!"

Before they retired, Adoram, the master of the King's tribute, undertook to go north to see the Hittite lords, and try and win their support away from their kinswoman Bathsheva and her son.

Soon the house was plunged in darkness. Avishag lay awake in a small chamber near the hall and listened to the sounds of the night. Old Naamah slept beside the door, her breath whistling softly through her nose. Now and then she muttered something unintelligible. In the women's wing one of the newborn twins began to wail and his brother promptly joined him. There was a pattering of feet and a murmur of soft voices, and the crying stopped. Outside the wind was rising and the horses, tethered behind the house, whinnied and stamped their hooves. Their strong smell came in gusts through the window lattice.

Avishag could not sleep. She kept seeing the faces and hearing the voices of the company she had been with before retiring. She would have enjoyed thinking about Kilav, the living image of the young David, his handsome looks and pleasant voice, but the others intruded. Though nothing had been said that need trouble her, yet she still felt disquiet. Perhaps it was the rising wind, presaging a storm, which troubled her mind and baffled sleep. Clutching her serpent amulet, she uttered a brief prayer to the goddess, the mother of all that lives. It eased her spirit and sleep began to spin its web about her. Just as she sank into a doze, a voice broke through the web. At once she was fully alert.

There were men behind the house, speaking together in the dark under the mulberry trees. Avishag rose and went to the window. The wind had a sharp edge and heavy clouds were scudding across the sky. She could hear the voices of two or three men, but could not make out the words. Who were they? She was weary, and said to herself that they must be the men who tended the horses. But the voices sounded familiar…

Just as she was about to return to her pallet, the speakers drew nearer to the house. She recognized the voice of Adoniyah, of Yonadav and – surprisingly – of Ahimaaz the Levite. They were speaking in Judean, but by this time Avishag could follow every word.

"…in Hebron, then," came the voice of the King's son, unusually low and grave. "And bring the horn of oil, Ahimaaz."

"But do not leave the King's city until you receive word from my messenger!" Yonadav admonished the Levite. "Zadok your father is not one of us. If he looked for the horn and found it not, he would raise the alarm."

"Ira is with us," said Ahimaaz, and his voice, too, was slow and grave, unlike his usual donkey's bray. "Though the people call him Eviatar, he is not like the old one, who was faint-hearted."

"Yoav will send word when all is made ready in Hebron," the old counsellor repeated carefully. "Gird yourself with patience, Adoniyah my son. Make no move before you hear from the sons of Zeruiah. Then we shall each know what to do." The younger men murmured their assent, and they went their separate ways.

Avishag remained by the window, though her body longed to sleep. The wind continued to rise, bearing the glad scent of rain. In a little while it came nearer, there was a rushing sound in the boughs of the mulberry trees, and then the downpour began. Once again she prayed, this time on her knees. She begged the Queen of Heaven for wisdom to help her serve the King in the best way she could, and beseeched her to intercede with her son, the lord of the storms, to lavish his gifts upon the parched earth.

She knew at once that something was amiss in the King's house. There were no outward signs – the Philistine guards were at their stations around the wall, while in the forecourt the servants were unloading baskets of kindling and provisions, which had just been brought up by a string of asses. And yet something was not right. She slid from her mule and, without stopping to remove her muddied mantle or to put on her shoes, she ran into the house. In the antechamber before the hall she met Benaiah, the Lion-slayer, who in the absence of the sons of Zeruiah, had been charged with the defence of the King's city. He came forward and with a grave air took the girl by the arm and led her inside.

"The King is ailing," he said quietly. "No one must know of this, not even the women in their house. I have sent for the sons of Zeruiah and likewise for Yonadav and the scribes. But it is you the King has been asking for. Make haste and go to him – he lies in his sleeping chamber above… But stop here a moment. He must not see that you are fearful."

Avishag's heart was beating hard, but she closed her eyes and called up all her strength. She thought about the King, his look when he ordered her to stay on at Adoniyah's house, and when he turned and waved to her under the mulberry trees. Benaiah waited. She opened her eyes and nodded, her heart having steadied.

"I shall go to the King now," she said quietly, and the old warrior led the way to the upper storey.

The King was lying propped up on bolsters and pillows, his hands crossed on his chest and his eyes shut. His face was flushed and moist and Avishag sighed with relief. It was not his former ailment then, not the sudden loss of movement in his limbs, but a fever. Though a fever may also threaten life, there was less danger in it than if the King were once again enfeebled and bedridden for a long time.

Outside the chamber she questioned Benaiah closely. When did the King fall ill? Had the Great Lady been told? Did the messengers he had sent to the sons of Zeruiah know about the King's sickness?

Benaiah replied that the King had felt chilled and feverish soon after he returned from Adoniyah's house. The Great Lady saw him and brought him a potion, which made him feel better, but then he asked to be left alone. Naamah had been nursing him while they awaited Avishag's return. As for the others – Benaiah had sent for them in the name of the King, saying nothing about the sickness.

"I shall speak to the Great Lady myself," said Avishag. "When the others arrive, send word and I shall prepare the King. It is only a slight fever and he will soon be well again…"

Recalling the lady Ephrat's words the previous night, she added, "We must tread softly, Benaiah, and remember, do not stir up the hornets' nest!"

Then she returned to the King's chamber.

The windows of heaven, which opened after the twins' birth-feast, let down torrents of rain. The cisterns were soon brimming with water and the gullies rang with rushing streams. Down in the desert, sudden floods swept through the dry ravines, carrying off tents and goats that had not been moved out of their paths in time.

The wise woman, Eglah the Edomite, was summoned from Siloam to the King's bedside. The chamber was filled with her reek, but her potions cooled the King's fever, and the leaves and other things she burned in her curious earthen pot helped to revive him. She chanted prayers in her tongue – taking care not to name Chemosh, her god, for there was an ancient rivalry between him and his brother Yah, the Lord of Judah and David's house. For three days she prepared the King's food with her own hands, and would not let even Naamah come near her as she crouched over the potage, stirring and muttering. As the King's health improved, she began to teach Avishag some of her secrets. The girl aroused her curiosity, and before leaving the King's house she again offered to make her disciple. Avishag thanked her for the honour and neither accepted nor refused the offer. The crone put out a claw-like finger and touched the serpent amulet on Avishag's breast. "Come when you will, my daughter," she said, "while you wear this sign."

"They will tear my kingdom apart!" the King exclaimed in a rage.

While he lay ill, the King fretted that his sons, seeing that he was bedridden, would turn fiercely upon each other. Even while he was burning with fever, he warned his captains and counsellors to keep a close watch on the rival princes and their followers.

Avishag meant to report to her master what she had heard at Adoniyah's house only when he returned to good health. But seeing that he would not relinquish the reins of his kingdom, even while he felt very ill, she told him everything. The King listened to her without a word, his countenance grimmer than she had ever seen.

Suddenly he cried out in a terrible voice: "They will tear my kingdom apart!" Alarmed to see him so enraged, Avishag implored him to remain calm. "My lord, they cannot achieve their purpose if you are healthy and well and know their every move!"

At her urging, the King relented and lay back. "It has come to this, then," he said more quietly, glaring at the ceiling. "Even the sons of Zeruiah conspire behind my back!"

"If it please my lord – " she began, hesitantly, and stopped.

"Speak, Avishag! To whom should I listen, if not to you?"

"The sons of Zeruiah are not conspiring against my lord. Though they lay plans with Adoniyah, even going so far as having the priests anoint him – it is but to stop the Great Lady and her son from doing likewise. They trust that it is my lord's wish that Adoniyah reign after…" She faltered, reluctant to speak of the time when he would not be among the living.

"So I have said," the King replied after a moment's thought. "But if Adoniyah were anointed by a connivance and without my blessing, Bathsheva would summon her kinsmen and the followers of Yedidiah in Ephraim, and while the breath is still in me, before I am gathered unto my fathers, the kingdom will be torn in two – just as it was when Ishbaal ben Saul reigned over Israel and I over Judah… No and again no! The heir to my kingdom must not be anointed in secret, and so give rise to further plots and rebellions. I shall do what must be done, so help me Yah!"

In the morning, the King, though not quite free of his fever, bathed and had his hair and beard dressed, and put on his royal gown. Then he made his way to the great hall, leaning upon Avishag's arm. He sat on the lion-footed chair and faced the assembly he had summoned. When the sons of Zeruiah stepped forward to stand at his side, he waved them back. Only Avishag and Benaiah the Lion-slayer stood beside him. Thus he sat, glaring at the assembly, gripping the arms of his chair to rein in his rage.

Before him, in a respectful attitude, stood the Great Lady, her son Yedidiah-Shlomo, Yonadav the counsellor, Adoniyah ben Haggith, the sons of Zeruiah, the high priest Ira-Eviatar and Ahimaaz ben Zadok the Levite. Behind them and along the walls were others of the King's court, such as the scribes, the master of the King's tribute and Ittai the Gittite. Suddenly the sun, which had scarcely been seen for some days, broke through the clouds and filled the hall with a sparkling light, but the faces of those assembled remained sombre.

"Where is Nathan? I have summoned him also," said the King.

"If you please, my lord," Seraiah the scribe came forward, "a messenger was sent to the seer in Kiryat Yearim, but he was away from home. No one could say – "

"Very well! I shall speak to him when he deigns to come to the King's house." The King paused and looked over the heads of the assembly towards the open doorway. Through it could be seen the flank of the Mount of Olives, the trees gleaming silvery in the sun. Avishag saw that his forehead was pale and moist with the effort and she trembled for him.

"I was a shepherd in the fields of Bethlehem," he began, speaking in his elder's voice, "when the god of the Forefathers sent me to the aid of King Saul. Old Samuel saw me in Ramah and foretold that I would reign over the tribes of Israel and Judah. And so, after many a battle, it came to pass. For seven years I reigned over Judah in Hebron, and for thirty years over Israel and Judah together, from my seat here in Jerusalem, the ancient abode of El Elyon. Twice I faced a rebellion and twice God lent strength to my arm, so that I overcame my enemies, those who sprang from my loins and those from the House of Joseph…"

He broke off. He made as if to turn to Avishag but stopped and turned instead to Benaiah.

"Water!" he said in a low voice.

The old warrior brought the King a cup of water and stood by while he drank. David sipped slowly, his eyes roving over the still figures in the hall. When he returned the cup to Benaiah he smiled: "Though it came not from the well of Bethlehem, it was sweet water from the hand of my brother, the Lion-slayer!"

Then he went on. "Now Jerusalem is a mighty city in the land, and with its shrines and oracles, a site of pilgrimage, rivalling the great high places for sacrifices and worship. From Dan in the north to Beersheba in the south, our tribes are at peace, each man under his vine and his fig tree. The tribes of Israel and Judah are as one, a great nation under the sun. And all this," he concluded in a fierce, powerful voice, "with the help of the Elohim, has been my doing!"

Strength came to him as he spoke. He leaned forward, raised his hand and looked sternly at his two sons – the stalwart Adoni-yah, with his copper beard and warrior's shoulders – and the slender youth Yedidiah-Shlomo, whose black beard had lately fledged on his chin and cheeks. They both cast down their eyes, not daring to look at their wrathful father.

"When the time comes, I shall proclaim my heir at the shrine of the Ark, before the Elohim and in the sight of the people. I shall swear an oath and the elders of Israel and Judah will be my witnesses as I make sacrifice to the Elohim of the Forefathers."

He paused, and even in the silence his sons kept their heads down. Then he went on sharply, "But I am not yet ready to join the dwellers under the earth! Therefore let there be no more conferring and conspiring in my house. And if any one conspires to anoint the future king while there is yet breath in my body – as Yah is my witness, I shall cut him down!"

Like a storm which comes roaring up from the distant sea, shaking and drenching every living thing, then moves on, leaving the world clean and chastened – so had the King's wrath chastened the rival princes and their followers and left them thoughtful and restrained. There was a quietness about the King's house, while he recovered from his fever and from the effort of chastising his unruly family and holding his kingdom together. All of the King's house and clan knew what had happened that morning in the hall, and the women in their quarter were quietly gleeful. The older women, who remembered Bathsheva's entry into the King's life and had despised her ever since, were angered by her ambition for her son. But the younger women were enticed by the Great lady's generosity, and took a growing interest in her son. Shlomo, lately grown taller, his shoulders broader, was sometimes seen walking in the garden, stopping to speak to the old Tyrian slave who tended it, patting the tame doe and her fawn and listening to the birds which nested in the trees and in the clefts of the rocks.

Adoniyah's Egyptian wife Titipah, who did not realize that the boy prince was her husband's rival for the throne, showed him open favour. She no longer kept apart from the rest of the women, but only Naamah and Avishag had patience enough to listen to her strange speech and to unravel her odd imaginings, but no one took the trouble to enlighten her about the rivalries that threatened the Kingdom. She too liked to stroll in the garden, where she was followed by a Kushite maid dandling her merry little girl, who struggled and cried to get down. It was there she met Shlomo, who spoke to her with his wonted courtesy – and in her own tongue! Thereafter Titipah sang his praises to all would listen.

All the while Adoniyah also strove to show himself a docile son. He came up often from his house in the dell, and helped the King judge the people. He conferred with his father, the captains and counsellors, about the levies and tributes and about the prosperous trade with Tyre and Philistia. Iron and horses figured largely in their conferences, for in them lay the strength of a kingdom. And there was much talk about the harvests, which produced the country's renowned oil, flour, honey and wine, and which were traded to neighbours and allies in return for their goods.

Yonadav, too, frequented the King's house, being more lively and forthcoming than he had been for some years. Eager to show the King that he was not conspiring with Adoniyah, he sometimes found fault with this prince. The sons of Zeruiah, seeing that they had acted hastily in the matter of the anointing, removed themselves with their best warriors to the outer reaches of the Kingdom. Wars and skirmishes among the neighbouring kings had to be kept from spilling into David's kingdom. Meanwhile, the defence of the King's city remained in the hands of Benaiah the Lion-slayer, though he often begged the King to let him return to his house in the desert, where his young Moabite wife awaited him. But it was the Great Lady herself who took the King's outburst most to heart.

"My sister," she addressed Avishag one day, when the King's house had returned to its accustomed ways, "my little sister, nothing is ever hidden from your eyes. You know that the King made me a promise when Shlomo was born that he would reign after him. He spoke from the bitterness of his heart, saying that his elder sons had done wrong and were punished, and as for the son of the priest-ess – who would support him except a handful of his near kinsmen? That was how the King spoke fifteen years ago, when Shlomo was born. But are not these words still true today?"

Avishag made no answer. She gazed into her cup of wine-and-water, on which floated some scented petals, and gave silent thanks that the young prince was not in the chamber with them. For though the Great Lady spoke delicately, weighing every word with care as one weighs grains of gold, she was a poor listener, while her son could hear the thoughts of men as plainly as their speech.

"We have done nothing," she went on, "I and Shlomo and those who champion his cause, to deserve the King's wrath. We trust in the King and in the promise he made, though the people do not know of it. But the followers of the priestess' son conspired to have him anointed, thus laying claim to the throne even while the King lives. Yet the King has not sworn an oath before the gods…"

And herein lies your strength, thought Avishag. While the King refrains from swearing an oath to place Adoniyah on his throne, Shlomo and his mother can gather supporters as a flowering bush gathers bees. Their great wealth and Shlomo's growing renown for wisdom served them well.

Bathsheva cut a tender morsel of meat and offered it to Avishag with a smile. "You are silent, my sister, but your wisdom, which far exceeds your years, tells you that no one in this house, no one in all the Kingdom, prays for the King's life as do I and my son."

The Hittite slave lighting Avishag's way back to the King's apartment heard her laughing softly to herself. He wondered if he should report this to his mistress, but when he returned the Great Lady had retired to her own sleeping chamber, and by the morning he had forgotten all about it.

Chapter seven

The great storm was followed by another long dry spell. The winter moon waxed and waned with scarcely a cloud in the sky. Once again the people flocked to the high places and lavished offerings to Baal Zaphon, lord of the winds, dispenser of rain. But the land, which had greened after the storm, began to languish under the relentless sun. The people grew restive and looked towards the King's city, murmuring that the King was too old. A younger king, one who had strength in his loins, might better propitiate the Elohim, so that the crops would not fail. In the fields and orchards of Judah mention was often made of Adoniyah and the many children he had fathered, chiefly the new twin boys.

The drovers who carried food and provender to the King's house also brought the rumours from the villages. The keeper of the stores passed them on, and soon the house was abuzz with anxious whispers. Only the Great Lady appeared unmoved. And the King, though he had recovered from his fever, he was still weak, and his captains and counsellors tried to keep him in good cheer. For her part, Avishag resolved to keep nothing from him, but before she could say anything about the rumours, the King decreed a day of prayer and sacrifices throughout the kingdom. He urged the priestesses to do their utmost, for Baal Zaphon was known to favour their worship.

When the day dawned, the heavens were as clear and burnished as they had been throughout the month. All day long the bellowing of the sacrificial beasts, the chanting of the priests and columns of acrid smoke rose from Araunah's threshing-floor and from the northern summit. Then, as the sun began to go down, a cloud no bigger than a man's hand came up to meet it. The throng, which had gathered about the shrines, saw it and held their breath. As the sun sank below the flaming horizon an evening breeze rose and grew stronger. A soft murmur rose from the multitude of upturned faces, and then very quietly, almost on tiptoe so as not to disturb the gods at their work, the people dispersed to their homes. That night the rains came back, winter returned, the grateful earth drank and quenched her thirst. The crops were saved.

"What then is the task of the King?" Avishag questioned her oldest friend.

Though she had refused to be his wife, she had not lost Ira's good will and support. At first he kept away from the King's house, and when he saw her he greeted her coldly. But after a while he took to wife the daughter of a priest of Nob, and was content. Avishag could again turn to him whenever she was perplexed, knowing him to be as devoted to the King as she was.

"It is the King's task to judge the people and to be their captain in time of war," he replied evenly.

"And does not King David judge the people, or has he failed to lead them in war? Even now, if need be, he could triumph over their enemies!" she replied, indignant on her lord's behalf. "Yet when the rains failed the King was blamed, as though being old and frail he was holding them back."

For once, Ira was at a loss for an answer. The King was the ruler, he said slowly, a great captain and judge – but he was not a priest, for all that he wore the *ephod* before the altar.

"Did his weakness keep the heavens shut?" he wondered, twisting the ends of his beard. "I have heard that there are nations ruled by women, priestesses of the great goddess, and the warriors obey them. And surely a barren woman would not remain long on the throne, or misfortune would follow. So it has been with the Hittites, though doubtless the Great Lady knows more about their ways... But this is not a fit matter for a Levite high priest to speak of," he finished sternly.

"Who should reign after the King?" Avishag asked quickly.

"Adoniyah ben Haggith!" came the prompt reply.

"Even though the King promised the Great Lady that her son would inherit his throne?"

Ira was startled. "Did he make such a promise?" he asked in alarm.

They were in the forecourt, which a mild wintry sun was drying after a downpour. Their heavy woollen mantles and stout shoes made their pacing slow and stately, for all their youth.

Avishag repeated to her friend what the Great Lady had told her about the promise that the King made when Shlomo – that is, Yedidiah – was born, and what the King had said from the bitterness of his heart.

"'I did not know," said Ira, his brow dark with disquiet. "It is true that Yedidiah was born soon after Amnon was slain by the servants of Absalom at the sheep-shearing feast. Then Absalom fled to his mother's father, the King of Geshur, and Tamar hung herself from the roof-beam of his house... All this have I heard time and again from the mouth of my master, Eviatar, whose name I now bear. Perhaps the King was so downcast by the crimes of his children that he renounced them all, wishing to start anew with the son borne him by the lady Bathsheva..."

"But as yet he has sworn no oath, Ira! He has not vowed to put Yedidiah on his throne after him."

"No," said the Levite gloomily. "But even a promise has to be unmade, not set aside carelessly. Avishag, my sister, this is a grave matter you have revealed to me. For if the King made a promise, albeit in bitterness of soul, and discarded it later, Adoniyah might suffer for it. But if the King should keep his promise and proclaim the Hittite woman's son his heir, the people of Judah will rend his kingdom apart as a lion rends a sheep to devour it!"

Avishag was deeply vexed by all she had heard of late. She saw that the louder the Judeans and their allies declared for Adoniyah, the greater grew the Israelites' resolve to put the King's youngest son upon the throne. Moreover, the two princes had their supporters within the King's city – indeed, within his very house… While the King was strong and the land was fruitful and at peace, the rival princes could only plot and plan, but no harm was done. But no sooner did the King's grip weaken, than they and their followers began to circle about his house, as vultures hover over a stumbling bullock. Who could keep them at bay? And who would advise the King and urge him to proclaim his heir, once and for all, at the shrine of the Ark, as he had said he would? The Levites sided with the Judeans, as did the King's captains and kinsmen. But she recalled hearing Yonadav warning Ahimaaz, that night in the valley of Rephaim, that his father, Zadok the High Priest, was not of their mind. And as for Nathan the Seer, no one knew where he stood in the matter. He had put a curse upon the first son borne by Bathsheva, but had shown no enmity to the second. And what of the King's old companion, Benaiah the Lion-slayer? Taciturn and grave, he had taken no side in the recent upheaval. Whom did he favour? He was still at the King's house while the sons of Zeruiah were away, and had sent for his young wife and their children. Avishag resolved to speak with him as she had spoken with Ira.

"There's a giant in the forecourt! Come and see, Avishag!"

The forecourt was filling with onlookers, and children pushed forward to stare at the visitors. The lord of Gaza had arrived with his company, one of whom was a giant. Clad in the short gown favoured by highborn Philistines, but helmeted and shod like a warrior, he was a fearsome sight. The tallest man's head reached no higher than his shoulder, and his legs were as thick as the waist of a youth. He walked sedately behind his master, holding a large feathered canopy over his head to shade him from the sun.

It was a fine-looking company, brightly attired and bejewelled, their beards close trimmed and their hair braided. When the Lion-slayer came out to greet them in the King's name and bring them into his presence, his dark garb and uncombed hair and beard made him look like a wild man. He cast a glance at the giant and nodded pleasantly, as though he knew him well. Then he ushered them into the house, and only their mules and servants remained in the forecourt to be stared at.

Later, Avishag was called to attend the King when he dined with the visitors. Yonadav sat at the King's side, and Benaiah stood behind him, where the sons of Zeruiah were wont to stand. The Philistines ate daintily, holding the food in their fingertips and taking small sips from their beakers. With their fine apparel and jewels, their dressed hair and delicate gestures, they were more like high-born women, like the lady Titipah or Bathsheva, than the men of Judah and Israel.

But for all their fine airs, they were hardheaded men and had come, so the Gazan lord said, to speak with the King about the defence of their coastal kingdom from the marauding bands that infested the desert. Their city of Gaza was a thriving port and a way station for caravans to and from the Land of the Nile. Moreover, they traded with Kaphtor, the cradle of the Sea People, and even remoter islands. For the Philistines were no longer the warriors they had been in the days of Saul ben Kish. Allied with the Judeans and Moabites, they had grown fat and prosperous and had lost their taste for war and conquests. But they had no treaty with the tribes of Israel, and now that the King was old and the land was rife with rumours of his sons' rivalry, they had grown uneasy.

So much Avishag learned from the talk at the King's table. Though the Gazans clothed their speech with many flowery phrases, it was plain to see that they were seeking assurances from the King that his heir would abide by the treaty between them and the

Judeans. The King, seated on his lion-footed chair, wearing his gown of fine, white wool and the golden chaplet on his head, spoke firmly and kindly to them.

"My son will honour our treaty," he said. "Has he not lately enjoyed the hospitality of your realm? There will be no war between my kingdom and yours, my brother of Philistia."

Whether the King's mellow words set their minds at ease, Avishag did not know. No doubt they had hoped to see the heir to the throne for themselves, and perhaps sow the seeds of a future treaty, if need be. But neither of the princes, whose names were on everyone's lips, was present.

As the day wore on, Avishag watched the giant, who stood unmoving as a pillar behind his master. He looked neither left nor right, nor even at the dancing and singing maids sent for by Yonadav to entertain the assembly. Though he was of huge stature, he had not a look of strength but of weight – a tree, not a bull. In battle, she thought, he would strike terror by his presence, but would not be agile enough to contend with skilled warriors. It was strange to see that though his master looked like a household image, small and bedizened, the giant submitted to his orders like a great mule driven by a child.

The lord of Gaza and his attendants were lodged in the new wing of the King's house, but others of the company were taken to the houses of Adoram and Yonadav in the city.

"Are the giants Philistines, my lord?" Avishag asked the King later that evening when they were alone.

"No," he replied. "The giants are Anakim, descendants of the mighty men of ancient times. It is said that in those days the sons of the Elohim paired with the daughters of men and begat the mighty men. Very few of their offspring remain. Some are still living among the Philistines, but the bravest of them perished at the hands of my warriors of Judah, in the battle of Gob. They were four brothers, the sons of Rafah, the giantess. Saph was slain by Sibechai, Goliath by my townsman Elhanan and Ish-Madon by my brother's son Yonatan. I fought with Yishbi, a giant clad in brass from head to foot – his spear alone weighed as much as a man – and though my sword pierced his armour at the waist, and I blinded him with my javelin, yet he almost killed me. Blood was pouring from my head and my thigh and my strength was ebbing, but Avishai ben Zeruiah came to my aid and with our two swords we cut the giant down. After that battle my captains swore an oath to the elders of Israel that I would go no more to the forefront of the battle... For the Israelites felt secure behind my shield, and feared to lose it, as a child fears to be abandoned by its mother. Have I not said that they are fickle as water?"

The King sighed. "But my son Adoniyah shall win their trust and keep my kingdom together."

To turn his mind from the cares that weighed upon him, she asked, "Why, my lord, is Benaiah called the Lion-slayer?"

Nothing pleased the King more than to recall the days of his youth and the exploits of his captains. "Benaiah ben Yehoiada was doubly a lion-slayer, my child! And when we are all gathered unto our fathers, his name will shine like a beacon, for none of my warriors was so valiant as he. Give me a little more of the warm wine, my child, and wrap the coverlet around my shoulders...

"It is the custom of Moab," he went on, "to celebrate a new reign with battles between the lion-men and warriors who come to challenge them. The Ariels, as the lion-men are called, wear lion pelts with the heads of the beasts over their own. It is an awesome sight! Whether they really are the offspring of lions, I do not know, but the sight of them turns bold hearts to water. When Zippor ben Raddai inherited his father's throne of Moab, I and my warriors went to his feast and took part in the games, for we of the Calebite clan of Judah are kin to Moab. But when the first lion-man hailed us in the name of their god Chemosh, jeering at our Lord Yah, his brother in heaven, Benaiah alone of all of my warriors dared to step forward. He stood up and fought with the Ariel and slew him. Then, though the ground was red with blood, he fought with yet another lion-man and slew him also! The mountains rang with the cheers of my warriors, and King Zippor himself hung the necklet of lion's-teeth around Benaiah's neck. And so he came to be known as the Lion-slayer... But that is not all. One day, in the tenth year of my reign in Jerusalem, in the coldest month, snow fell upon the mountains. Have you ever seen snow, Avishag?"

"Only from afar, my lord. On the summit of Lebanon."

"It was a hard winter that year. When the snow fell it lay thick upon the ground, filling the gullies and hiding the paths and roads. In the city few ventured out of doors, for the cold was fierce and there were pitfalls under the snow. Soon the ravening beasts came out of their lairs – wolves, jackals and leopards, seeking prey for their whelps, for the small creatures had all gone to ground. All at once there was an uproar in the city – a lion was seen prowling on the mountainside! The people were fearful. 'Let the Lion-slayer fight him!' they cried. 'Send for the Lion-slayer!'

"At first I would not let him go. The Ariels he had killed in Moab were men, not wild beasts, and for all his prowess, Benaiah was not like Samson the Danite, a child of the Sun by a mortal woman, who could tear apart a lion as though it were a little goat-kid...The lion had fallen through the snow into a pit near the Shechem gate, and was struggling to climb out. His roars terrified the people, who redoubled the cry for Benaiah... He was young then – as were we all – and a mighty man to look at. He put on stout shoes and took his armour, his sword and javelin and went out. We followed him, armed and ready to come to his aid, but it was he who went into the pit and fought with the lion and slew him. But the beast tore his arm, and it has hung withered and powerless ever since.

"That is why," the King finished sleepily, "Benaiah ben Yehoi-ada is called the Lion-slayer. For not only did he slay the two Ariels at Moab, but also the lion in the pit on the day of the snow. Yet some say that even he did not measure up to the three warriors who fetched water for me from the well of Bethlehem... I shall tell you about them some time."

The King sighed and closed his eyes.

Three large ravens sat on the wall near the gate and watched the King and his company riding out of the city on their way to the oasis of Ein Gedi. The riders looked away from the birds, which rarely speak unless their eyes are met – all save Shlomo, who gazed directly at them. Meeting the prince's eyes, the leading raven raised its head and cawed loud and sharp – once, twice, three times. The other two birds bowed and moved a pace or two away.

The Great Lady was displeased. She urged her mule forward and spoke to her son in a low voice. He hung his head docilely but did not reply. Avishag, whose slow mule kept her back at the end of the procession, wondered what Shlomo had learned from the ravens. But he did not speak and she did not question him.

They had scarcely rested from the journey and begun to enjoy the warmth of the oasis and the comforts of Yonadav's estate, when a breathless runner arrived from the King's city. So dire were his tidings that Yonadav feared to report them to the King and took counsel with the women. A great calamity had occurred – David's oldest companion, his kinsman, Avishai ben Zeruiah, was dead!

The King had gone hunting with Ittai the Gittite and some menservants. Thus the whole house heard the dire news before he did, and waited for their lord's return in silence. Avishag was dismayed. She agreed to break the grievous report to the King, and feared that the blow would crush him. She saw that the Great Lady was secretly exulting, though she kept her eyes lowered. Avishai had been an even greater enemy to the Hittite widow than his brother Yoav.

As soon as he saw the waiting assembly the King knew that some misfortune had happened, though the ragged and dusty runner was kept out of sight. The King's face, which had flushed in the desert sun, turned pale.

"Who has died?" he asked. "Is it my son Adoniyah?" His voice began firmly but broke upon his son's name.

"No, my lord!" said Avishag. "All your sons are alive and well. It is an old companion and kinsman of my lord who has died. It is Avishai ben Zeruiah."

The King reached out a hand and Avishag took it and led him

to the dais in the hall and made him lean on the bolsters. His face was grey and his hands turned cold in hers. Refusing the warmed wine she offered him, he rent his gown and ruffled his hair and beard. Yonadav, who was also looking stricken, gave his kinsman and lord a handful of ashes to throw on his head, then he too rent his gown and threw ashes on his head and face. Seeing them thus, the women of their clan began to wail for the dead warrior. Then the tears began to flow from the eyes of King. He buried his face in his hands and wept for his lifelong companion.

It was a mournful procession that returned to Jerusalem. The King did not ride in front. Too dispirited even to hold the bridle, he let Ittai lead his mule gently on the sinuous path up the mountainside. Avishag, riding close behind him, saw his bowed back jogged by the beast's stride and his head drooping forward. His sorrow moved her to tears. Proceeding slowly, they broke their journey at a Kenite encampment in the desert, where they stayed overnight. They entered the city at dawn, the rising sun stretching their shadows before them.

The King and all his house followed Avishai's bier to Bethlehem, to bury him in his fathers' sepulchre beside his brother Asahel, who was slain many years before by King Saul's captain, Avner ben Ner. The procession increased as it went, until it covered the earth as far as the eye could see. Wailing and flinging dust upon their heads, the mourners reached the burial ground, but its boundary could not contain them all, and so few heard the King's lament for his kinsman and companion. Before returning to his city, the King ordered a pillar to be erected on the site and his lament to be engraved on it, as he had done at the burial of Saul and Jonathan. Of the three sons of Zeruiah, Avishai alone had neither sons nor daughters in Judah, only in Gath. His Gittite sons – two handsome men, garbed in the Philistine manner in short gowns and with their hair in braids – kissed the King's hands and thanked him for the honour shown to their father. It was said that they were great men in Philistia, and had taken wives from the house of Achish, lord of Gath. Though they were of the clan of Caleb, they claimed no share in their patrimony, but were content to live in their mother's country.

All Judah and Jerusalem mourned Avishai ben Zeruiah. Even they of Ephraim and Benjamin passed the forty days of mourning in quietness, refraining from all celebrations. Tyre, Gath, Rabbah of the Ammonites, Edom and Moab, all sent emissaries to console the grieving King on the death of his sister's son.

But the King remained low-spirited. Morning and evening, throughout the forty days of mourning, he offered libations to Yah in Jerusalem, prostrating himself before the god of the Forefathers. He did not wish to see anyone save his kinsmen and companions of old – Yoav, the remaining son of Zeruiah, Yonadav, Benaiah the Lion-slayer, Zadok the Levite and Ittai the Gittite. Of the women, none but Naamah and Avishag could approach him, but he scarcely spoke to them. Remembering Naamah's story of how the King had grieved for his infant son when he was gravely ill, and rose and recovered after the child died, Avishag was puzzled by the depth of his grief at this time.

Avishag crouched on a rocky ledge near the tabernacle, as she had done every morning since the burial of Avishai. Huddled in her great mantle against the chill wind, she watched the men at their worship. The old warriors stood around the great altar, their hoary heads bowed, their gnarled and scarred hands lifted in prayer. So few of them were left! Most of their companions had died. How many more years would they remain under the sun?

The old warriors were not alone at the shrine. Standing behind them in a respectful attitude were the younger men of the King's house, come to make mourning offerings to the god of Judah. Adoniyah came early, as he did every day, for Avishai had been like a father to him. But this morning Yedidiah-Shlomo had come too, bearing a golden censer filled with sweet incense. The King embraced his youngest son and blessed him for honouring Avishai, despite the enmity between his mother and the warrior. David's other sons had come to Jerusalem to partake in the mourning rites – Kilav ben

Abigail, Shefatiah ben Avital, Yitream the Edomite and Yafia, the son of old Temimah, the living widow. By chance, Absalom's only child Tamar, whom he had named after his ravished sister, was present, too, having just arrived from Geshur with her nurse. A fine-looking girl who favoured her dead father, she remained in the King's fort and did not set foot in the women's house.

Shlomo caught sight of Avishag on the ledge. When he had burned the incense and made obeisance to God, he came and stood beside her. Together they watched the company at the shrine.

"These were the men," said the young prince in a low voice, "whose very names spread terror far and wide. Each of these warriors was like an army with banners, turning the hearts of their enemies to water... But look, Avishag – now they are old and weary and a child could overpower them all."

"A child, my lord? A child overpower all of them?" She exclaimed, annoyed by his words, which seemed to slight her lord.

Shlomo laughed softly.

"Nay, my sister. I meant no disrespect! There is strength yet in their ancient sinews and skill in their wielding of weapons. It was sadness which made me speak this way, sadness that even the greatest warrior must come to this, like an aged lion whose teeth are blunted and whose roar no longer terrifies... Even the weapons they wielded in the days of their prowess have long ago turned to dust, as have the bones of the giants they felled."

They watched the rites in silence, and then the young prince took Avishag's arm. "Come, my sister. It is cold and the rain is about to fall. Let us return to the house."

Seeing that the men at the shrine were also turning to go, she gave in and they walked back to the King's house. The rain began to fall as soon as they reached the gatehouse. Resolved to wait there for the King, she stopped and Shlomo stopped with her.

His manner was so mild that she dared to question him. "My lord, if you please – what did you learn from the raven?"

Shlomo looked into her eyes for a moment before he

answered: "There were three ravens on the wall, Avishag. One spoke and the others bowed. And see, now of the three sons of Zeruiah only one remains among the living. The other two have joined the dwellers in the nether world."

Avishag smiled. "Are you saying, my lord, that the runner who brought us the news that Avishai ben Zeruiah was dead need not have come? You knew of his death from the raven?"

"Do not mock me, my fair one! No, I did not know who had died. The omens do not speak as men do, but he who heeds them is forewarned. The ravens foretold the death of one who was one of three. I thought it would be one of the three sons of Zeruiah."

Avishag shivered. There were other questions on her tongue, but she knew not how to voice them. Then they heard the King's company coming up the path and Shlomo recalled her to her duty.

"My father will be weary and cold. He must not fall ill now!"

Avishag bowed to Shlomo and went to meet the King.

Avishag and Ada, Benaiah's young Moabite wife, were playing with Ada's children under the flowering almond trees in the garden, when an uproar rose beyond the King's house. In a trice, all the women, maidservants and slaves hurried to the forecourt. Avishag and Ada took the children in their arms and followed the others.

In the forecourt stood a chariot drawn by a pair of horses, which stamped and pranced on the paving stones. The crowd stood back, afraid of the beasts, which were bigger than any mule. Cries of admiration mingled with yelps of fear when the Philistine charioteer, grinning under his leathern helmet, twitched the bridle on the horses' backs.

It was the chariot which Kilav ben Abigail had brought as a gift for Adoniyah at the birth feast of the twins. But Kilav himself was not be seen – he had gone into the hall to bow to his father. Two of his servants stood unmoving by the chariot, awaiting their lord. Such a sight had never been seen in the King's fort.

"What means this, my sister?" asked the Moabite, hugging her small daughter to her breast. "Why are they all agog?" Her older child, a stout little lad, pulled Avishag by the hand, eager to approach the chariot.

"It means, Ada my sister, that the King's son Adoniyah ben Haggith desires to reign after his father," Avishag replied, her nostrils widening as the scent of the horses reached her. This was a bold move indeed!

"And shall he do so?" the Moabite asked. "Benaiah says the King wavers and does not proclaim his heir. Perhaps he will anoint his youngest son, Shlomo?"

Urged by the charioteer, the horses took a few paces forward, raising squeals and laughter in the forecourt. Suddenly Avishag knew whose chariot she had seen driving across the plain of Jezreel when she was scarcely bigger than the child at her side. It had been Absalom, the King's beloved son, returning from Geshur three years after the slaying of Amnon. Did he not ride in a chariot to Jerusalem, and soon after, did he not lead the revolt against his father…? Was Adoniyah about to do the same, now that the King's strength was failing? Why could he not wait patiently at his father's side? Had he heard about the King's promise to Bathsheva?

Ira-Eviatar assured her that there was no talk of rebellion. "It is only that the passing of Avishai ben Zeruiah recalled to mind the King's old age. No, he is not ancient, and may live ten years more. But it is time to give the people a sign that when he is gathered unto his fathers they will not be left without a captain. Adoniyah does well to show himself strong and bold."

"Why do you favour Adoniyah, Ira?" Avishag felt bold enough to ask. "Has Shlomo no merit to commend him?"

"His name alone, my sister, tells you why. Shlomo is not a Hebrew name, it is neither Judean nor Israelite. Though the King calls him Yedidiah, he goes by the name his mother gave him. Were he to rule in Jerusalem, it would no longer be the city of David, of Judah and of Yah."

"Yet it was the city of El Elyon before this time."

"El Elyon is but another name for our god, Avishag. Yah is

El Elyon, as he is El Shaddai. The Elohim of the Forefathers, of the tribes of Israel and of Judah, are but the many titles of our god. The shrines of the Ark, of Yah, of the Cherubim, of El Elyon, and all their oracles – why are they all in Jerusalem, if not for the glory of the Elohim?"

"And the Ashera?" she asked, thinking about her promise to Dinah. "Have you no fear of the goddess, Ira?"

"Let other nations worship the goddess! As Edom and Moab serve Chemosh, and Ammon the Moloch, so do some nations worship the Queen of Heaven above all gods. The Hittites call her Arinna... But we are the people of Yah, of the living Elohim of Judah and Israel."

"And will Adoniyah remove the Ashera from her summit?" She held her breath while Ira pondered uneasily.

"No," he replied at last. "It would imperil his kingdom to offend her."

When the King rose from mourning for Avishai ben Zeruiah he bathed and changed his clothes, permitted his hair and beard to be dressed and sat on his throne. For a whole week he sat in judgement, and for another week he conferred with his counsellors, scribes and recorders. Wearied at last of the company of men, he commanded a feast for his household.

"Let us have music, singers and dancers, wine and fine meats," he said to Naamah and Avishag. "I am not yet so aged that my eyes cannot see nor my mouth taste dainties nor my heart take pleasure in song. Before I send Absalom's child, Tamar, to her kinsmen in Geshur, I wish to see her laughing and dancing under my roof. Until now the maid has seen nothing but mourning and sadness in this place."

Young Tamar's arrival had soothed the King's heart even in his grief. He was often tormented by his memories of Absalom. At times, the recollection of the insult to his throne and the rape of his wives fired him with wrath, as though it had happened yesterday. At other times he would rail against Yoav, who had killed the rebellious prince, saying aloud that he wished he had ceded his throne to his beloved son without a battle.

At the feast, he seated Adoniyah ben Haggith beside him, and made sure that both the Egyptian and the Benjamite wives of the prince were in the hall. Bathsheva made no demur. After taking her seat near the King, she nodded her head and smiled at Adoniyah's wives. But Avishag saw that her hands were clenched as tightly as her rings allowed.

"Where is your son, Bathsheva?" asked the King. "Where is Yedidiah?"

The Great Lady begged the King's indulgence – Shlomo had gone to Gilloh, she said, to comfort his aged teacher whose wife had died.

"Indeed, my lord, it was the wife, a Chaldean, who instructed Shlomo in the knowledge of stars and constellations… She foretold the day of her own death – and many other things…"

They had all eaten a great deal of fine food and grown merry with good wine and ale, and the singers and dancers had begun to play, when the young prince entered the hall. Calm and stately, he went up to his father and bowed low, begging forgiveness for his late arrival. Then he clapped his hands and his manservant came up and gave him a bundle wrapped in fine linen. Silence fell in the hall while the young prince uncovered the gift he had brought the King.

It was a shining golden bowl, which bore the signs of the constellations embossed around its rim, and the stars of heaven engraved within.

"See, my lord," Shlomo said, his voice ringing clearly in the hushed hall, "when the bowl is held thus, with the sign of the sun to the east and the moon to the west, the stars and constellations take their places as they do in the heavens."

A gasp went around the hall while Bathsheva glowed with pride.

"It was made at my behest, my lord, my father, in the exact

form as the clay bowl upon which I was taught the knowledge of the heavens. If it please my lord, may this small gift gladden your heart with the blessing of the host of heaven."

While Shlomo spoke, Adoniyah's countenance darkened and he stood up. For a moment Avishag thought that he would leap on his younger brother, who looked like a sprig of myrtle before an oak tree. But then his brow cleared, and he spoke indulgently.

"Behold a learned lad, my lord father! We shall have no need of stargazers from Mesopotamia, nor of wizards from Egypt, having so wise a diviner in our household."

Shlomo thanked his elder brother and took his place in the hall – not beside his mother, who rose to greet him, but beside Tamar, the lovely maiden from Geshur. The King, who was greatly taken with the golden bowl and its signs, sent Naamah to bring the young prince the best meats and wine. Then the singers and dancers began again, and the hall was filled with their din.

Seeing Shlomo gazing at Tamar with a lustful eye troubled Avishag, though why she could not say. Shlomo had already fathered a child by one of the maidservants in his mother's household, but had not yet taken a wife. But Tamar was no maidservant. Would he ask for the hand of his dead brother's daughter?

The thought lingered in her mind, troubling her till she asked the King about it. Was it likely that Yedidiah would seek to marry Absalom's daughter? And would the King allow it? Her heart fluttered while she waited for the King's reply.

"It would please me, but not his mother," the King answered at length. "Bathsheva now seeks to ally her son with the leading clans in Judah. She has sent messengers to Baalei Yehudah, to ask Nahash ben Yeter for the hand of his daughter for Yedidiah. It is time the lad took a wife."

Since rising from the mourning for Avishai, the King was calm but sparing of words. He conferred with his counsellors and gave them their orders, judged his people and watched over his household, as in times past. But Avishag saw that he often closed his eyes with weariness and that his heart had grown heavy. After Tamar left to return to the house of her kinsman the King of Geshur, her mules and servants laden with gifts from Jerusalem, there was no more talk of feasts, of singers and dancers and dainty meats.

Spring arrived and the land was astir with the early harvests. Adoni-yah, having driven his chariot about the King's city – though the horses were less sure-footed than an ass or a mule in the steep alleys – drove it at last to his estate in the valley of Rephaim. Some of the King's captains and counsellors also departed to oversee their own fields and flocks; and Bathsheba and her son left for Shechem. Without the rival princes and their followers, the King's house went about its everyday chores. The ominous cloud that had hung over it during the presence of the opposing camps lifted, allowing the King's house a calm respite. Even the spirit of the King lifted when his contentious sons had departed.

"Let us go to Bethlehem!" he announced one morning, when dawn filled the chamber with a rosy light.

"I have a great desire to dip the bread of Bethlehem in the good oil from our press, to dine with my kinsmen under their roofs… Avishag, my child, I shall show you the fields where I watched my father's flocks."

He had not been in such good cheer since their last sojourn in Ein Gedi. He smiled while she dressed his hair and beard, which were now white as milk, and he sang, though his voice was unsteady.

> *"Come let us get up early to the vineyards, let us see if the vine flourish, whether the tender grape appear and the pomegranates bud forth…"*

"*Take us the foxes, the little foxes, that spoil the vines,*" Avishag sang in response, *"for our vines have tender grapes!*"

And as she sang she began to plan a secret scheme in her mind.

For the first time since coming to the King's house, more than three years before, she laid a plan of her own, unknown to the King.

When the King arrived in Bethlehem, people ran from their fields and orchards, sheepfolds and barns to greet him. The festivities began at once. David's kinsmen vied with each other for the honour of receiving him and his company under their roofs, and the elders entreated him to sit at their head at the town gate, if only to hear a single plaintiff. All over Bethlehem calves and sheep were slaughtered, jars of wine and pots of butter broached and bread freshly baked, to provide a worthy feast for the King.

It was at the house of David's kinswoman Edrei, the daughter-in-law of his brother Eliav, that the company supped and rested from their journey. In the evening there was singing and dancing on the threshing-floor. Edrei's youngest and prettiest daughter played the viol and sang the renowned love song that David had composed in the Carmel, when his men fought Nabal's servants and he had courted Abigail.

> *"Behold, thou art fair, my love, behold, thou art fair! Thou hast dove's eyes within thy locks. Thy hair is a flock of goats that appear from the Mount of Gilead. Thy teeth are like a flock of sheep that are even shorn, which came up from the washing... Thou hast ravished my heart, my sister, my spouse, with one of thine eyes! Until the day break and the shadows flee away I will get me to the mountain of myrrh and to the hill of frankincense..."*

When she finished singing she laid down the viol and ran and hid her face in her mother's shoulder. Her name was Yehoadan, and she was not yet spoken for.

"She will be a worthy Judean wife for my son Yedidiah," the King said genially to his hosts. "If she be willing... Why do you look downcast, Avishag?"

"I am not downcast, my lord!" she replied with forced gaiety. "It was my lord's song, so sweetly sung, that moved me."

The following morning the King sat with the elders of Bethlehem at the gate and heard two plaintiffs. One was an old man who had known Jesse, the King's father. Having no sons, and his daughters having gone to live in Moab, he had given his house and field to his brother's sons in return for his keep. Now they had driven him out, and he cried to the elders for justice. The brother's sons had tried to evade judgement, but hearing that the King himself was sitting at the gate, they put on their finest clothes and came and bowed to the King and the elders.

They spoke in low voices, while their uncle, crouching by the plaintiffs' stone, shouted and whined ceaselessly. But it soon became apparent that the younger men had good cause to put their uncle out of the house, for he had become foul and lewd. Some women who stood around the circle of judgement affirmed that he was unfit to live in a house with a family. The King heard them all gravely, but he took pity on the old man, for the sake of his father's memory. He ordered the nephews to build a small house for the old man outside the town, and made them swear an oath to keep him in comfort so long as he kept out of their way.

The next to plead was a widow woman who said she had come from afar to seek the King's justice. She was a Danite who had married a Judean, who left her a vineyard and a daughter. Now, she said, two brothers were vying for the maiden's hand and inheritance, each claiming that her father had promised her to him.

"And while they contend for my daughter's hand, the vineyard languishes." Her speech bore no trace of her long sojourn in Judea.

"And your daughter – cannot she choose between the brothers?"

"No, my lord. She says she cares not which one she weds, for each has some virtues to commend him, and some faults that must be overlooked."

The King looked at the elders, who were seated to his left and right in the half-circle, but none of them knew the woman or her story.

"Did not the girl's father give a pledge to one or the other of the brothers?" the King asked.

"My lord, each has a small pledge that was given him in private. But no oath was taken before witnesses."

The King grew impatient.

"It is your misfortune, woman, to be the widow of a man who knew not his own mind! It is likewise the misfortune of your daughter, and of the vineyard, and of the two brothers!"

Here he paused and his brow darkened. The woman waited calmly by the plaintiffs' stone. She had the tall stature and fair face of a Danite, and her manner was that of a great woman, not a poor widow.

"Then hear my judgement, woman, and all ye who may bear witness to it," the King announced. "Before the Elohim of Judah and Israel, I order you to give your daughter to the eldest brother. There being nothing to choose between them, it would go easier for the younger to cede to the elder, than for the elder to the younger… Go now, woman, and prepare the marriage feast."

"It was you, Avishag, was it not, who sent that Danite widow to me?"

For the first time since she came to him, Avishag had angered the King. She bowed very low and whispered a plea for forgiveness.

"Who else had a hand in it?" he demanded.

"None other, my lord!… The woman is a Danite from the north, the wife of a kinsman of mine. I met her when she came to Jerusalem to make a burnt offering at the shrine of the Ark, to plead for her only daughter, who is barren…"

"Oh Avishag!" The King's anger passed and he laughed. Avishag fell to her knees and hid her face in the hem of his gown, giving silent thanks to the goddess.

"You will have me choose Adoniyah, then, he being the elder? Or was there some other purpose behind your game?" But Avishag kept her head down and did not reply.

Then King sighed deeply. "Arise, my child," he said at last. "I promise I shall answer the woman's plea. The vineyard shall not languish."

It was a cold spring morning. The sun hid behind a veil of mist. A little rain had fallen in the night and the inhabitants of the King's city rose unwillingly from their warm beds. Suddenly rams' horns sounded on all sides, dismal hoots that sent shivers down men's backs. Was it a call to arms, the men wondered aloud, while children slipped from their mothers' grasp and ran outdoors. Then the King's criers passed through the alleys and summoned the populace, even those who were neither of Judah nor of Israel, to come to Araunah's threshing floor. In a little while the paths leading to the shrine were thronged with people huddled in mantles and shawls against the chill. As they walked, they questioned one another: Was the King summoning his people to war? And with whom? Surely not with the Ammonites again!

When they had filled the precinct and its surroundings, the King arrived, leaning on a staff, followed by a large company. Everyone gasped when he removed the shawl with which he had muffled his head, uncovering a chaplet of solid gold set with precious stones. It had never been seen outside the hall of the King's house. Then the Levites placed a high backed, carved chair on the pavement before the tabernacle and the King sat on it, staff in hand. A hush fell upon the multitude and the King addressed God lifted his face to the heavens and spoke in his native Judean:

"Lord Yah, God of the Forefathers, who ridest upon the Cherubim! Who am I, and what is my house, that thou hast brought me this far? Thou didst take thy servant from the sheepfold, from behind the flocks, to rule over thy people. Hear my oath! Hear me, ye Elohim of the Children of Israel, who did take the kingdom from Saul ben Kish and his house, and gave it unto me and my house. Hear my oath! My brothers of Judah and of Israel, ye shall bear witness to the oath that I swear at this shrine, before the Ark and the Cherubim."

He paused and looked around him. On his right stood his son Adoniyah, looking strong and noble in his striped gown, on his left the young Eviatar in his garb of high priest. Such was the silence that the birds were heard singing their morning song. For a moment he wished he were back in Bethlehem, among his kin, having nothing but some fields and sheep to bequeath... Yet here he was, and here were the people awaiting his oath. Old though he was, he was still their captain and their judge. It was he who had joined together the houses of Israel and of Judah, and had made the kingdom strong and prosperous. He who had brought the Ark and the Cherubim to Jerusalem and made it a great city in the land. These recollections gave him strength and he rose from his seat and bowed very low before the tabernacle. The multitude drew a deep breath and waited.

"I am old and shall soon be gathered unto my fathers," the King went on in his strong elder's voice. "But the Kingdom of Judah and Israel shall abide, as Thou hast promised. Bless my son Adoniyah, who stands before Thee, and who shall be ruler after me, to lead the people and judge them in righteousness. Before God and men, I take my oath that my son Adoniyah, who was born to the priestess Haggith, shall sit on my throne after me."

A loud murmur swept over the assembly. Eviatar approached the altar, while his acolytes threw upon it a fettered white yearling calf. He raised high the sacrificial knife and brought it down swiftly, slitting the animal's throat, so skilfully that its blood gushed cleanly and ran down the channel to the edge of the pavement. He filled a brass bowl with blood and marked the King's forehead and right hand, then did the same with Adoniyah. Then he prostrated himself before the Ark, stood up and with a faggot of burning flax set fire to the oiled kindling under the dead beast. The flames sprang high and the Levites sprinkled them with sweet incense. The King and Adoniyah also prostrated themselves and cast incense on the flames. Then they left the shrine and returned to the King's house, leaving behind them a column of acrid black smoke rising to heaven in the windless and sunless morning. They did not hear the shrill arguments that broke out among the Judeans, Israelites and others as they walked back to their houses.

"The deed is done!"

"Done and fulfilled! From first to last!"

"Now for the anointing ceremony."

"And it must be soon, before they of Israel take counsel together to thwart our King's choice."

"Let them murmur and whine, for that has always been their way! As soon as the smallest skirmish approaches their fat fields, they will come to our King Adoniyah, grovelling and whining, as they did to his father: 'Are you not flesh of our flesh, bone of our bone? Deliver us from our enemies or we shall perish!'"

The speaker, Ahimaaz ben Zadok the Levite, stooped low and imitated the speech and manner of an old Benjamite beggar, and his listeners laughed till the tears ran into their beards.

But Avishag, who had witnessed the oath, and herself poured the celebratory wine for the King and Adoniyah when they returned to the house, did not exult. She saw that the King, seated on the lion-footed throne, was weary of the day's events and only remained in the hall to honour his son. A great feast had been prepared and the hall was filled with the jubilant followers of Adoniyah. Yoav ben Zeruiah had brought his wife and sons from Tekoa, arousing the curiosity of the King's household who had not seen them before. Moreover, Yoav was seen smiling and laughing – a rare sight. Even grave Benaiah, the Lion-slayer, was unusually gay and drank much wine in honour of the future king. The lady Ephrat, Yonadav's sister, was there with her family, as were all the foremost elders of the clan of Caleb. Edrei, the King's kinswoman from Bethlehem, had brought her daughter Yehoadan, who had so charmed the King when she sang his love-song.

Avishag recalled the King saying that the little maid would be a worthy Judean bride for his son Yedidiah, and that the thought had displeased her. But where was the young prince, and where was his mother? Were they in their apartments in the upper storey, or had they left the city? Seeing the exultant faces of the King's captains and counsellors, Avishag thought that they knew the whereabouts of the rival prince and the Great Lady, and were untroubled by it. Were they really so confident that Shlomo could not undo what had been done that morning?

At the King's behest, she served Adoniyah as she served him, cutting his meat and pouring his wine from the King's own vessels. The prince, whose countenance had flushed dark as a pomegranate, seized her hand and looked into her eyes.

"Will you drink with me, Avishag? Your blessing shall be with me always."

Titipah, Adoniyah's Egyptian wife, who was seated on a hassock at his side, laughed and clapped her beautiful hands to see Avishag so honoured. Hannah, the Benjamite wife, sitting beside the Egyptian, looked on gravely. The King having nodded consent, Avishag took the prince's cup and drank to his life.

"Are you content, Avishag?" the King asked her when she returned to his side. "It was your doing that I swore the oath today."

"You do me too great an honour, my lord."

"My house has not seen so many joyous faces for a long time, yet you are not rejoicing… Why are you so solemn?"

Adoniyah's eyes were on her, and though she knew that he could not hear her words amid the revelry in the hall, she did not dare to speak about her fears for Shlomo. The thought that the hotheads among the Judeans might even now be conspiring to do away with him chilled her heart. She said to herself that surely the King would not allow any harm come to his beloved Yedidiah, nor to Bathsheva, the last wife of his bosom. But she remembered that even in the prime of his reign he had been unable to save the life of Absalom, though he had warned his captains not to harm his rebellious son. Did he not say that the sons of Zeruiah were too hard for him..?

But Avishag had learned to dissemble, and now she hid her fears behind a cheerful mien which deceived the King. There was nothing else she could do.

Chapter eight

The day after the swearing of the oath Avishag went to look for the Great Lady and her son. There was a strange Philistine guard standing outside the door leading to their apartments. They had gone to Shechem, he said, and taken their Hittite servants with them.

Avishag did not believe this. The Great Lady never set forth from the city without a caravan of mules and asses, slaves and maid-servants. Nor would Shlomo so humble himself as to pass stealth-ily through the gates of the King's city. And yet Bathsheva's entire household had disappeared as though blown away by the wind.

The ceremony of the oath must have exhausted the King's remaining powers, and he became like an old man who desires only to sit in the shade and listen to the chirp of the grasshoppers. The scribes turned away plaintiffs and supplicants and sent them to Adoniyah, who sat in judgement, sometimes at his house in the valley of Rephaim and sometimes in Hebron. Now that he was con-firmed as the next king, the prince drove everywhere in his chariot, while his men rode on caparisoned mules. Wherever they went they cried, "Make way for the King's heir Adoniyah!"

"Just like Absalom!" sighed old Naamah, and at once clapped her hand to her mouth. Then she added fervently, "Yah's blessing on Adoniyah – long may he live!"

The King was content to pass his days in the garden or on his roof, often in the company of Yonadav and the lady Ephrat, or Yehoshafat the recorder, and Avishag forbore to speak to him of anything but everyday matters. She feared for Shlomo, and her conscience troubled her. She knew that it was her doing – but for her ruse with the false widow woman, which prompted the King to take the oath, Shlomo and his mother would have remained safe under their roof. She was amazed that the women's house, which a trifling matter could set abuzz like a swarm of bees, remained unmoved by the absence of the Great Lady, the young prince and all their servants.

"What have we to do with them?" said the women scornfully, when Avishag mentioned the emptiness in the Great Lady's quarters. "What is it to us if they choose to remove themselves to Shechem? If Bathsheva did not even bid you farewell, you who found favour in her eyes and supped with her and her son – why would she take leave of us, whom she scarcely deigned to see?"

As her anxiety grew, Avishag took counsel with the Levite. Though he was pleased about the King's oath, she knew that he wished no harm to come to the young prince. But all Eviatar would say was, "Yedidiah is alive, and so is his mother." When she tried to question him further, he admonished her: "Why do you trouble yourself about them, Avishag? Do you not know that the King suffered calamity after calamity at the hands of our Israelite brothers? They followed Absalom and they followed Sheva ben Bichri, and even chose the lame and foolish Meribaal for a king… My master, old Eviatar, was wont to say that David dealt too gently with the House of Joseph. Perhaps he should have remained in Hebron, to rule over the Israelites from the ancient city of Yah and of Judah. For it was chiefly to please them that he set his throne and the Ark in this city, which lies between the lands of Judah and Benjamin."

"But must Shlomo pay with his life for the wrongdoing of the Israelites? Is he not also the King's son, and one to whom the King promised the throne, albeit in bitterness of heart?"

"The King will undo that promise when Adoniyah is anointed," was all the Levite would say on that point.

"Ira," she asked – for she never called him by his old master's name – "Ira, does the King know where the Great Lady and her son are held?"

The Levite frowned and did not reply. He bade her farewell and hastened away, saying he could hear his acolyte calling his name. He had never been so abrupt with her, and Avishag's anxiety increased.

The moon of Ziv waxed full and on the northern summit the priestesses were celebrating with music and dancing. Listening to their revelry in the night, Avishag thought of the Great Lady and her devotion to the goddess, whom the Hittites call Arinna. But it was Shlomo who was constantly in her thoughts. Prostrating herself before the mother of all living, she prayed for his life and vowed that she would not rest until she knew what had befallen him. If by the month's end no word came, she would entreat the King for help.

Word was brought her by none other than the King's son Kilav. He came to the city with a gift for his brother Adoniyah from the lord of Ekron – two fine mares and their foals. The King welcomed him gladly and bade him remain at his house for some days.

Whenever Avishag saw Kilav she thought he was the King himself, restored to youth and vigour, so much did he favour his father. In her secret heart, she thought that were he to ask for her hand she would not refuse him.

In the morning, when the King and Kilav, with Yehoshafat the recorder, were sitting at their ease in the shade of a spreading fig tree in the garden, Avishag went to the garden wall and looked out towards the wilderness of Judea. She thought of the journeys to Ein Gedi, and her talk with Shlomo that night on the shore of the salt sea. She heard his voice saying, "I shall build me a winter house in Ein Gedi, and a garden with all manner of trees, and a pond to attract the birds. I shall spend my winters here, with my wives and my companions…" A shiver went through her and the view misted before her eyes.

"Is it well with you, Avishag, my sister?" She turned and saw Kilav standing beside her.

Avishag smiled. "Well indeed, my lord! And is all well with you and your house?"

"I beg you, do not call me lord, my sister! I am no prince, while you are the King's right hand."

Gazing at the distant mountains, he said in a low voice, "I bring you word from one who went away a month ago." He touched her shoulder. "Do not start. Let us speak together quietly, thus… My brother Yedidiah and his mother are in Mahanaim. They are safe, though they may not leave the stronghold."

Amazed by his words, she collected herself and replied quietly, "Mahanaim? Is it not across the Jordan?" Her thoughts had never turned that way. It was Shechem she been thinking of, or failing that, the Hittite country in the north.

"It is east of Gilead, a short ride from the Jordan. They have been entrusted to Kimham, the son of Barzillai, the Gileadite elder who provisioned and aided the King at the time of Absalom's uprising."

She wanted to turn and look at him, but caution made her gaze at the wilderness, which was still fresh and green, as the sun had not yet parched the earth. Below them, on the hillside, a flock of goats grazed on the grasses and thistles, while the boy who herded them lay supine in the shade of a castor bush.

"I did not know where they were, Kilav," she said softly. "The guard at their door said they had gone to Shechem, but I did not believe him. I feared that they were dead… Does the King know?"

Kilav rested his hands, the strong hands of a charioteer and forge-master, on top of the stonewall. "The King said only, Deal gently with my son Yedidiah. But remembering that he had said those very words when Absalom rose up against him, yet Yoav ben Zeruiah did not scruple to slay him, my father made us all swear an oath that not a hair of Yedidiah's head or his mother's should fall."

A large dog pushed its way between them, sniffing at Kilav's garments, which smelled strongly of horses. Avishag thought about Shlomo, and the way he had with all the creatures of the earth and sky. At a word from him a dog would lie down and remain so until released by another word.

"Did Adoniyah also swear this oath?"

"Yes, my sister, he swore... Do not fear. As soon as Adoniyah ben Haggith is anointed, our little brother and his mother will be free to return."

No more was said that morning, for a maidservant came to tell Avishag that Adoram, the master of the King's tribute, had come and was waiting in the hall.

Later that day Kilav described to Avishag how the Great Lady and Shlomo were taken in the night by Yoav ben Zeruiah and a dozen of his warriors and carried to the Gilead and across the river. There, in the old stronghold of Mahanaim, they were met by Kimham, the son of Barzillai the Gildeadite, who bade them welcome. Though they were confined to the citadel, their host was kind and generous with Bathsheva and her son. "Kimham's mother was a Hittite, like Bathsheva," said Kilav. "He will let no harm come to the Lady or to Yedidiah."

Kilav had accompanied them to Mahanaim. "The Jordan was still swollen and the fords were impassable. We therefore had to go south and cross the wilderness to Edom, then turn northwards and follow the eastern shore of the salt sea and the bank of the Jordan, till we arrived in Mahanaim seven days later."

"And the Lady's Hittite servants, Kilav?" asked Avishag. "Where are they?"

"Three are with them – the steward, Yedidiah's manservant

and one of his mother's handmaidens. The others are held under guard. They are not far from here."

Avishag had faith in Kilav, for as well as resembling his father, there was about him something of Ornan, her elder brother. He loved Shlomo as Ornan loved her, like a big brother. At length she asked: "Were the Great Lady and Shlomo very much afraid, Kilav, when Yoav and his men took them away in the night? Did they think they would be killed?"

"I did not see them until the next day, when they reached the Kenite encampment at Zorim. Then they were calm and said little. I heard my little brother speak softly to his mother in the Hittite tongue. Hearing him, she raised her head and smiled."

The King's household remained unconcerned by the absence of the Great Lady and her son. Only Titipah, Adoniyah's Egyptian wife, and the Tyrian gardener who tended the King's garden, spoke to Avishag about Shlomo. Filled with foreboding and unwilling to deceive them, she said only that he would doubtless return to Jerusalem before long.

Spring became summer. All over the land the people laboured in the fields and vineyards and few plaintiffs came to seek justice at the King's gate. The counsellors and scribes went to their estates, and even Adoniyah was rarely seen at the King's house.

It was a quiet time in Jerusalem. The Levite priests went forth to hold sacrifices at the ancient high places – some to Beth-El, some to Gilgal and Mizpah – leaving the shrine of the Ark to be served by a single priest and his acolyte. But the Ashera on the northern summit was diligently attended, and her altar and that of her consort El Elyon were never without offerings.

The King seemed content with the quietness of his days. He had stopped his sons from tearing his kingdom apart, and now, he said, the yoke of kingship might rest more easily on his shoulders. He still conferred with his captains and the master of the tribute, and passed long hours with Yehoshafat the recorder. The emissaries of Tyre, Moab, Edom and Gath he saw in the garden bower, for he called their kings brothers. Others, who came from Aram Damascus, or from Rabbah of the Ammonites, were received in the hall. Seated on his lion-footed throne, the gold circlet on his head, he spoke to them in a measured voice and a stern mien. Whenever Adoniyah was in the King's city, he sat beside his father and took part in the councils.

With the Great Lady away, the King passed all his nights in his sleeping chamber. But he slept less than before, and often lingered on the roof until the midnight watch, gazing at his city and the valley below. At such times Avishag had only to ask, and he would gladly speak about the former days, recalling the companions of his youth, the perils they had known and the joys. But he never spoke about the Great Lady or her son, and Avishag forbore to mention them.

When she was not at the King's side, Avishag helped Naamah to nurse Temimah, who was gravely ill. Something was consuming the innards of the old concubine, causing her a pain worse than the pangs of childbirth. After a while her agony abated and her cries no longer resounded in the women's house, but she was too weak to rise from her couch. Eglah, the wise woman from Siloam, had done all she could to heal her, but it was too late – the seed of death had sprouted in her bowels and could not be purged away. The Edomite therefore prepared a potion that eased Temimah's pain and made her drowsy. From time to time her eyes would open and she would gaze searchingly at Avishag, who nursed her as gently as a daughter.

"Why is your spirit so low, my child?" she asked one morning. "Has anything happened in the house since I fell ill?"

Avishag was taken aback. She had hidden her anxiety from all eyes, but had not troubled to do so in the sick woman's chamber.

"Mother," she said softly, holding Temimah's bony hands in hers, "I fear for Shlomo's life…" And she recounted all that had happened since the King's oath.

A smile flitted over the dying woman's face. "So love has come to you at last," she whispered. "I told Naamah that the days of your virginity were numbered."

Avishag was vexed but did not gainsay her. She turned away and began rubbing Temimah's feet, to soothe her. When she looked back, the old woman's eyes had again closed in sleep.

Another day, Temimah, whose life was ebbing fast, motioned to Avishag to come close. "When I have gone the way of all the earth," she gasped, "you must tell the King… tell him…" Her voice was so low that Avishag had to bend close to her mouth. The smell of death was upon her and the maid held her breath.

"Tell the King – Absalom did not touch me. He bade me wash his feet and dress his hair and beard, but he did not touch me… He lay with the first woman that was brought to him, the little Moabite who had but lately come to the house. The others he did not touch…"

"Mother! Why did you not say this to the King? Was he ever told?"

The old woman shook her head slightly, her face ashen with the effort of speaking. "Whether Absalom lay with us or not, the injury was done… The people saw the tent upon the roof, saw Absalom enter and saw us taken in to him, one by one… But when I am dead, you may tell the King."

Temimah died that night. Her son Yafia, who had not seen her since the outrage, when he was a mere boy, came to bury her in the sepulchre of her Jebusite fathers on the Mount of Olives. But he begged the King's leave to pass the days of mourning at his home in Maon. Avishag resolved to tell the King what Temimah had said, but time passed and she held her peace.

Beneath the quietness of the long summer days a new tempest was brewing, but only the keenest ears heard its early rumblings. When the fifth moon waxed full, priestesses gathered from all the nearby shrines and groves to celebrate the holy night around the ancient Ashera on the north summit. The King gave Avishag leave to spend the night in their company, in the worship of the goddess.

"I shall pray to the Queen of Heaven to bless my lord's house," Avishag promised the King before she set out.

The celebration lasted all night, and ended when the first light of the sun touched the head of the Ashera. Then the women who had come to take part in the rites went home, dazed and happy, leaning on each other in their weariness. The priestesses gathered in the nearby grove house to eat their morning meal, and Avishag – whom they honoured since the oracle was brought to Jerusalem at her urging – remained to break bread with them.

There she heard that there had been skirmishes in Mount Ephraim, which had been quelled swiftly and harshly by Judean warriors and their Philistine allies. Blood had been spilt and some men of Ephraim, with Hittite support, had taken to the wilderness.

"They do not wish to be ruled by Adoniyah ben Haggith, nor to be led by the Yah-worshipping Levites," said a priestess, whose speech reminded Avishag of her native country. "The elders of Benjamin may be willing to place their necks under the yoke of Judah, but not the men of Ephraim. Does not the King know this?"

Avishag was taken aback. Long ago she had repeated to the King her grandfather's warning, but those words weighed little, when his counsellors of Judah and the Levites were speaking otherwise, day after day. Now the fear that had been smouldering in her heart flared up like a summer blaze.

"Were the skirmishes only in Mount Ephraim, or also in Jezreel and the Galilee?" she asked, trembling. But no one could tell her where the rising had been, nor which of the clans of Israel had taken part in it.

As she walked back to the King's house the tears blinded her and she stumbled and fell on the path. Her palms were cut by the stones and the hurt released the sobs she had been holding back. She sat down on a rock and wept bitterly.

Before going into the King's house she bathed her hands and face at the cistern in the forecourt. She smoothed her garments and hair and was about to enter the hall, when a maidservant came and whispered to her that someone was awaiting her behind the gatehouse.

It was her brother Ornan.

He was ragged and dusty and his head was muffled as though he had been winnowing. He did not remove his headcloth even while he hugged her. Avishag begged him to come into the King's house, but he refused.

"No one must know that I have come to Jerusalem," he said in a low voice, speaking through the cloth. "Go into the house and let no one see that you are troubled... When can you come out to meet me, and where?"

Avishag was at a loss. Where could she hide her brother in the King's city? And how could she leave the King's house to meet him in secret? She was weary after the night's celebrations and her thoughts fluttered aimlessly. At length she said, "Do you see the village on yonder hillside, to the south and east of the King's city? It is Siloam. There, not far from the spring, you shall see a great terebinth oak, and in its shade a hut. A wise woman by the name of Eglah the Edomite dwells there, who is known to me. Tell her I sent you and bide with her till I come."

She would have liked to send some victuals or other gifts to the wise woman, to secure her good will, but Ornan would not wait.

"Tell Eglah that when I come I shall reward her kindness," she said, hugging her brother, her eyes brimming. He left her then, making his way swiftly downhill, through the wild olives and castor bushes. A moment later he was out of sight.

The King was kind and sent Avishag to rest after the holy night's vigil. The next morning, the King and the Lion-slayer went hunting for partridge and quail in the valley of Kidron, and Avishag led a mule out of the stable and rode to Siloam with gifts for Eglah in her saddlebag.

Eglah's serving lad was at the well. When he saw Avishag he ran to the hut to announce her coming. The wise woman was away from home, but she had provided her guest with a pallet, water ewer, bread and figs.

"Why do you hide your face, Ornan?" Avishag asked, fearfully, for his head was still swathed in the cloth. "Are you wounded?"

"No, not wounded... I shall show you." His face flushed dark when he removed the cloth and Avishag gasped – his beard had been cut off, leaving mere stubble on his cheeks.

"Who did this, my brother?"

"The Judeans, my sister, Adoniyah's warriors! They captured us and cut off not only our beards but our gowns, up to the buttocks... They jeered at us, saying the next time they would cut higher."

Now he told his sister all that had happened since the King's oath. When the Israelites heard that Adoniyah ben Haggith would soon rule over them, aided by Judah's Philistine allies and the Levites, the elders of the clans held a council in Baal Hazor. The Benjamites counselled patience – King David was yet alive, they said, and might heed the protests of the Israelites, if these were put to him firmly and honourably. For the Benjamites are afraid of Judah, being a small tribe that had been all but destroyed in the days of the Judges. Though their own House of Saul was extinguished by David, they had lately been placated by the burial of the impaled men and by Adoniyah's marriage to a Benjamite woman. But the Ephraimites were very hot against Judah and Adoniyah, and the Israelites of the north, who were allied with the Hittites, tended after Shlomo. The elders deliberated for three days, some calling for an uprising while others proposed entreating King David to undo his oath. At length they resolved to send messengers to the King, to implore him to choose another heir.

"But whom would you have as king?" Avishag asked her brother, and at once remembered that this was the very question for which her grandfather had rebuked once, but did not answer.

"Some have said Shefatiah ben Avital," Ornan replied, rubbing his face. The loss of his beard troubled him, but to Avishag he looked as he did in the far-off days, when she was a little child and his beard had just begun to sprout. "Shefatiah is a great man in his country, an elder and a judge, and his mother is an Israelite. But if the King chose Shlomo, the Children of Israel would keep their peace... Is it true, my sister, that he and his mother are held captive in a stronghold in Judea?"

"They are captive, Ornan, but not in Judea," she answered, afraid to say any more. "But tell me what happened to the messengers."

"There were ten of us, one from each of the foremost clans, strong young men, for the elders feared that Yoav ben Zeruiah and his warriors would try to capture us. We kept to the mountains, hoping to reach the King's city by way of Benjamin. But no sooner did we pass Shechem than a company of Judean and Gittite warriors fell upon us from the forest and brought us before their captain, a young man of Judah whom they called Ben-Shafan. He it was who ordered the outrage... Then they gave us back our mules and saddlebags, saying, 'Go back where you came from! Tell your elders: If you rise up against King David or his heir Adoniyah, there shall be none left in Ephraim that pisses against the wall!'"

As he spoke, Ornan clenched and unclenched his hands, furious and helpless.

There was a silence. Outside the hut the Edomite lad was watering Avishag's mule and speaking to it in his tongue. Inside it was dark and hot and there were sharp smells from Eglah's store of herbs and other things.

"My sister, you are our hope," Ornan said softly. "You have the ear of the King, and you alone can sway him, if swayed he may yet be. Surely he does not wish the kingdom he has put together to be rent in two! Speak to him, Avishag! Tell him what you have seen and heard. Let me go back with a word of hope for our people..." And Ornan hid his face in his hands and wept. Avishag had never seen him cry, and it wrenched her heart. She knelt before him and embraced him till he recovered.

After a while she asked, "Was blood spilt in Mount Ephraim? The priestesses said that there have been skirmishes and some men fled to the wilderness."

"So I heard in Gibeah, where I stopped on my way here. But I do not know who the men were, or if any of them died."

He rose and bathed his face in a basin and swathed his head again.

"I cannot remain here," he said, taking her by the hand. "All day people come to the old woman for advice and potions. I shall go into the country of Benjamin, and bide there until the new moon. Then I shall come to the King's house in the guise of a Canaanite pedlar, saying that I bring a gift to you from your mother, and you shall tell me the King's answer."

It was not an easy task that lay before her. Before the oath, Avishag had felt free to speak to the King about his sons and his kingdom. When she sent him the false widow in Bethlehem it was but a parable, such as the elders and wise women tell, to urge him to decide. But since the oath, the King had withdrawn even from her. He made no mention of the Great Lady or her son, and she forbore to speak of them until he did. She did not even tell him Temimah's dying words, for they were a reminder of a rebellious son and the kingdom in peril. How could she now disclose what his captains and counsellors had hidden from him?

If only there were someone with whom she could take counsel before speaking to the King! But all of the King's house sided with Adoniyah, with the rule of Judah over Israel. Had none of them foreseen the outcome? Yet if the King had chosen Shlomo, as he had once promised the Great Lady, would not the people of Judah have taken up arms and marched on Jerusalem to stop him? "Never will the son of the Hittite widow rule over us!" was the rallying cry of the sons of Zeruiah and others of the clan of Caleb. The King was greater than all of them, for he had brought together the tribes of Israel and Judah, and made them perforce into one nation under the sun. But now he was old and weary and could no longer bend them to his will.

The King did not perceive that Avishag was distressed. She served him as she always did, and he was content with her wise and loyal stewardship. His thoughts dwelt on the past and shrank from the future. He spoke often of Saul and Jonathan, as though they had not been dead these thirty-three years. He spoke also of Michal, whose pride and bitterness still galled him. The days of Ziklag and of

Gath, the days of his kingship over Judah in Hebron, these images were in his thoughts morning and evening. Amnon, Tamar and Absalom he recalled only as children, before the calamities which befell them and him.

And yet, though it would shatter the calm of his declining days, she knew it was her duty to speak to him, to disclose what his counsellors and captains were keeping hidden. She must tell him of the trouble that was brewing in Israel.

One evening after supper – it was three days after Ornan's furtive visit – the King climbed up to the roof and Avishag went with him. They were met by a strange sight – the sun had just sunk behind the mountains to the west, and whole dome of heaven was stained blood red. Down in the city people clustered on the roofs and in the streets, staring up at the ominous sight. In the courtyard below someone whimpered in terror.

The King remained calm.

"It is not so rare or dreadful a sight as you think, my child," he said to Avishag, who was gazing anxiously at the crimson firmament. "In the southern wilderness such a sky may be seen after a day of dust storms…"

But as he watched he too grew uneasy. The light was fading, but the heavens remained red as blood even as the stars came into view.

Suddenly Ittai the Gittite came up and, keeping his eyes lowered, approached the King. "Nathan the Seer is come, my lord," he whispered and hurriedly retired to a corner of the roof. Like all the Philistines of the King's guard, Ittai feared Nathan worse than an armed enemy or a ravening beast. Caught between the ominous heavens and the Hebrew prophet, the old warrior cowered like a slave.

At a sign from the King, Avishag went to the head of the stairs and met the old seer when he came up. She waited quietly till he recovered his breath and then led him to the roof arbour, where the King was reclining on a couch. She was glad that he appeared not to see or hear her, but went directly to the King and bowed.

"Blessed be your coming to my house, Nathan," the King

said equably. "It has been a long time since you honoured us with a visit."

The old prophet drew his mantle of skins closer, as though he felt cold. "Thou seest the signs in the heavens above, my lord," he croaked, pointing at the sky. But there was no force in his voice and face, and all at once Avishag lost her fear of him; he was merely a strange old man.

"I see a red sunset, prophet. What it betokens I know not, but doubtless you shall tell me."

The King's calm reply revealed his late disdain for the seer. This was no Samuel, whose appearance even after death had struck terror in King Saul's stalwart heart.

"My lord, I cannot say…"

"What? Has God cast you off, that you no longer speak for him?" the King taunted, but at once felt remorseful.

"Sit you down, ancient companion! Avishag will give you cool water with date-honey to refresh you, and I shall listen to your every word."

Nathan hesitated, then sat down on a hassock and accepted a cup of water from Avishag's hand. While he drank, Ittai came out of his corner and scuttled around the roof to the stairs. The King saw him and laughed.

"My lord," Nathan began in a stronger voice, "thy kingdom shakes, as a tree is shaken by a great wind that seeks to uproot it. The Israelites are up in arms, and thy captains are even now crushing them. The omens in the heavens have been sent to warn thee –"

The King broke in. "What dream is this you have dreamed, prophet? There is no trouble in my kingdom! All is quiet between Dan and Beersheba." The King spoke evenly, but he sat up and Avishag saw his hands clench.

"No, my lord, it is not a dream but the truth of truths! After thine oath to put Adoniyah on the throne, the Israelite elders gathered in Baal Hazor. Some called for an uprising, to thwart thy choice of heir. In the end they sent hither ten messengers, one from each great clan, to beseech thee to undo the oath."

"No messengers have come to me... Avishag, is this true?" he asked, raising his hand to silence the seer.

Trembling, for her world seemed to be falling apart, she fell on her knees before the King. "True, my lord. It is three days since I heard about it from my brother Ornan... I feared to tell you, my lord!"

"Where is your brother now? Why did he not come to me?"

"He was ashamed to appear before my lord in his condition. Also, he feared for his life in this city... Forgive me, my lord!"

Nathan opened his mouth, but the King did not let him speak. Night had fallen and now two slaves came up bearing lighted lamps. When they left, Avishag told the King all that she had heard from the priestesses and Ornan. The King rose and began to pace to and fro on the roof. Then he stopped and spoke to the girl, who was still on her knees.

"Am I so fierce a master, Avishag, that you feared to tell me the truth? I know that smooth-tongued counsellors lie, and some old warriors believe their ways are better than mine..."

He raised his hands to the star-strewn heavens. "Oh Lord Yah!" he cried. "Deliver me from lying lips, from deceitful tongues! Woe is me – I am for peace, but when I speak, they are for war!"

Those were the verses he had sung when driven from his city by Absalom's revolt. Though stung by his rebuke, she was glad to hear these words from his lips. So he was neither too old nor too weary to save his kingdom from being drenched in blood!

"What say you, prophet? Is not Adoniyah, the son of Haggith, a priestess of Yah, the rightful heir to my throne?"

"My lord, Adoniyah is thine eldest son, and a true son of Judah. He serves our Lord Yah with all his heart. He is a stalwart warrior who can lead the host and win..."

"Why then do you mumble your words so, prophet, as though they tasted salty in your mouth? Speak plainly!"

The grim old seer seemed subdued. He wavered and at length said, "It is not the will of God that Adoniyah follow thee on the throne, for if he lose half the kingdom so will our Lord Yah. Thou hast made Jerusalem the city of Yah and the heart of a great kingdom, for the tribes of Israel have learned to honour thee and worship our god; but they will not submit to the son of Haggith and to his followers, to the Calebites and the Levites. Like the Egyptian calf they worship, they will kick over the pot and spill the milk."

A shrunken red moon had risen and hung over the King's city. Nathan had his back to it, or doubtless he would have taken cover. Avishag was dismayed to hear him speak as though the Lord Yah were the only god for the King's people. Like Eviatar the Levite, he sought to impose Yah's rule upon the whole kingdom, though he went about it in a different way. Did they not see that Jerusalem was a great high place for all the host of heaven and its queen? However, she kept her peace, for Nathan was opening the King's eyes to the perils of Adoniyah's rule, better than she or her brother could have done.

The King stood by the parapet and looked out over the city, the hills and vales, towards Hebron. Down in the city cooking fires were still burning in many inner yards and oil lamps flickered on roofs, to ward off the evening's fearful portents. The guards and the household were unusually quiet, and the wailing of jackals could be heard from the valley of Hinnom. The seer sat motionless, his head hanging low on his breast. His bonnet of skins had fallen off, exposing a bald pate amid the shaggy locks. At last the King turned back and said to them, "Better is a poor and wise child than an old and foolish king who will not be admonished. Avishag, bring your brother to me when he returns. Old man, the Lord Yah has sent you to me in time. Do not go back to Kiryat Yearim but bide here a while, for I shall have need of you. And let neither one of you speak to a soul about it, for a bird of the air might carry the word!"

But could the King's oath be undone? Ira could have answered this question, but he had declared himself for Adoniyah and was not to be trusted at such a time.

The King made no move to disavow his choice, but quietly took counsel with those of his men who were not of the camp of

Adoniyah. Such were the old priest Zadok, Adoram, the master of the tribute, and Benaiah the Lion-slayer. They came one by one and sat with the King under the spreading fig tree in the garden, sipping wine-and-water and speaking together in low voices. At such times the King sent the recorders and scribes away on diverse errands, and only Ittai the Gittite and Avishag attended him. The lady Ephrat, Yonadav's sister, had left the King's city some days before and returned to Hebron, and Adoniyah's camp were untroubled, assured that all would go well, now that the King was slowly relinquishing the reins of the kingdom. The prince himself travelled around the land in his chariot, accompanied by horsemen and bowmen.

Every morning, before the sun rose, Avishag walked up the path to the northern summit to burn incense to the Ashera and to the oracle of Shiloh. She was known to be a favourite of the priestesses, and no one wondered at her zeal, or else thought it was in the King's service that she went there daily. She went there not only to seek the goddess' help, but to speak with the priestesses, who had eyes and ears all over the land. Each of them had kinsmen and clan, and to their grove came gifts and petitions from Dan in the north to Beersheba in the south.

The weightiest question she put to them was soon answered.

"A solemn oath may be untied," said Meulah, one of the oldest priestesses. She was the daughter of Nimshi, the Gibeonite high priest, and was held to be the wisest of them all. "But the rite of untying is long and hard for an old man."

Then she told Avishag how it might be done. Avishag trembled to think of the King enduring such a trial as this. And what if he did not endure…?

"Should not the young prince be brought back before all this is done?" asked Avishag.

"That is for the King to say," replied Meulah. "While he is under the oath the goddess will give no sign."

Avishag understood that the priestesses wished to keep out of the smouldering war between the camp of Judah and the camp of the Israelites. But their preference was clear: under the reign of

Adoniyah ben Haggith, the Levites would hold sway in Jerusalem. All the other rites would be hard pressed to assure that they did not suffer neglect. But under Shlomo, the Levites and the Judean hotheads would be kept in place, and Jerusalem would remain as it had always been – a centre of worship for all men and women and all rites.

Her heart was very heavy. With her Danite widow ruse she had urged the King to make known his choice of heir, not thinking that the Israelites would rise up, nor that Adoniyah's captains and followers would be so heavy-handed. She had forgotten her grandfather's warning. Moreover, Shlomo, for all his grace and wisdom, was much disliked by the Judeans, and not all his mother's gifts and blandishments served to win them over.

Yet, thought Avishag, the King could have prevailed over his kinsmen to accept his youngest son, more readily than his captains could subdue the sullen Israelites. And Shlomo, if he were to be king, would keep the Levites in check.

But now time was short. Every day rumours of skirmishes in the north reached the ears of the priestesses and made them all fearful.

Ornan returned as he had promised, on the eve of the new moon. As the day drew to a close, a maidservant came to Avishag, saying that a Canaanite pedlar had come from Jezreel bringing a gift to her from her mother. When she went down, Avishag saw how Ornan sought to efface himself in the lengthening shadows in the forecourt. Clad in a dusty cloak, he stood humbly by the gate, holding a laden ass by the halter. She yearned to run and embrace him, but seeing the soldiers and servants about, she walked towards him sedately, biting her lip.

Pretending to examine his wares, she told him in a low voice to go at once to the house of Oved-Edom, west of the King's city. He was to remain there and await word from the King.

"Is not Oved-Edom a Gittite, an ally of Judah?" asked Ornan in a low voice, muffled by the head cloth.

"Oved-Edom is the King's man, brother, a kinsman of Ittai. Fear nothing," she said firmly, "but go to his house and give him this pledge." She put a leather pouch in his hand, as though in payment for his wares. In it was a piece of scarlet cord with a pottery bead, bearing the imprint of a crouching lion – the emblem of Judah and its scion King David.

"The King knows about the skirmishes in Ephraim and wishes to hear from your lips all that has happened." Looking into his eyes she added, "He is good and wise, Ornan! He will not let Adoniyah's camp tear his kingdom apart and drench it in blood. But he does not wish to crush them by violence, for that might break up the kingdom another way."

"I have faith in the King," Ornan replied in a low voice,"but I do not trust his men, neither the Judeans nor the Philistines."

"Have faith in me, then, my brother!" she urged. "Go now!"

She stood at the gate and watched him lead his beast down the steep path. Her heart was in her mouth, and she felt more alone than ever before. Was she doing the right thing? What right had she to interfere in the choice of the next king? What if Adoniyah really were the rightful heir, and Shlomo the intruder, pushed forward by his scheming, ambitious mother? But she had turned away from Adoniyah and his camp and there was no turning back.

Early the next morning the King rode out of the city. With him went Avishag, Ittai the Gittite, Benaiah the Lion-slayer and two lads bearing bows and quivers. Turning west from the valley of Kidron, they made their way slowly towards the western hills, stopping only once to rest under some trees by the wayside. Few words were spoken. Partridges and hoopoes rose from the thickets, gazelles darted across their path and hyraxes peered at them from the rocks, but the lads were not allowed to draw a single arrow from their quivers. The three old men did not spare a glance for the creatures that at other times they delighted to hunt. The sun was high in the heavens when they reached the estate of Oved-Edom and rode through the gate.

Oved-Edom himself, a heavy old man who had been King

David's armour bearer in years gone by, came out to greet them. Tears poured from his eyes as he bowed low and helped his old captain alight from his mule. A throng of women and children surrounded the visitors, shouting and ululating with excitement as they were led inside. There, their feet were bathed and they rested from their journey, while the household prepared a fit repast for the King.

Oved-Edom had hidden the Israelite in the house of the oil-press, and now he sent to fetch him. When Ornan entered the chamber and saw the Lion-slayer at the King's side, he recoiled. The old warrior was a Judean, though not of the Calebite clan – would he not side with Adoniyah, as did most of his people? Seemingly he did not, for the King trusted him.

The room was full of bustling women, some carrying out basins of water and others loading the board with wine, bread and meat.

"Sit you down, Ben Baanah," the King said to Avishag's brother, who bowed low before him. "We shall share bread and wine while I rest from my journey, for I am no longer young. But you are young, and have been here a while. Tell me and my old companion, Benaiah ben Yehoiada, all that befell you and the other emissaries of Ephraim."

When Ornan unwound his head cloth and revealed his almost beardless face, the King frowned. He knew that to the men of the north a beardless man was a man without honour. They had little truck with smooth-shaven people, like some of the highborn Philistines, or the sleek Egyptians who despised the hirsute, wool-clad men of these lands.

Ornan recounted what he had told Avishag. He described the gathering of the elders, and the diverse counsels that were given, some calling for an uprising and others for petitioning the King. Then he told how the Judean warriors captured the emissaries in the forest, and what their captain Ben-Shafan had said.

"And where are the others now, my son?" asked the King, who had not touched a morsel while the young man spoke.

"Two are in the country of Benjamin, awaiting my return. The others have gone back to their homes…. My lord, the men of Ephraim are much aggrieved. If Adoniyah does not punish Ben-Shafan and his men and make amends for their acts, there will be no end of bloodletting between his men and ours. I crave your indulgence, my lord. Your goodness and forbearance are known throughout the land, but we fear Adoniyah ben Haggith."

"Will the men of Israel accept Adoniyah if he punished Ben-Shafan and made amends for the insult to the emissaries?"

There was silence. The King and Benaiah exchanged glances. Ornan hung his head and seemed lost in thought.

"My lord, I fear they will not," he said at length. His eyes, which resembled Avishag's eyes, moved the King to trust him. "Too much has come to pass between the captains of Judah and the Israelites. The sons of Zeruiah and their men have lorded over us, until the shepherds and the villagers tremble at the sound of their names. They pass through our country like a swarm of locusts, stripping it bare. And Adoniyah – forgive me, my lord – he has told our elders he would chastise us with scorpions, to punish us for past uprisings…"

The Lion-slayer spoke up. "Adoniyah's sting is sharp, but if he were king, he would rule justly and even-handedly."

"If you please, my lord," Ornan retorted stoutly, "we care neither for his sting nor for his honey."

The King nodded and his eyes smiled. It was an apt reply.

"Under the sceptre of David we have known prosperity and peace," the young Jezreelite went on. "It is true that there have been uprisings, and foolish counsels, but the tribes of Israel are content with your rule, my lord king, and pray to the Elohim that the son of Jesse live forever."

"And yet you complain against my captains and kinsmen!"

Ornan was undaunted. "My lord's captains may wrong us, but the King himself is good and just; and so we live. But if captains and king alike lay heavy hands on us, our lives would not be worth an olive stone."

"Whom, then, would you have as king after me?" asked the King. Avishag stared at the patterns on the floor and tried to still her trembling; her brother's answer might sway the Kingdom. But Ornan shook his head.

"It is not for me to say, my lord."

The King sighed and leaned back on the bolster. Avishag had told him that the Israelites spoke of Shefatiah ben Avital as one whom they would accept – and so would the Judeans, if pressed. But he knew that Shefatiah was a weakling, given to childish pleasures and easily swayed. Compared to Adoniyah, Shefatiah was a broken reed… The Israelites had foolishly put the inept Meribaal on Saul's throne – he was not about to pass his kingdom to an inept man of his own seed. He drew a deep breath, and his glance fell on Avishag. The girl's eyes were upon him, bright as polished onyx, intent and as though willing him to speak. All at once he knew what was on her mind, and wondered that he had not divined it before. He nodded to her to come close.

"It is Yedidiah, is it not, my child, whom you would have me declare as my heir?" he said softly.

She was taken aback. Though she had willed him to think of Shlomo, she was abashed to hear him say so. The King might think it was her woman's heart that swayed her judgement. Her face burned and she hung her head.

"It is not for me to say, my lord," she replied, echoing her brother.

But the King persisted. Avishag was no wilful maiden, who cries as her eyes alight on a comely young man, He is my heart's desire, father, I will have none but him! Nor was she hostile to the Judeans. What then was in her mind?

"You have been at my side, Avishag," he said, speaking as though they were alone, "day and night, summer and winter, in my city and without. My sons, too, are known to you, the first and the last, and you are wise beyond your years. Speak your mind, my child. Is the younger more fit to rule than the elder?"

No one moved. The servants had left the room and Oved-

Edom had taken his kinsman Ittai to see his infant great-grandson. The question weighed heavily on the girl and she touched the serpent amulet on her chest. The eyes of the King, of Benaiah and her brother were upon her.

"No, my lord," she replied. "I cannot say that Shlomo is more fit to rule the Kingdom. Adoniyah is a great and valiant man, while Shlomo is young and untried. But, my lord, Adoniyah knows that the people of Israel fear him and loathe his followers, yet he has done nothing to placate them and to check his warriors. Under his shield, too, the Levites have mocked the priests of Ephraim, and who will resist them when he reigns? Your son Yedidiah is neither a Judean nor an Israelite – he is Shlomo, and there is none like him. Though he is young, yet nothing escapes his eye. He sees what others do not see and hears what they do not hear. If it be your will and your command to make him your heir, my lord, he will be a great king after you, and make your kingdom still greater."

She paused for breath, surprised by her own confidence. Then she added very softly, "But only if the Judeans accept him, my lord. Only if the Judeans accept him."

Her heart fluttered in her breast. Never before had she spoken so boldly, as though she were a grey-bearded counsellor. With lowered eyes, she took his hand and pressed it to her forehead. She knew that her words about the Judeans stung him. She had heard him say that since the fall of Absalom, the Calebites had grown too mighty and proud. But could he curb them now?

The King had no doubt.

"The Judeans," he said firmly, "will do my bidding. They are my flesh and my bone, and I have brought them this far... They will obey!"

Silence fell in the cool, shadowy room. The three men and the maid thought their own thoughts. Outside, a woman was lowering a brass pitcher into the cistern, and it clanged against the stony sides as it tumbled down to the water. The King lifted his head and listened as if the sounds spoke to him. His face was pale and set, and the room remained silent for a long time.

The King would have gone back to his city that day, but Avishag prevailed on him to rest and ride back in the morning, in the coolness of dawn. But Ornan departed with Benaiah, accompanied by one of the lads and two of Oved-Edom's sons. They went north, avoiding the city, heading for Gibeah of the Benjamites, where Ornan's companions awaited him.

In the morning, riding with his men towards the rising sun, the King thought about the task that lay before him, as fateful as any he had faced in his long life. He must turn his fellow Judeans from Adoniyah's side to that of Shlomo, the son of the Hittite widow. He must bend the stiff-necked Calebites to his will, though but a few months had passed since his solemn oath to place the son of Haggith on the throne.

One by one they passed before his eyes – Yonadav, his wily kinsman, as subtle and devious a man as the great Ahitophel; Yoav, the last of the sons of Zeruiah, a great captain, hard and gnarled and utterly faithful – though he it was who had speared the young Absalom, when he had hung helpless between heaven and earth... And proud Ephrat, and the Levites, and, first and foremost, Adoniyah himself – a valiant man, haughty, masterful, a leader of men...

Was Yedidiah, or Shlomo, as they all called him, a kingly man? Was he not, as Adoniyah had said at the feast, a stargazer, a learned mage? All his other sons had born arms before they were thirteen years of age, but not Yedidiah, whose hands were as smooth as a pampered woman's... If only he could place Adoniyah on the throne and set Shlomo beside him, as his counsellor! But it was not to be. The lion of Judah would never be counselled by the Hittite leopard.

A great weariness fell upon him, and he wished he could ride on to Bethlehem, sit under his father's fig tree and sing and play upon the shepherd's pipe for Eliav's children. Then he recalled that the fig tree had been struck by lightning many years before, and Eliav's children were greybeards like himself, or else dwelt under the earth with the Forefathers. He spurred his mule forward. Ittai and Avishag and the archers followed. Soon they came within sight of

Jerusalem, shimmering in the morning light. The King sighed. His city appeared to him like a millstone, and himself an aged bullock condemned to turn its wheel till his dying day.

"Lord Yah, God of my forefathers, thou who hast girded me with strength to battle, deliver me from the strivings of my people…" Thus he had prayed more times than he could remember. Surely the Lord Yah would not fail him now, but would support his lifted arms till the day was done.

Then he saw a troop of Philistine guards come out of the southern gate to meet him and escort him back to the King's fort, for which he had to thank the faithful Ittai. Once back in his hall, he sent for Nathan the Seer and for Zadok, the High Priest, for it was they who would lead him through the untying of his oath. But on Avishag he laid the weightiest task, one he could entrust to no other hands.

"Go to Mahanaim, Avishag," he bade her, as if she were one of his captains, "and bring back my son Yedidiah."

Chapter nine

The shadows of night were gathering, though in the west the sky was still aglow. The evening star, which they of the north called Ashtarot, gleamed in the twilight, awaiting the rising of the moon. The only sounds were the hooves of the mules and asses, the jingle of their reins and the muted clang of the guards' arms. Not a word was spoken after they came out of the narrow defile through the mountains and into the open plain of Ayalon. Beside Avishag rode two of the guards of the King's house, chosen by Ittai and commended by the King. Behind them rode six young Benjamite men from Gibeah, who had joined them outside the city. They had been sent by the Lion-slayer, who had gone back and was now at the King's side.

Only the priestesses knew that the King had sent Avishag from Jerusalem on a secret errand. It was assumed by the members of the King's house that she had withdrawn to the grove in fulfilment of a vow, and if any doubted it, none was so bold as to question it.

A runner had been sent to Kilav ben Abigail, to alert him of her coming and bid him prepare for a long journey. Soon she would see him, and together they would turn east and north, to Mahanaim in the Gilead, across the Jordan. But where was Kilav? As darkness fell, owls and bats sallied from the trees and flitted silently over their heads. The mules and asses slowed their pace.

"Mistress," said Itamar, the Gittite guard on her right, speaking close to her ear, "we had best camp here, under these trees."

"Was there not an inn about these parts, with a Danite innkeeper?" asked Avishag. "It cannot be far from this place."

"It is not here, but at the Valley Gate, mistress," he replied. "It is another road we have taken, for fear of spies. We shall start again at first light and be at the meeting-place before the sun is high."

Avishag wanted to ride on. She had hoped to meet Kilav before the day was done, not pass the night in the open, with only the guards about her; but soon it was too dark to go on, for the very road could not be seen.

It was an fearsome night. The virgin moon had no sooner risen than she set again, and darkness lay thick upon them. They kindled a small fire to keep off the wild beasts, but dared not build it higher. There were wild men, too, in these parts, robbers who preyed upon the rich caravans that crossed the land from Aram to Egypt, from Ammon to Philistia. Avishag lay on a heap of cloaks and thought about the King, his sons and the kingdom. If she failed in her mission, if Adoniyah and his men seized the throne in opposition to the King, there would be war. Bad days would return, as it had been when the house of David and the house of Saul fought each other all over the land, or when the uprisings drove the King from his city. Shlomo must be brought back swiftly and proclaimed the heir before the eyes of all the people, though the Judeans would murmur and chafe at this. In the end they would obey the King and accept whichever of his sons he chose to put on his throne. But she remembered, too, another dark night when she heard Ahimaaz the Levite, the son of Zadok the High Priest, boast that the horn of the oil of anointing was held in readiness for Adoniyah, and her heart misgave her.

The King no longer had with him his old captains and companions, who had fought his battles and done the hard deeds on his behalf, who willingly risked their lives to bring him water from the well of Bethlehem, and one by one reduced all his enemies. Some already dwelt with the Forefathers under the earth, and of those who lived all but one were for Adoniyah. His trusted counsellors likewise were of his own clan, and despised the son of the Hittite widow. Those who were with him today, Nathan the Seer, Zadok the High Priest and Benaiah the Lion-slayer, were no match for such as Yonadav and Ira, Ephrat and Yoav. There was only one man in the land who might outwit them all, but he was young and untried and in captivity... These thoughts drove the sleep from her eyes and she grew restless in the lingering night, falling into slumber a little before dawn. At first light Itamar waked her, and in a little while they were on their way again.

The broad plain of Ayalon lay before them, veiled in a light mist. Here many battles had been fought in ancient times, where now flourished fields of wheat and barley, olive orchards and vine-yards.

Here too, amid the groves and pools, a little way from the high road, stood an ancient temple of the Moon, to which people flocked from far and wide. Touching the serpent amulet at her throat, Avishag vowed in her heart that if the goddess prospered her way, she would return to the famed shrine and offer a fine sacrifice on its altar. But now the sun rose, filling the valley with radiance, and she spurred her mule on, towards Haroshet Pelishtim, the place of the iron-forge that was Kilav ben David's domain.

Suddenly Itamar halted and pointed. "There he is, mistress – behold, there is the King's son!" he cried excitedly, for he too had feared that the Judeans would fall upon them before the appointed meeting with Kilav and his men. And there were the chariots, rush-ing furiously forward, banners flying, dust rising, brass shields gleaming in the morning light.

Kilav leaped from his chariot and ran to Avishag. He took her hand and she dismounted. She felt she had never been so happy to see any man. The strong odour of horses that hung about him reminded her of their last talk together in the King's garden.

"Is it well with my father, Avishag?" he asked eagerly. "The King's runner said he bade me follow you wheresoever you lead, with chariots and horses and men. But he did not say why or to what purpose."

They stood in the shade of a great tamarisk, whose boughs were festooned with votary strips of cloth. A cup of water from a skin offered by a manservant refreshed her, and she told Kilav what the King had commanded them do.

"Unless Shlomo is anointed before the eyes of all the people, Adoniyah ben Haggith will inherit the King's throne. Then the Israelites will rise up and the land will be drenched in blood. Already there are skirmishes in Mount Ephraim between the men of Israel and the Judean warriors... Oh Kilav, we must not linger here, but must go at once to Mahanaim and bring back the King's son before the month's end."

"But the men of Judah, will they accept Yedidiah, or Shlomo as you call him? Does my father the King forget how staunch they are for the son of Haggith?"

"He has not forgotten, Kilav. No one knows this better than he. Yet he trusts that they will obey his will at the last, and so must we obey him and do as he bids us. I shall tell you about my brother Ornan and what befell the emissaries of Ephraim, for we have a long journey before us. Call your men, Kilav, and let us away!"

While they spoke, the Gittite guards from Jerusalem told Kilav's men about their mission. The Philistines from the coast stared curiously at the maid who was to lead them and their captain across the land on a secret mission for King David. The Benjamites stood apart from them all, awed and silent. Skilled bowmen and hunters in their own country, they were unaccustomed to dealing with Philistines, and were amazed by the sight of the chariots and horses. Kilav helped Avishag mount his chariot and then went to the Benjamites and spoke to them kindly. His handsome countenance and gentle words set them at ease. But they were mounted on asses, and would be hard put to keep up with the horses and chariots.

He therefore told them to go to the spring of Harod, at the foot of Mount Gilboa, and there await the return of his company. From there they would ride together back to the King's city.

Their troop of three chariots, accompanied by riders on twelve horses and four mules, drew all eyes. For two days they rode north through the lowlands, between the mountains and the seacoast, past villages and encampments, walled and open cities. And everywhere the people gathered along the road and stared at them with awe. Avishag stood beside Kilav in his chariot, and the wind sang in her ears. Though she was anxious about her mission, uneasy about the King and uncertain about the future of Shlomo, the swift journey at Kilav's side filled her with a strange new joy.

They passed the first night in a Kenite encampment, where Kilav was received as though he were the King. Avishag was led to the women's hut beyond the camels' pen, and shown great honour, as befitted a king's emissary. The Kenites never took part in the wars which now and then raged in the land, but offered bread and the milk and cheese of she-camels – for they ate no meat – and the shelter of their big black tents to whoever came in peace and surrendered their arms to the women's keeping. That was why in a corner of the tent where the women feasted Avishag lay a mound of bows and quivers, swords, javelins and bucklers.

In the morning, the weapons were returned to the men and the company mounted the chariots, the horses and mules and went on its way, their saddlebags stuffed with bread, cheeses and dried summer fruits. They rode north, Kilav having sworn that they would be in Taanach before the day was done.

Word of their coming spread through the House of Joseph, and all the Israelites clamoured to welcome them, though it soon appeared that they thought it was King David himself who was riding through the land. Kilav assured the elders that he was only the King's son by Abigail the Jezreelite, sent on a mission to the kingdoms of the north.

"And the maid?" they asked. "Is she the King's daughter?"

Kilav touched her shoulder. "She is my sister. Her hand has been sought in marriage, but I may say no more…"

While they rode, Avishag told Kilav all that had gone before – the skirmishes in Mount Ephraim, the evil deed that was done to the ten emissaries of the Israelites, and how Nathan the Seer had come to see the King on the night when the sky was red, and warned him that his kingdom would be riven in two and Judah and the Lord Yah would lose its northern half to the Israelites, if the son of Haggith should inherit the throne.

"May the Lord Yah prosper our way, then, my sister. I fear the Judeans will take it ill."

They passed the second night in the house of Hazael, the lord of Taanach, who lodged them in his great stone hall, upon couches and bolsters, and gave them fine meats and purple wine. But in all that splendour there was not the peace they had found in the Kenite encampment, where they supped on the simple fare of the tent dwellers, amid the snorting of the camels.

On the third day, they turned east and began to wend their way through the rich valleys between the mountains. They passed so near Shunem, that Avishag thought she could hear the piping of its shepherds and the voices of its children. Had Ornan reached home since she saw him last at the house of Oved-Edom? Her heart grew heavy, and she longed to call a halt and descend from the chariot, to walk through the groves and fields to her father's house, and be once more the child she was before she ever went to the King's city. As the chariot rumbled on, she recalled the song sung by the maidens of her village when one of their company was betrothed:

> *"Return, return, O Shunammite, return, return, that we may look upon thee… How beautiful are thy feet with shoes, O great man's daughter..! How fair and how pleasant art thou, O love!…"*

But she was no longer the Shunammite. She was the King's steward and emissary, as Eliezer had been to Abraham the Hebrew.

The shadows were lengthening when they reached the river Jordan. The bank was hidden behind a thicket of reeds and willows, but the horses and mules, scenting water, stepped forward eagerly. When the company reached the bank and dismounted, the beasts lowered their heads and drank deep, and Avishag and the men bathed their hands and feet and splashed water on their heads. The goatskins were filled afresh, and the men gathered sweet ripe figs in a basket.

When they had rested a little, said Kilav, they were to ride north until they reached a ford, and before the day was done they would be on the other side.

Suddenly the twang of a bowstring broke the stillness. An arrow flew through a willow tree. The men sprang to their feet, and at once the air was filled with shouts and the clashing of brass. Strange men rushed at them from behind the reeds, waving spears and javelins and calling imprecations. Only four of Kilav's men were armed, the others had left their weapons beside the chariots. These four now moved forward and tried to beat back the attackers, while the rest ran to the chariots and picked up their swords and bucklers.

Kilav pushed Avishag behind one of the chariots. Then, he too seized a spear and buckler and rushed at the attackers. A fierce fight was raging, the men bellowed threats and cried out in pain when they were struck. Avishag peered around the side of the chariot and saw that the attackers were fighting with javelins and spears. There were ten of them, Judean warriors by their garments and arms. The battle was hot. Blood ran from the shoulder of Achan, Kilav's armour-bearer. Itamar was fighting nearby with a great scarred warrior who, with a spear in one hand and a javelin with the other, was driving him back towards the chariots. The horses were stamping, rearing and neighing in fear, and the confusion was dreadful. Kilav, who had rushed forward, roaring imprecations against the King's enemies, was fighting near the bank.

There was a long javelin lying on the floor of the chariot, made of stout wood with a sharp brazen point. Avishag picked it up and hefted it. It was as tall as she and weighty, and she held it close, meaning to fend off any attempt to seize her. Nearby, Itamar was being driven back by a Judean warrior, whose javelin he kept thrusting aside with his sword, but he was unable to close with him. A moment later his sword broke, and the adversary raised his spear and was about to run him through. Avishag saw that the Gittite would perish and ran to his side, brandishing the javelin with both hands. The warrior, seeing a maid rushing at him with a javelin, stopped and lowered his arms. Better be taken captive than felled by a woman. Itamar took the javelin from her hands and thrust it into the man's waist through the leather girdle. It did not go deep, but it stopped him in his tracks and he retreated.

The battle raged on, and Avishag refused to withdraw again behind the chariots. But she had no weapon, and could only stand by and see the blood spurt and hear the cries of the men and the screams of the beasts. Itamar, armed with the javelin she had handed him, was in the thick of it, but she could not see Kilav or Achan, who were on the farther side. Little by little the attackers appeared to be losing. One of them lay on the ground nearby, writhing and groaning with pain, while the blood welled from his side and drenched the dust. His spear lay at his feet, forgotten. She crept forward and with a swift movement seized it and stepped back. He did not notice, but drew up his knees and moaned. She saw that he would not rise again. Armed with his spear, she ran behind the chariots and to the other side, and there she saw Kilav and Achan, shoulder to shoulder, fending off three of the attackers who were driving them to the water's edge. She burst out from behind the chariots, waving the spear and shouting.

"In the name of King David!" she cried. "Make way for the King's emissaries!"

The attackers were so amazed by the sight of a young woman in a bloodied gown, her hair flying loose, that they stopped and gaped. In a trice, Kilav's men fell upon them and disarmed them. The battle was over.

Two of the attackers were dying and others were bleeding but able to stand. On the King's side, too, there were injuries, but none so bad as to hinder them from going on. But who were the attack-ers? Their captain, a high-shouldered man with the dark looks of a Kushite, stared fiercely at Kilav and Avishag and remained silent. It was only when Achan prodded him with his sword that he replied, sullenly:

"We are Judeans, sent by Yuval ben Shafan to watch the passes of the Jordan."

"And did Ben Shafan order you to fall upon the King's emis-saries?" asked Avishag.

"It is our task to keep peace in Israel, in the name of King David and our Lord Yah… I did not know you were on the King's errand."

"What shall we do with them?" said Kilav in the end, when he had learned all he wished to know.

"Kill them!" said Achan. He was wounded in his shoulders and legs, and his blood attracted flies and gnats, which stung him.

"Leave them here," said Itamar. "Without their weapons they can do no harm." He had lived long among the Judeans and did not wish to have the blood of their men upon his head.

"What say you, Avishag?" asked Kilav.

"Cut off their beards, my brother," she said, her heart swelling. "Then send them on their way." She had told him what Ben Shafan had done to her brother and the other Israelite emissaries, and Kilav was pleased. He, too, thought this a fitting punishment. Soon there was a heap of cut hair lying on the ground, and the eight Judean warriors, abashed and beaten, crept away.

By now the evening shadows were gathering, and they did not reach the ford before nightfall. They were weary and their wounds hurt. Avishag bathed their wounds with water from the Jordan and dressed them as best she could. They slept in the grove of a horned god whose name they did not know, who was served by an ancient, mute priest who showed no alarm at their appearance. When they made a fire they gave him some of their food, which he nibbled quickly with his remaining teeth, then disappeared among the trees. The men made a circle around Avishag, whom they were now calling "my lady". But she was shaken and anxious. Too many days had passed since she left Jerusalem, time enough for Adoniyah and his men to thwart the King's will.

"There will be songs sung about you, my sister," said Kilav, before sleep overtook them.

"The songs will only be sung in Shlomo's kingdom, my brother," she said. "Not in the kingdom of Adoniyah ben Haggith!" She thought about King Saul, and how in his distress he had found a wise woman who raised the spirit of old Samuel from under the earth, for him to consult. If only she could go now and consult the prophetess Dinah... But it was not to be.

They slept. In the morning, Kilav poured some wine on the horned god's altar, to thank him for letting them shelter in his grove overnight. Then they rode on until they reached the shallow ford. Before the sun was in mid-heaven, they had crossed the Jordan and were riding towards the citadel of Mahanaim, the estate of Kimham ben Barzillai, the greatest man in Gilead.

Kimham himself came out to meet them. He was an old man, heavy of body and limb. Though the day was hot, he was wrapped in a bordered mantle of fine wool. As they stepped down from the chariot, he embraced Kilav and Avishag alike, as though she were also the King's child. Walking slowly between them, resting his heavy arms across their shoulders, he led them through the gate of the citadel into the forecourt, and ordered his house steward to see to the men and the beasts.

They were a sorry sight, their robes besmirched with blood and dust, and the maidservants and slaves quickly took them in hand. Though they wished to go directly to the young prince, neither Kilav nor Avishag could deny their host, and submitted to his servants.

Avishag found it hard to sit quietly while the maidservants ministered to her with basins of water, jars of ointment and fresh gowns. She bathed and dressed with haste, dismissed the women and returned to the hall. There she found Kilav, washed and clad in clean garments, seated beside the lord of the citadel. Servants were bringing in platters laden with food and jars of wine.

"If you please, my lord," she said, bowing to the old man. "We thank you for all your kindness in welcoming us, but we have been a long time on the King's errand and must not tarry. Is not the King's son, Shlomo, under your roof?"

Kimham was taken aback. "Yedidiah and the lady Bathsheva are lodged in my summer house," he replied. "I shall send a servant to ask them to come here."

"No, my lord. If you please, it is for us to go them. We must go and speak to Shlomo ben David, who is to reign in Jerusalem after his father."

It was as though the King's voice spoke from her mouth. Not another word was said. The old man rose from his seat and, leaning on the arm of his steward, led them from the hall. The whole household, men, women and children, watched in silence as their master led the visitors through the orchard behind the main house and to the summer house beyond. It lay within the wall, amid a grove of date palms that gave it shade.

As they drew near, a man came out of the door. It was the Great Lady's house-steward, the old Hittite servant who had gone into captivity with his mistress. Seeing him, Avishag's spirit left her. Suddenly, she was not the King's emissary, but the Jezreelite maiden whom the Great Lady and her son treated graciously.

Kilav spoke to the old Hittite servant. "Go tell your master that we have come from the King."

They followed him into the house and waited in the outer chamber. Avishag's knees weakened. She wished she could step back and hide behind Kilav's back, as befitted a young maid in a stranger's house. But it was not to be.

The prince and his mother entered the chamber. They stood side by side and waited for the visitors to speak. Shlomo was taller than Avishag remembered, and his beard had grown thick and black.

His eyes glittered and his nostrils flared, but he said nothing. The Great Lady was calm and as richly apparelled as ever she had been in the King's house.

Kilav and Kimham stepped forward and bowed deep, and Avishag followed them, as in a dream. But Shlomo knew which of them was his father's emissary.

"So you have come, my sister," he said to Avishag. "I have been waiting for you." And he took her hands in his.

"My lord," she said in a low, uncertain voice, for her strength had not returned. "The King your father bids you to come back to his city. You are to reign after him."

The Great Lady gasped. Shlomo had been expecting Avishag and her tidings, but she had not.

Her breast heaved and her eyes filled with tears, and she turned away, unwilling to let the visitors see her weep.

"Mother," her son said gently, "I must hasten back, and shall ride in my brother's chariot. You must wait here under Kimham's roof, and come to the King's city when I have taken my place there."

Kimham, who had not uttered a word since Avishag bade him take them to the summerhouse, now bowed low and swore to the young prince that his mother would be safe and at ease under his roof. He added that, just as his own father Barzillai had served the King when he was in flight from the rebels, and was remembered when the kingdom was restored, so he and his son would doubtless be remembered when Shlomo ben David sat on his throne.

Shlomo had indeed been expecting emissaries from his father. His mother's spies, mingling with Kimham's servants, had brought word of the skirmishes in Mount Ephraim. He had had his servants watch from the roof and from the high palm-trees for the sight of chariots. When word came that a young woman arrived with them, he knew that it was Avishag – for who could it be but she?

All this and other things he told the maid in Jerusalem, many days later. But on the journey to the King's city they had few words together. After their meeting in the summerhouse of Kimham the Gileadite, she kept away from the young prince, nor did he seek her out. She rode on a mule among Kilav's men in the middle of the caravan, while the King's sons rode in the two forward chariots, with their armour-bearers and charioteers. Kimham's son Jared, a young warrior and priest, rode in the third chariot with one of his men, but he could not tear his gaze from Avishag, whose beauty overwhelmed his senses.

The Benjamite bowmen, who awaited them, as they had been ordered, at the spring of Harod, had raised many more men from the House of Joseph, and as they moved through the country the host that accompanied the young prince to his father's city grew larger day by day. The land of Ephraim swarmed with Judeans warriors and their allies, but after losing two skirmishes they withdrew into the forest and did not confront Shlomo's troops.

So great was the acclaim which met the caravan in the country of Benjamin, that they made little progress from dawn to dusk, and halted in Gibeah. Shlomo wanted to ride on to Jerusalem, after sending runners to tell the King that he was on his way. But Kilav demurred.

"Our father has doubtless heard that you are near," he said, "but we do not know the whereabouts of our brother Adoniyah and his followers. Let us send a messenger to speak to the King, and to find out if it is best for us to approach the city from the north or from the south."

Shlomo was content to heed his elder brother's advice. He had been wary at first, remembering that Kilav had taken part in carrying him and his mother into captivity. But he saw that Avishag trusted him, and moreover that he was clearly pleased to bring him back, and forgave him. For Shlomo had never doubted that his time would come, that he would be king in Jerusalem – the stars and the portents had all foretold as much. This, too, he would tell Avishag when the time came.

The elders of Benjamin rejoiced at the arrival of the King's younger son. They threw open their houses, broached their best casks and killed the fattest cattle of their flock to feast him and his company. That night the King's sons and Avishag supped with Yerahmeel, the chief of the Benjamite elders, and his wife Hamutal, who was a great woman in Gibeah.

When they had eaten and drunk their fill, the elder spoke of the fears and hopes of the Benjamites, being a small tribe whose country lay between Judah and Israel, and who did not wish to quarrel with either side. The King had dealt with them honourably, he said. It was not the King, said his wife Hamutal, nor even Adoniyah ben Haggith whom they feared and loathed, but the sons of Zeruiah. The Benjamites had never forgiven Yoav for treacherously slaying their great captain Avner ben Ner.

"Avner saw that our people were greatly troubled by the war between the followers of Saul and the followers of David, for much of it raged in our country," she told the visitors. "Therefore he sent messengers to Hebron, where David reigned over Judah, saying, 'Make league with me, Ben Yishai, and I shall bring all Israel to your side.' David consented, and Avner spoke to the elders of the House of Joseph, and they all agreed with him to join Israel with Judah and make of it one kingdom under David ben Yishai and his sons forever. But when Avner and his men returned from Hebron, where they had celebrated the new agreement, Yoav ben Zeruiah met him upon the way, by the well of Sirah. 'Come back with me to Hebron,' he said to Avner, 'for the King wishes to speak with you again.' And he took him aside, as though to speak with him in secret, and thrust his sword between his ribs and slew him where he stood!" Hamutal voice broke, with anger rather than grief. She turned to her left and sprinkled some wine on the ground, to appease the spirit of the dead she had spoken of.

Her words cast gloom upon the assembly, and Yerahmeel added hastily: "But the King was angry with Yoav for this terrible deed. He disavowed him before all the people, and rent his clothes and fasted, and buried Avner with great honour in Hebron."

"So he did," said Shlomo equably, "for he honoured Avner ben Ner as a great warrior, a man of renown... The sons of Zeruiah have indeed been hard men, harder and harsher than my father the King. But those days are long past, Benjamite. There is no war now between Judah and the House of Joseph, nor shall there be when I am king."

Hamutal was pleased with these words and clapped her hands for the singers and dancers to enter and play for the visitors. But as their din filled the hall, and good cheer returned, Avishag pondered the tale just told. Hard men, indeed, were the sons of Zeruiah, and so the King often called them. Yet they had served him well, binding his contentious kingdom together, and taking the spilt blood upon their own heads, to spare him...

But the visitors were weary and before long they took their leave of the elder and his wife, and followed the torchbearers to the guesthouse. The larger chamber was given to Shlomo, and the smaller ones to Kilav and Avishag. Before they retired, Kilav spoke softly to Avishag.

"'It is all true, my sister, what Hammutal has said. Yoav did slay Avner, who was a better man than he. But it was not without cause. He was avenging the death of his own brother Asahel, whom Avner had slain in Gibeon... Oh, my sister, pray that such evil times do not return. May God make my little brother Yedidiah as wise as the Forefather Joseph – who, it is said, held all Egypt together when the bad years came upon it."

Avishag stopped in the doorway and turned to Kilav. Their eyes met in the flickering light of the windblown torches. Again she thought that he looked like the King in his young days, and a wistful desire overcame her. A part of her wanted to surrender to him, as though thereby she could reach her master's youthful manhood, but another part held back. For he was not the young David – he was Kilav, a good man but not the anointed king with a spark of God burning in him. Not for him had the goddess destined her. She touched the serpent amulet on her breast and tore her gaze away from him. As she went into the chamber that was set aside for her use, she felt his eyes following her.

That night Avishag dreamt that she had arrived all alone at Deborah's Palm. She entered the tabernacle and though it was utterly dark she could see clearly that the opening leading to the inner sanctuary had become as wide as the portal to the King's hall. As she walked towards it and into the cavern, her footsteps were slow and ponderous, as though she had grown very heavy. Inside the cavern, Nehushtan the brazen serpent gleamed on its staff, and its eyes followed Avishag as she approached the brazier to sprinkle the flames with the frankincense she had brought in her cupped hands. The cavern had grown immense and she was about to remark on it, when she heard the voice of the prophetess, speaking from behind the Nehushtan. It seemed she was speaking in some language that Avishag did not know, but thought it was the language of Egypt. Suddenly she grew fearful – the prophetess was telling her what to do, but how could she obey her command when she did not understand it? Then she realized that it was the serpent's voice, not the prophetess', and this was the reason she could not understand the words. She saw that Shlomo was standing beside her, and he took the frankincense from her hands and sprinkled it on the flames. At once a bright light burst from the brazier, as bright as the light of day, and the great serpent lowered its head from the staff, till its flicking tongue reached Shlomo's outstretched hand, and licked it. Shlomo turned to her, smiling, and touched her breast with the hand that the serpent had licked. A shudder went through her, and she woke up. Clearly she had been given a sign that she was on the right way, and when her spirit grew calmer she felt greatly reassured. Only later that day did she discover that she had lost the amulet that had protected her since her first year in the King's service.

In the morning, Kilav chose one of the King's guard and ordered him to run ahead of their company to the city and inform the King of their approach. But Avishag spoke up.

"Let me go to the King, my brother," she reasoned, "and let Itamar come with me."

Now that they were so near, her fears were all for the King. He was surrounded by the followers of Adoniyah, both within the city and in Judea. Moreover, the long rite of untying of the oath, which he had hoped to complete before Shlomo's return, was a taxing one for a man of his years.

The King's two sons hesitated to let her go. Even accompanied by Itamar and other men, if the Judeans knew of her part in bringing back the son of Hittite widow, her life would be forfeit as soon as she approached their camp. But she pleaded and won. The sun was just rising when she rode out of Gibeah with Itamar and two other Philistine guards. Behind them rode two Benjamite warriors, dressed as hunters in wild beast skins, their bows slung over their shoulders.

Avishag wished to go first to the northern summit, there to take counsel with the priestesses, who would surely know all that was taking place in the King's city and household. But Itamar urged that they turn west and approach the city through the valley of Kidron, as though they had come from the plains. There they would meet his companions of the King's guard, who would see them safely through the gate and into the King's fort. Avishag agreed and so they circled the city at a distance, and reached the valley of Kidron when the sun had passed mid-heaven. It was a hot day, windless and dusty, the sky hanging low over the land. On such days men and beasts alike sought shade and water, but they kept going until they reached the southern gate.

There was not a guard to be seen, only the beggars and pedlars were there, such as always clustered near the gate, driven back by the guards whenever any great person entered or left the city. Opposite the gate, in the shade of a carob tree, stood a wandering prophet, shaggy and naked but for a leather girdle, shouting and waving his arms, ignored by all. But where were the guards?

Avishag and her companions halted. The Benjamites, unfamiliar with the city gate, saw nothing amiss and drew up.

"Bide here a while, my lady," said Itamar in a low voice. "I shall seek my companions within the gate… It has never been left unguarded!"

Avishag looked about her, to see what caused this extraordinary sight. But apart from the prophet, whose voice rose and fell and whose beard was spattered with foam, the people who dawdled near the gate and those who went through it gave no sign that anything was amiss. And yet, the King's city was unguarded!

It was all she could do not to follow Itamar through the gate, and try to reach the King's fort unaccompanied. Full of misgivings, she waited, flanked by the Benjamites, who were only made uneasy by the prophet's ranting. Nothing could be seen through the gate, for the wall turned behind it – a cunning device the King had learned from the Hittites. But of what use was it, if it was left unguarded?

At last she could bear it no longer and spurred her mule forward. The Benjamites followed close behind, and as they went through the turn of the gateway they saw Itamar, on foot, hurrying to meet them.

"My lady," he said, speaking low, "there are a few men within, and some are guarding the King's fort. But many of the Philistine guards are in Hebron, sent there by Yoav ben Zeruiah… My mule is stubborn and will not leave her old stall, now she has found it again. I shall take another and we shall ride together to the King's house!"

The path leading from the gate up to the King's house had never seemed so long and arduous as now. Her weary and thirsty beast kept stopping and needed to be spurred on. The people of the city, young and old, got in the way. A wailing procession, accompanying a dead man on a litter, crowded the path and would not step aside even when the Benjamites struck at them with their staves. At length they reached the upper level, where the approach to the King's fort was watched over by a handful of guards.

Seeing Avishag and Itamar they came forward and greeted them sombrely.

"Have you come from Hebron?" asked their captain.

"Not we," said Itamar. "We were on the King's errand in the north... Why do you ask about Hebron, my brother?"

"The King's son has gone there, and Yoav with all but a handful of our men –"

Adoniyah! The horn of the oil of anointing! The thought flashed through Avishag's mind.

"And the Levites?" she asked. "Have the Levite priests gone to Hebron also?"

"Aye, mistress! There are great rites and celebrations afoot."

She did not stop to hear more, but rode on as fast as she could. When the mule would not obey her, she sprang from the saddle and ran. Two guards who were leaning against the pillars of the gate drew themselves up and made to stop her, but she called to them, "It is I, Avishag of the King's house!" and they stepped aside.

Inside the forecourt, the King's household seemed unchanged. With almost no breath in her body, she called to the first servants she saw, "Is it well with the King? Where is he?"

"The King is in the upper chambers," replied a young maidservant, carrying two great jars of water on her shoulders. "Old Naamah is with him... Have you come from Hebron, mistress?"

She ran on, into the fort and through the hall to the upper storey. At the door of the King's sleeping chamber she ran into old Naamah.

"The King – is it well with the King, Naamah?" she gasped.

"Avishag, my child, why are you here? Were you not bidden to Hebron?"

Without answering the old woman she ran into her master's chamber. He was lying on his couch, seemingly asleep, but when she fell to her knees beside him and burst into tears, he opened his eyes.

"I had not thought to see your face, my child," he whispered. "And have you brought my son Yedidiah with you?"

She knew then that his days were numbered, for he spoke to

her in his native Judean, having forgotten that she was a Jezreelite. She kissed his hands and bathed them with her tears.

"Aye, my lord. Your son Yedidiah is on his way, and a great host has come with him, to see him anointed as your heir."

She understood that the King did not know that on this very day Adoniyah ben Haggith was celebrating his own anointing in Hebron, amid much pomp and ceremony, surrounded by the Levites and the elders of Judah. All the King's captains and counsellors were there, and even the last surviving son of Zeruiah had left him. The Lion-slayer was nowhere to be seen.

Chapter ten

Yonadav was riding to Hebron. His mule was a big beast, broad-backed and slow, and his two servants helped him to alight often, to rest under a shady tree by the wayside. Still, the journey tired him, and he wished he had stayed under his own roof in the King's city.

The road to Hebron swarmed with people from all over the land. A company of Philistines rode up from the plains, highborn men from the Five Cities. Clean-shaven and bejewelled, they fanned themselves against the heat and the flies, and laughed at everything they saw. Close behind them a Moabite caravan came up from across the Jordan. Gorgeous women in bright gowns and gold ornaments lolled on camel-borne litters, while the men rode in front, sitting in leather saddles on tall black asses, looking like crows in their dark cloaks and head-cloths. Two fearsome warriors, dressed in lion-skins and flourishing brazen javelins, rode ahead on tall red mules.

Yonadav's servants were cheered by these sights. The older one, a Hebrew slave, kept raising his hands to heaven and praising the Lord Yah for his greatness. The younger one, a fresh-faced Canaanite lad, laughed merrily at the thought of the feasting to come. But

Yonadav himself was ill at ease. All the people he saw on the way to Hebron were Judeans or their allies. There were no Israelites among them – not even of Benjamin, though Adoniyah had taken a daughter of that tribe to wife. Nor did he see any visitors from the north – no Aramaeans, Tyrians, Hittites or Danites…

Soon they were engulfed by the throng that pressed against the city gate. The dust and din rose to heaven. Beasts stamped and snorted, men shouted and women screamed. Yonadav could neither move forward nor draw back. His old servant was swallowed up by the crowd, and the young one clung to him in terror. Then a Gittite guard from the King's house saw Yonadav and came to his rescue. Striking at the crowd with his pike, he cleared a path for him, crying, "Make way for the King's kinsman!" and led him into the city.

After a while he reached his sister Ephrat's house, a big compound of chambers and courtyards in the heart of Hebron. Her house-steward met him and led him to the fine chamber she had prepared for him. Exhausted and uneasy, he sank down on the couch and closed his eyes. But before sleep overcame him the lady Ephrat bustled into the room.

She kissed him on both cheeks and then saw that he did not share her gladness. "Why are you downcast, Yonadav?" she cried aloud in her broad Judean-Moabite speech. "Is it not a great day for our house? Do you not rejoice at the anointing of the son of David and of Haggith, here in the city of the Forefathers?"

Yonadav muttered that he was weary and all his bones ached. Abashed, she shouted for the servants to bathe his feet and bring him refreshments. Then she left him, for many other guests were coming to lodge under her roof – not least, the son of the King of Moab, a kinsman of hers from the days when she was his uncle's wife.

The city was in a tumult of preparations for the anointing of Adoniyah. The Calebites were there in force, and with them a score of Levites, led by the high priest Ira-Eviatar and Ahimaaz, the son of Zadok. Many of the Philistine guards had been brought from Jerusalem by Yoav ben Zeruiah, and other allies of the House of David gathered in Hebron to witness Adoniyah's anointing – not merely the Moabites and Philistines, but Edomites, Ammonites and others of lesser nations. Grandest of all were two high Egyptian lords, with their servants and guards, who were on their way back to the Land of the Nile from a royal mission to the King of Aram Damascus. Rumours of great events in the land of Judah had drawn them to Hebron, and their scribe was seen writing down everything that he saw on rolls of fine stuff that was neither cloth nor parchment.

Yonadav kept to his chamber, but his sister came in often and told him all that was happening in her house and in the city. The great ceremony would take place in a day or two, she said. The Levites had already purified the precinct and altar at the east wall, in readiness for the rites.

"And is all quiet in the north?" he asked. "Are the Israelites at peace, content to see Adoniyah ben Haggith made ruler over them?"

Ephrat gave her brother a puzzled look: "I have heard that there were some small skirmishes in Mount Ephraim, my brother, but all is quiet there now... What is it you fear, brother? They of Ephraim have long submitted to our rule. What other king can they have over them? There is none left of the house of Saul, and of David's sons none but Adoniyah is fit to rule. Shefatiah ben Avital is of little account, and as for the boy prince, the wise child of the Hittite widow – he is a callow lad, quite unfit to lead the people! No, my brother, even the Israelite elders are not so foolish as to put their fate into such tender hands as his!"

Yonadav fingered his beard, which he kept trimmed and oiled. He murmured a brief prayer of thanks to the Lord Yah, but his heart was still vexed. There was much that his sister did not know.

"Do you not see that some are missing who should be here?" he asked her. "Where is the seer Nathan? And Kilav ben Abigail – why has he not come to see his brother anointed? And Benaiah, the Lion-slayer? And what of Adoram, and Zadok the priest?"

Ephrat recovered her wits. "Zadok the priest? Did not the King decree that one high priest of the Levites must remain in Jerusalem at all times?"

"But the others!" snapped her brother peevishly. "Can you not see that without them there is something amiss? I left Jerusalem without seeing the King, and now my heart misgives me. I trusted Yoav ben Zeruiah and Ahimaaz, who said that the King blessed the anointing of Adoniyah, though he was too frail to come and witness it with his own eyes…" He shook his head angrily. "To spare my old bones, I did not ride up to the King's house, and did not hear it from David's own lips!"

Ephrat was dismayed. Her brother, though never a brave man, was renowned for his wisdom. Was there something amiss about the great event that was going forward in Hebron? But she could not linger to speak with him. She had to attend to the guests and the preparations for the ceremony. Her many kinsmen and kinswomen looked to her to make the celebration as lavish and princely as she knew how.

Yonadav bestirred himself and came out of his chamber. He walked through an inner courtyard full of saddlebags and provisions to a staircase that led up to the roof. He climbed up, panting for breath, and then stood and looked around him. The wind was blowing from the west, bringing a hint of the rains to come. It was, doubtless, an auspicious season for the anointing of a new king… Hebron was where he had passed the years of his young manhood, at the side of his great kinsman, and like him left several offspring among its populace… Looking around the city and its environs, he saw many riders and beasts, and in a nearby field some young warriors were staging mock battles. The wind carried the sound of their clashing weapons and their shrill war cries. Nearer the city wall some youths in short kilts were unharnessing the horses from two iron chariots and leading them to the watering trough beside the well.

The sight of the chariots reminded him again of Kilav ben Abigail. It was he who had given Adoniyah his first royal chariot and brought him fine horses from the plains… Yet he had not come to witness the anointing. Thinking about Kilav put the old man in mind of Avishag, whom he had seen more than once speaking with the King's son. Why was she not in Hebron? The young she-steward was David's eyes and ears, yet he had not sent her to Hebron to see his heir anointed!

And now another question came into his mind. Why Hebron? Why was the great rite being celebrated in the heart of Judea, when David had chosen Jerusalem as the seat of his rule over the joint kingdom of Judah and Israel? It could not be the presence of the Great Lady and her son that repelled the Judean faction, for they had been sent away these many days… Yonadav pondered all these questions and then sighed. He knew now what he had to do.

Early the next morning, well before sunrise, a small company of one mule and two asses, rode out of the gate of Hebron and headed back to Jerusalem. It was Yonadav with his two servants. He had not even made his excuses to the lady Ephrat.

When she saw that he had left she grew fearful and sent her steward to Adoniyah's house, to see what he could see and hear what he could hear. But nothing seemed amiss. Adoniyah was there and all his captains and counsellors, his wives and children. The only mishap was a mighty quarrel between the prince's wives, which, taken up by their servants, resulted in many broken jars and torn garments. But it had now been settled, and peace reigned under Adoniyah's roof.

Her good spirits restored, she exclaimed, "O Lord Yah, 'tis not I who am an old woman, but my brother Yonadav!" Then she cuffed a slave who had dared to enter the house in shoes and returned to her household duties.

Of all the King's men, only Ittai the Gittite was to be found in the King's house. Avishag met him on the stairs leading to the King's sleeping chamber.

"I dared not speak to the King about the gathering in Hebron," he said in a low voice, shaking his grizzled head. "The King's own kinsmen left, one by one, each one saying he was called away to his estate, or some such ruse…"

"But where are Benaiah and Nathan the Seer? Why are they not at the King's side?" she asked.

"They are not far, mistress. The seer is with the Levites, at the threshing-floor, and the Lion-slayer has gone out with the guards to make a round of the city... And there are many of my brother guards here, within the wall and on the nearby hills."

Avishag returned to the King's chamber and found him struggling to sit up on his couch.

"Were you here a little while ago, my child?" he asked, "or was it a dream I dreamt?"

"No, my lord, it was not a dream. I am back, and in a little while your sons Yedidiah and Kilav will be here, as you commanded."

"Help me, child. I have been lying here for too long..." But when he stood up he staggered and leaned on her shoulder.

Though she would have liked nothing better than to reassure the King and let him rest, Avishag knew that he had to show himself when Shlomo and the people with him arrived at the King's house. She called for wine-and-water and some nourishing broth, and when the King had eaten and seemed to feel stronger, she combed his hair and beard and helped him put on a fine mantle and his golden chaplet. She was about to summon Ittai to help the King go down to the hall, when Benaiah appeared on the threshold.

Together they helped the King down the narrow stairs to the great hall below. Benaiah wanted the King to take his place on the lion-footed throne, but Avishag knew that it would be some time before Shlomo and the others arrived. So they laid the bolsters and coverlets on the dais and the King reclined on them.

He seemed more refreshed, and now Avishag sat beside him and in a low voice told her lord and the Lion-Slayer all that had happened since she left. She tried to make little of the attack near the Jordan ford, but Benaiah had heard about it from runners sent by Kimham ben Barzillai.

"My lord, this maid took part in the fighting, and your son

Kilav had not enough words to praise her courage," he said, a smile warming his stern features. Avishag feared that the King would be distressed by the thought of the danger to her, but he seemed above all eager to hear how they had found his son Yedidiah.

"Yedidiah expected us, my lord," she said, "and wished to start on the journey to the King's city without delay. Only Kimham's urging us to rest a while kept us from setting out at once."

Then she described the journey, and how at every stop the people thronged around the young prince and shouted his praises. These stories took some time in the telling, for the King asked many questions about the places and the people encountered on the way, and still nothing was said about the events in Hebron. Avishag wondered if the King was really unaware that many of his household had gone there, or did not wish to hear about it. His eyes were on the open doors, awaiting the runners that would announce Shlomo's imminent arrival. But it was Yonadav who entered the hall, looking dusty and dishevelled.

Now the events in Hebron could no longer be ignored. As soon as he recovered his breath, Yonadav described what he had seen and heard in and around the Judean city, speaking more directly and simply than was his habit.

"It is our own kinsfolk, David," he said, forgetting, in his bitterness, his usual courtly manner, "who are bent on sundering the kingdom you put together. They expect the Israelites to rise up against them, and mean to crush them by force – or if they fail to do so, they will be content to rule over a kingdom of Judah alone…"

There was a silence. The King's face was awful to see – grim and pale, yet without the power that had in the past quickened his old frame and enabled him to impose his will. His brow was knotted and still he did not utter a word.

"And the King's city, my lord?" Avishag ventured to ask Yonadav. "Do they mean it to be the seat of a Judean king, or is Jerusalem to be ruled from Hebron?"

Her mind was on the Ashera and the grove of the priestesses

on the north summit. What would befall them and all of the King's city if there were to be a separate kingdom of Judah with its seat in Hebron?

Yonadav hesitated. He looked at her and at Benaiah, then turned to the King. "Whether Adoniyah proposes to rule in Hebron or in the King's city, I do not know. But I have heard the Levites speaking of a great temple to be built on yonder summit to house the Ark of Yah…" He pointed north, to where the altar of El Elyon and the grove of the Ashera had stood since time immemorial.

At that moment she knew with a certainty that she had done the right thing. Adoniyah and the Levites would despise the worship of the goddess and drive her devotees into a corner, but Shlomo would honour the goddess and the host of heaven.

By the time they approached the King's city, Shlomo's company had grown into thousands. The people who had followed him from the Gilead and Mount Ephraim were joined by numerous Benjamites, and as they began to march around the flank of the mountain so as to approach the King's city from the valley, a large number of Judeans joined them too. Whether these were swept up by the enthusiasm of the advancing throng, or were people with a grievance against the Calebite leaders of Adoniyah's camp, no one could say, but they knew their advantage and moved to the forefront of the march. At first their forward position provoked the displeasure of the Israelites, but Shlomo soothed his followers, saying, "Now we are entering the land of Judah, and our passage to the King's city will be all the easier with Judeans at our forefront."

The men repeated these words to each other, pleased with the wisdom of their young prince.

The Great Lady – who had refused to remain behind in Mahanaim and insisted on accompanying her son – was riding far behind the throng. She had her own company of Hittite and Philistine bowmen, as well as some young men from the leading northern Israelite families. Especially favoured was a Danite named Yair, who was believed to be a descendant of the legendary Samson. Not only was he head and shoulders taller than most men, he was very power-ful and was treated with great respect. He wore his hair knotted into seven braids, like his illustrious ancestor, and the sight of his great, commanding head inspired confidence in the other men. The night before their arrival at the King's city Yair was seen entering the Great Lady's tent, whence he emerged only at daybreak. But the Great Lady's handmaids dismissed all the sly remarks by declaring stoutly that Yair had merely lain across the opening of the tent to protect the prince's mother.

As the swelling caravan entered the green Valley of Hinnom, runners were sent to the city to announce the prince's arrival at the King's house. They had no sooner begun to run up the steep hillside than a company of Judean warriors appeared from behind a clump of wind-warped pines and challenged them. The runners were unarmed and might have been torn apart, but the leader of the Judean company caught sight of the throng that was advancing towards the city. He raised his hand and stopped his men, who had already drawn their swords.

"It is the King's son Yedidiah," he said, and his voice shook a little.

"What of it?" cried one of his men. "We are Adoniyah's men! He is being anointed in Hebron!"

"True, but this is not Hebron," replied the leader thoughtfully, torn between his allegiance to Adoniyah and his fear of the advancing host. He had once seen a clutch of bird hatchlings overrun by a swarm of locusts, which moved on, leaving a handful of little white bones behind. He made a sign to his men and they let go of the runners and withdrew quietly behind the trees. The runners cheered aloud, shouting, "Shlomo ben David!" and "Shlomo our king!" then lowered their heads and started running uphill again.

Now the prince gave the order to proceed further south so as to approach the fort from the city gate. The runners would reach the King's house well ahead, and give the household time to prepare for his arrival. When he reached the city gate he dismounted from his fine mule and made the rest of the way on foot. He had ridden in the chariot only to the border of Judea, then ordered Kilav to place both chariots in the rear of the caravan and ride beside him to the King's city on mule back. Now he urged Kilav to walk with him to the fort.

The gate of the King's house did not now seem abandoned, as it had been when Avishag arrived. Hundreds of people from the city and from Siloam swarmed there, and most of the King's household rushed out to see the young Shlomo-Yedidiah arrive at the head of a vast throng. The day had been hot and overcast, but now the sun broke through the low-hanging clouds when he and his brother Kilav entered the forecourt and the crowd likewise parted to let them pass, the women ululating and children shrieking with excitement. Though Shlomo was not tall, the awe and affection with which his people surrounded him made all eyes turn to him. He walked slowly, at a measured pace, and Kilav – who had seen the great lords of Philistia and Egyptian emissaries at their most ceremonious – smiled slightly and fell back a pace or two.

Standing in the doorway of the King's house were Benaiah the Lion-slayer and Yonadav, the King's cousin. Behind them stood Adoram, the master of the King's tribute, and Seraiah the scribe. They bowed to the young prince and Yonadav kissed him, and then led him inside into his father's presence. Kilav followed them in.

For many years to come storytellers would vie with one another in describing the scene when the old King David received his youngest son Shlomo – the name Yedidiah having fallen into oblivion – and placed his golden chaplet on the prince's raven locks. They would make no mention of the gathering in Hebron that was taking place at the same hour, the ceremonies in which the other prince, the former heir, Adoniyah, was anointed by Eviatar the Younger, and was wildly cheered by the Judeans and their supporters. They would also leave out the matter of the oath, which David had sworn and which should have been untied, but was not. It was never mentioned again, and being ignored it ceased to matter. What everyone remembered was the sudden, unseasonably heavy rain that fell soon after Shlomo's arrival at the King's house, auguring an early autumn and with it rich harvests and prosperity in the land.

Chapter eleven

The scent of Titipah's unguents and wigs still hung in the chamber. The Egyptian woman's belongings and her two Kushite handmaidens had been removed to Hebron, where Adoniyah gave her a house of her own beside his estate, but Avishag still sensed her presence in the rooms she had occupied. They were now her own – the first rooms she had ever had entirely to herself. Only the Great Lady, the young King's mother, had grander quarters.

Time passed, but Avishag was in a dream and could not account for the days and nights. Since the passing of the old King, at whose side she remained had till his last breath, she hardly knew where she was. At times, when she walked about the courtyards with their garden and trees, she fancied she was still the wild young Shunammite, and her eyes sought the young Ira in his goatskin apron, labouring over his master's meal on the roasting spit. Then she would also recall her village, her mother and the friends of her girlhood, and thought she could hear their voices and smell the wind carrying the scents of the tilled soil and the ripening grapes.

But a servant stepping respectfully out of her way would

bring her back to the present, to the King's city, the city that was now the seat of King Shlomo, the young man she had brought back from banishment. She had not seen him since the burial of her master, the old King. Kilav, too, had disappeared from sight – he had returned to the valley of Ayalon, to his horses and chariots. Benaiah the Lion-slayer had replaced Yoav ben Zeruiah as captain of the King's army, and was away from the city, moving about the country with a band of men, mostly Philistine, Hittite and Israelite, and a handful of Judeans, to secure the peace which had been all but shattered by the events in Hebron.

There was nothing for Avishag to do. One day she went to the grove and spent some time with the priestesses, who received her gladly and asked many questions about the young King. Avishag found that she could not speak about him. Her mind shied away from the memory of their encounter in Mahanaim, and the rest was coloured by her sorrow for the old King.

"My life has been broken in two," she said to Almah, one of the priestesses who had come up from Shiloh with the oracle and who had become her friend. "The true part was buried with the King."

Almah stroked her palms, which were lying idly in her lap.

"You are mourning," she said. "He was your father and mother and your master, and you were with him day and night for so long."

But Avishag knew it was more than mourning. Something had died, but something else was waiting to be born, and she was afraid to look either backward or forward. She returned to the King's house, yet it came to her that she could join the priestesses in the grove and serve the goddess. The goddess loved virgins, and if they conceived and gave birth while in her service, the children were especially blessed. But she could not bestir herself to do so, any more than she could go back to Shunem, though at times she dreamed about it.

More and more her thoughts veered back to the old King – not as he was in his last years, in the eyrie she had shared with him at the top of the house, but as the young man of his stories. She saw his memories as though they were her own. He was the young shepherd in the fields of Bethlehem who became King Saul's favourite, then had to flee from him. He and his men were haunting the wilderness like a pack of wolves, and he was a fearless warrior, a born captain, whose men would risk their lives for him, even to bring him water from the well at Bethlehem. He stood on the ledge before the mouth of the cave and cried out to the brooding king who sought to kill him, 'After whom has the King of Israel come out? After a dead dog, after a flea!'

How proudly he had repeated those words to her, and then shrugged his shoulders. And how he laughed to recall his feigned madness in the court of his friend Achish, king of Gath... He had loved many women, but declared that his love for Jonathan was greater than the love of women... Slender, bold, red-haired, with flashing, laughing eyes, he was the lover she had never had, and it filled her with pain to think that she had shared only his old age. Had it been she and not Michal who watched him leaping and dancing before the Ark, she would have laughed for joy and been proud of her lord who so displayed his devotion.

And now he was gone to his long home, and never again would she sing with him as she had done sometimes while she dressed his hair, or when they sat together on the roof – songs of love and of harvest, songs of longing and exaltation...

"*For love is strong as death; jealousy is cruel as the grave,*" was one of the courtship songs she had brought from Jezreel and had sung for him, and now, humming it to herself with tears in her eyes, she knew that it was death itself she was jealous of. The tears welled over and ran on her cheeks as she sat on the garden wall, enveloped in her mantle, while her gaze followed the flights of swallows wheeling and swooping across the evening sky.

From the moment of Shlomo's arrival at the King's house, Yonadav never left the King's side – neither the old King, until his peaceful death and his burial near the spring of Gihon, nor the young King

Shlomo, who was anointed on the same spot by Nathan the Seer and Zadok the Levite. Whether Yonadav's conscience smote him for having gone to Hebron at Adoniyah's bidding, or because he always strove to be present when momentous events were happening, he himself could not say. He knew that it was up to him to see out the last days of King David's reign and the first of Shlomo's, and to dictate their story to the scribes before others told their false tales.

He was sorry to see that no sooner was the old King dead and buried than Avishag the Shunammite withdrew into the women's house and was no longer seen in the King's hall. Not having been the old King's concubine, she was free to return to her father's house, if she so wished. Or she might stay and await the young King's decision as to her fate. In David's last years people called her the King's shadow, but she had been more – she had been his secret counsellor, his confidante and his most trusted friend. Yonadav doubted that Shlomo would let her depart, lest she fall into the wrong hands. But her position was indeterminate, and Yonadav was puzzled. From day to day, he proposed to call at the women's quarters – where, as the King's cousin, he was free to go – and speak to Avishag as they had done many times before the old King's death, but something held him back, and he spent all his time at the side of the young King.

Shlomo began his reign very quietly, consulting calmly with him, Yonadav, with Adoram and Benaiah, and leaving the latter to give the orders to the guard, which remained unchanged. He gave no order to bar those who had taken part in the events in Hebron – indeed, he made no mention of them. Every evening his mother, the Great Lady, came down and joined him in the hall, and when she spoke he listened to her most courteously.

For a few days, or perhaps weeks, it seemed as though nothing had changed. Then all at once, in one fell swoop, Shlomo purged his kingdom of all who would challenge his throne. It began suddenly, like a storm that breaks with a thunderclap.

One evening, when they had all supped and drunk wine, and had listened to an old Sidonite bard sing an ancient song of the sea, Bathsheva spoke up.

"My son," she began, "my lord king, I have a request to make of you."

The King, surprised, turned to her. "Speak, mother! Have I ever refused anything you have asked of me?"

"You know that I have been visiting my estate in Ephraim, my lord, to see that the steward did not neglect the shearing of our flocks. While I was at my house in Shechem a man came to see me, to beg the favour of my help in bringing a petition before you…"

Yonadav saw the King's face grow very still. The benign smile with which he had turned to his mother faded, and his eyes became hooded. "Who was this man, mother?" he asked in a low voice.

"It was Adoniyah, my lord… He came as a suppliant, on foot and wearing a coarse mantle." Her voice remained even, as though she was unaware of her son's ominous stillness. "It was as a humble petitioner that he sought my help. 'Speak to the King your son, I pray you, to give me Avishag the Shunammite to wife. The King will not deny you.' I promised him nothing, save that I would speak to you, my lord, and tell you of his petition."

Yonadav saw the King's handsome young face darken, his nostrils flare and his black brows knit together. At the sight, cold fear gripped his innards and he wished he were far away from Jerusalem.

"Why do you ask Avishag for Adoniyah?" the King replied in an iron voice, such as Yonadav had never heard, and to judge by her look, neither had his mother. All those who sat nearby froze in their seats. "Ask for him the kingdom also, for he is my elder brother! And for Eviatar the priest and for Yoav ben Zeruiah…"

Then he stood up and the entire company rose hastily to their feet.

"Mother," the King said coldly, "you are tired. It is time you went to your quarters and rested."

The Great Lady had turned very pale. Silently she bowed to

the King and walked out of the hall. It was, no doubt, the first time that she had ever been dismissed in such a manner, and Yonadav did not envy her servants tonight.

"Call Benaiah!" the King commanded without resuming his seat, and at once a runner was dispatched to the Lion-slayer's house in the city.

Before the night was out, the order was given for Adoniyah's slaying. Yonadav heard later that the sun had not yet risen when the elder prince was hauled out of his house in the valley of Rephaim and slain in the nearby mulberry grove, out of the sight of his wives and children. No honours were paid to him after death, and his burial was hurried and furtive. Mortal terror fell upon the Calebites, the Judean clan from which King David had sprung, and which had raised its head while he ruled over Judah and Israel. Many who had rallied to Adoniyah fled the country, some to the cities of the Philistines, some to their kinsmen in Moab and Edom. Some others perished.

Nor did this appease the King's fury. Having once unleashed his vengeance, he gave it free rein. Yoav ben Zeruiah, who had served King David all his life, but had rallied to Adoniyah, was next to die. It was a grisly end for the old warrior. Benaiah was loath to kill his old comrade, and tarried a while before setting out to do so. Yoav caught wind of it and fled to the tabernacle, where he seized the horns of the altar and clung to it as a baby clings to its mother's bosom. Later Yonadav heard tell that as Benaiah approached the altar and said to Yoav, "The King commands you to come forth," Yoav replied, "Nay, I will die here." Deeply distressed, the Lion-slayer sent word to the King, who thundered, "Do as he says, fall upon him and bury him!" Then Benaiah ran Yoav through with his spear.

Many were horrified by the spilling of human blood at the altar, and there were rumours of discontent in the King's city and throughout Judea. In the days that followed, Yonadav hardly ventured out of the King's house, not even to return to his own in the city, fearing that the anger at the King would be vented upon his own aged, corpulent self. In his heart of hearts he rejoiced that he had not attempted to see Avishag after the old King's death.

Later the King spoke to all his court, saying that the death of Yoav had cleansed the house of David of the innocent blood that he had shed.

"Yoav had slain two men more righteous and better than he," said Shlomo in ringing tones. "He slew them with the sword – my father David not knowing thereof – to wit, Avner ben Ner, captain of the host of Israel, and Amasa ben Jether, captain of the host of Judah. Their blood shall therefore return upon the head of Yoav, and upon the head of his seed for ever."

At the King's command, these words were repeated by criers all over the land, and whether it was his mention of both Amasa the Judean and Avner the Israelite, or because the people had come to realize that a firm hand had seized the reins of the kingdom, the murmurs began to die down. Yoav's body was taken from Jerusalem and buried at his own house in Tekoa. After this there were not many left on whom Shlomo wreaked vengeance. He summoned Eviatar the Levite – who had also once asked for Avishag's hand, but that was long before, and perhaps the King had not heard of it – and told him he deserved to die for his support of Adoniyah.

"Notwithstanding, I shall spare your life, because you bear the name of him who served my father the King faithfully through great vicissitudes for many years. But I banish you from Jerusalem forever. Go to the house of your fathers in Anathot and remain there till you die."

Ahimaaz, the bellicose, fleet-footed young Levite, was likewise spared, for the sake of his father Zadok the priest, but banished to the far north, to serve as a house priest to a Danite clan. Yonadav had always detested the rowdy, loud-mouthed young Levite and was pleased to see the back of him.

The last to fall was Shimei ben Gera, the Benjamite who had fought and reviled King David through much of his reign, and whom the King had spared in the weariness of his heart. Shlomo left him to last, as one leaves the hyena until the lion and the bear have been disposed of. Then he summoned Shimei to the King's house and commanded him to remain forever in Jerusalem:

"The day that you set foot outside my city you shall die."

Since Shimei's clan lived in the land of Benjamin, and he traded with the Philistines of Gath, Yonadav knew that it would not be long before Shimei, too, would be disposed of.

Like all the denizens of the women's quarters, Avishag heard about Adoniyah's fearful end, but not what had prompted it. That was known only to those who had been present in the hall and heard Bathsheva put Adoniyah's petition to her son, and they did not speak of it. The events in Hebron had borne their bitter fruit, as they had been sure to do sooner or later. Then came the news that Yoav ben Zeruiah had been slain at the tabernacle, and it was whispered that Benaiah the Lion-slayer was sick at heart and the King allowed him to return to his home in Edom to recover. Avishag, who had come to know and honour the Lion-slayer, pitied him with all her heart. It seemed it was not only her life which had been cleaved in two by the old King's death, but all the world she had known. The women, too, felt it, and were unwontedly quiet.

Avishag was sitting at the window of her apartment one evening as the sun was going down, gazing at a young maidservant who was suckling her baby under a sycamore. She heard slow, shuffling footsteps on the stairs and old Naamah appeared in her door, red in the face and out of breath.

"My daughter," she panted, "you are called… The King's mother, Bathsheva, bids you come to her."

Avishag's heart sank. She had not seen the King's mother since the old King's burial, and had no desire to climb up to her ornate apartment and hold empty talk with her. With a slight sigh, she rose and followed Naamah down to the courtyard. She did not change her dress, nor even washed her hands and face. If this displeased the Great Lady, perhaps she would not send for her again. A great weariness engulfed her.

But it was not Bathsheva who met her in the Great Lady's apartment. It was the young King, and when the old Hittite man-servant ushered her in, he came forward and took both her hands. "I have been waiting for you, my sister," he said, looking into her eyes.

Avishag bowed low. A turmoil began in her bosom and she could neither speak nor look up.

Shlomo's voice was as low and beguiling as it had been that dark night by the salt sea.

"*O my dove that art in the clefts of the rock...*" he said, speaking his father's favourite love song. He brought her hands to his lips, and when she still hung her head and did not reply, he touched her face and raised it.

"You know that my brother Adoniyah," he said, "has paid with his life for presuming to ask for you."

She looked up and saw his eyes, the long, black, luminous eyes that had gazed at her intently ever since he was a beardless lad. Filled with horror and an unbearable sweetness she whispered, "What are you saying, my lord?"

"I sent Benaiah to end his wretched, scheming, faithless life," Shlomo went on calmly, while his hands moved over her face and hair. "He deserved to die for what he did in Hebron and for plotting to kill me. But I let him live... till he asked for you. Then I knew he would never cease his efforts to take my place. Because you are the King's shadow, my dove – and I am the King now."

The following morning a small company rode out of the King's city and headed north towards Gibeah. There, on the site of King Saul's small fort that overlooked the road to the land of Ephraim, Shlomo had built himself a hunting lodge. It nestled in the woods beside an ancient grove with a sacred spring in its midst. There the company dismounted, and soon peace returned to the secluded place.

Avishag was a virgin and the King was young. He had desired her ever since he first saw her, and such was their love, that only words that celebrate all love, all ecstasy, since time immemorial, would do to describe it. Nothing came between them then – not affairs of the kingdom, nor memories of past years. Days and nights were as one, with the couch and the woods, food and wine, whispers of love and birdsong.

Were they there a week, a month or a year? Avishag could not tell. The past fell away from her like a shed garment, like a dream that is forgotten upon rising. All that existed was the young King, and she hungered and thirsted for him as he did for her. When they rested from the act of love, he drew from her all the songs of love she had ever known – those of her girlhood in Jezreel and those she had learned from the old King.

"Tell me, O thou whom my soul loveth," she sang, while he twined her tresses on his fingers, *"where thou feedest, where thou makest thy flocks to rest at noon?"* And she taught him the response: *"If thou know not, O thou fairest among women, go by way forth, by the footsteps of the flock, and feed thy kids beside the shepherds' tents…"*

She taught him the verse:

"As the lily among thorns, so is my love among the daughters," and she sang the retort, *"As the apple tree among the trees of the wood, so is my beloved among the sons. I sat down under his shadow with great delight, and his fruit was sweet to my taste…"*

She listened closely when he spoke to her of the marvels of faraway lands: Egypt upon its great river, the cedar-clad kingdoms of Lebanon, the far-flung empire of his kinsmen the Hittites. Of songs he knew little, but he taught her some love verses he had learned from the wife of his Tyrian teacher:

"Therefore came I forth to meet thee, diligently to seek thy face, and I have found thee. I have decked my bed with coverings of tapestry, with carved works, with fine linen of Egypt. I have perfumed my bed with myrrh, aloes, and cinnamon. Come, let us take our fill of love until the morning: let us solace ourselves with love."

Perhaps because it was a woman who had taught him these verses, Avishag did not engrave them in her memory.

The time came for the King to return to Jerusalem. Runners had been coming each day, bringing him word from Yonadav, Benaiah, Adoram, Zadok the priest and Ittai the Gittite, and taking back his commands, but this was no longer sufficient. It was then that he offered her all that his kingship could give.

"Remain here, beloved," he said, clasping her waist. "You shall lack for nothing, and I shall come to you whenever I can… Or you may return to the city with me and be the King's shadow, as you were with my father. You shall have your own quarters in the King's house, and a household of your own, being the King's counsellor… Or you may be my wife – yes, my sister, my dove! Not the first wife, for I shall marry a daughter of Egypt, and daughters of the kings of Tyre, Sidon and the Hittite kings, as well as one of Judah. They will secure my kingdom, as a fortress wall secures a city. But you shall be my best-beloved wife, and no one shall take your place. This I swear…"

Avishag did not reply at once. She knew she could not bear to be always at his side as she had been with his father, only to part from him at nightfall when he went to lie with one of his wives, nor to be herself one of his wives, though he gave her the first fruits of his love. That which might have been bearable had she married Kilav, would have meant anguish with Shlomo.

One last night remained to them in Gibeah, and they never slept.

"Allow me to return to the city with you, my beloved," she said when dawn broke and the first light fell on their couch. "But if you please, my lord, I shall retire to the grove and serve the goddess with my sisters the grove priestesses." Her tears fell on his face and he did not brush them away. His eyes were full of love, but she knew that already he was filled with thoughts of returning to the city and to his kingship.

"I shall send for you," he said gravely, holding her hands, when they stood face to face at the gate of the city. "The grove will not swallow you up as the earth swallowed Korah! Rather I shall make your grove the foremost in the land, beloved, while you dwell in it."

With these words echoing in her ears, assuring her that the goddess had indeed brought her all this way, Avishag mounted her mule and rode up the hillside, towards the grove.

When the year turned again, and spring was in the land, Avishag bore a son. She named him Nadiv, but he would be known all his life as Ben Avishag. When he was seven weeks old, she took him to the King's house and showed him to his father. No one saw them, because Shlomo sent everyone out of the hall and remained alone with Avishag and his son for so long, that his servants grew alarmed and listened at the door. All they could hear was a soft murmuring as of doves, and they withdrew quietly till Avishag departed with her infant.

When she had weaned Nadiv, Avishag sent for the scribe Ahiah and ordered him to write the words that she would say to him. He had to come and go many times before it was all written down, and before she was satisfied. Though she was never again alone with the King, the words of her great song nourished her love and fed its flame all the days of her life.

"The song of songs, which is Solomon's," is how it begins. *"Let him kiss me with the kisses of his mouth, for thy love is better than wine...."*

Avishag the Shunammite –
Bedwarmer or eminence grise?

There are not many interesting female characters in the Old Testament. The action is dominated by men, with women at best appearing in supporting roles. There are a few intriguing exceptions – Tamar, who seduced her father-in-law Judah so as to keep her place in the clan; Deborah the Prophetess, who led the Israelite tribes in battle; Queen Jezebel, the effective ruler of the kingdom of Israel during the reign of her husband, King Ahab; Naomi and Ruth, whose mutual devotion flies in the face of the stereotype mother-in-law... But it was a decidedly patriarchal world, though there are hints in the text that women were not quite as passive and insignificant as the later editors of the Bible, Jews and Christians alike, would have them.

Avishag the Shunammite is referred to in less than two-dozen sentences in the First Book of Kings. Nevertheless, she must have played an important role, albeit behind the scenes, in the court of King David and his son Solomon in Jerusalem. From being a mere bedwarmer to the aged David, this "fair damsel" advanced to become his housekeeper, or steward (*sokhenet* in the Hebrew original). She was not his concubine. After David's death, Prince Adoni-yah's request for her hand in marriage infuriated the young King Solomon, who saw it as a design on the throne itself and ordered his older brother's execution. Why? The text does not explain. There is something elusive, tantalizing, in this brief glimpse of the young woman, who is described as exceedingly beautiful.

The story of Avishag the Shunammite is especially intriguing in the context of her time and place – the reigns of David and Solomon in Jerusalem in the 10th century B.C.

What do we really know about King David?

Forget the innumerable paintings and Michelangelo's statue, the tradition that David wrote the Psalms, and other popular legends; set aside the modern novels, which portray this Middle-Eastern bandit-king of 3,000 years ago as a wisecracking modern Jew, a sort of early Woody Allen (Joseph Heller's *God Knows*), or as a Germanic machiavellian prince (Stefan Heim's *The King David Report*).

Let us confine ourselves to the Old Testament – the Book of Samuel and the opening chapters of 1 Kings, as well as the relevant, if garbled, chapters in the Book of Chronicles. This is our only source, and from it we must glean the solid nuggets of information, weigh conflicting statements against each other, and leave question marks where doubts arise. For example, did David kill Goliath, as described in the charming fairy-tale-like Chapter 17 of 1 Samuel – or was it his townsman Elhanan ben Yaari (11 Samuel 21:19)? Was Zeruiah, the mother of his three devoted captains, David's sister – i.e., the daughter of Jesse (1 Chronicles 2:16) – or was she the daughter of someone called Nahash (perhaps the King of Ammon – 11 Samuel 17:25)? In any case, it is best to read the original Hebrew text, because all the translations are quite flawed, sometimes through misunderstanding, but often deliberately, to make the ancient text conform to later ideologies.

As you read you begin to wonder if a single person could have done all the things that are ascribed to David. Is it possible that the little shepherd from Bethlehem, the youth who played the "harp" (actually a kind of lyre) to soothe the sick mind of King Saul, also killed Goliath, and also became a great general, and also married the king's daughter, and composed the marvellous lament for Saul and Jonathan, and went over to the Philistines, and also pretended to go mad in the court of Gath, and bred a huge and contentious family, and captured Jerusalem from the Jebusites, and also made it his capital, and fled from it for fear of his son Absalom – whom he later mourned so memorably – and fled again for fear of Sheba ben

Bichri, and seduced Bathsheba and sent her husband to the "hottest battle" to be killed, and had the beautiful Shunammite sleep "in his bosom" without "knowing her," and had his late-born son by Bathsheba, Yedidiah-Solomon, anointed in his own lifetime to prevent the seizure of the throne by his older son Adoniyah... Even given that he lived to be seventy, a great old age in those days, it does seem a lot of action to fit into one lifetime.

And then there are the seeming contradictions in his character. He had idols in his house, though he worshipped Jehovah and went to great lengths to establish his shrine in Jerusalem. He fought against the "uncircumcised" Philistines (and personally circumcised 200 of them, by way of bride-price to King Saul for Michal), but had no compunction about fighting *for* the Philistines on occasion, and only the scruples of Achish, the lord of Gath, prevented him from fighting in their ranks against his own people. Later, his palace guard in Jerusalem consisted entirely of Philistine mercenaries. He was as chivalrous as a medieval knight, never failing in respect for the life and person of the reigning monarch, Saul, who was trying to kill him; refusing to drink the water from the well of Bethlehem, because his captains had risked their lives fetching it; sparing the life of a man who had abused him when he was down on his luck, and rewarding his faithful supporters. But he also made a habit of leaving the nasty work to his captains, while publicly protesting that he was unable to restrain them. He was always a sucker for beautiful women, fell in love repeatedly and showed himself incapable of refusing them anything, yet had a passionate affair with Jonathan, whose love, he declared, was "wonderful, passing the love of women." Ruthless with his devoted captains, he was a foolishly doting father to his own children – Amnon, who raped his own sister Tamar, Absalom, who tried to depose him, Adoniyah, who tried to force his hand in the matter of the succession.

What else does the Bible tell us about David? That he was his father Yishai's (Jesse's) seventh and last-born son, that he was a handsome redhead with beautiful eyes, and that he loathed disabled people ("the blind and the halt"), possibly because they could be neither warriors nor priests. That is a lot of information about an individual who lived three thousand years ago. It adds up to a rich, rounded portrait that we intuitively accept as historical. We feel closer to King David than to many medieval figures – for example, Richard the Lionheart, who lived a mere eight centuries ago.

But the text leaves some mysteries unsolved, not only because of conflicting statements, as in the reference to Goliath, but because we are told too little. One question that comes to mind is: Why did David choose his late-born son Solomon to succeed him? What was so special about the son of the widow of Uriah the Hittite? The original and obvious heir, Absalom, a grandson on his mother's side of the king of Geshur, was dead – but what was wrong with Adoniyah? Had David promised the succession to Bathsheba's son? And even if he had, was the promise – made presumably at the height of his infatuation with her – so binding that he had to keep it even at the risk of another coup d'état?

The status of Avishag the Shunammite is also mysterious. The beautiful young virgin was brought to the old king to warm him in the cold nights of Jerusalem. It is stated explicitly that David did not have sexual intercourse with her, and that she became the steward of his house. Since she was not a royal concubine, there would have been no lèse majesty in marrying her after the King's death. Yet when Adoniyah asked his young brother, King Solomon, to give him the Shunammite for a wife – presumably as a sort of consolation-prize for losing the throne – Solomon was enraged, shouted that Adoniyah would next demand the crown for himself, and ordered his assassination... What made the former bedwarmer-*cum*-housekeeper so important, that asking for her hand was tantamount to a plot against the throne?

These are but two of the mysteries that intrigued me when I read and reread the story of King David. I have the advantage of reading it in Hebrew, so I know – for example – that when the Philistines left their "idols" on the field of battle in the valley of Rephaim,

David and his men did not "burn them," as the King James Version says, but carted them away like any spoils of war. This is only one of innumerable "improvements" which Christian translators sought to make in the ancient text.

Located between the two great civilizations of the ancient Near East – Mesopotamia and Egypt – the Land of Canaan (later called Judea and Israel, and by the Romans from the 2nd century A.D. onwards – Palestine) was a patchwork of small nations, nomadic tribes and city-states, ruled by numerous kings and warlords. The Book of Samuel describes how David fashioned a kingdom from the unruly tribes of Judah and Israel, and made Jerusalem its capital. It also says that under David's successor, Solomon, the kingdom flourished and allied itself with the great powers to its north and south. At this time the culture that gave birth to the Bible – and thereby affected the history of the world – began to take shape. Later, both Jewish and Christian writers would project their own ideas and mores onto that early Hebrew kingdom, depicting it as quite out of step with its era. But the historical truth is that King David – if he existed – was a minor Semitic king in a barbaric age, and to portray him otherwise is anachronistic.

Reading the Bible with a fresh eye, ignoring all that one has been told about it, one discovers a world very unlike its traditional representations, whether renaissance art, Hollywood movies or school drama productions. *Yahweh* (Jehovah), a.k.a. *Elohim* (which means *gods,* in the plural), the Lord of Hosts, etc., was a Judean/ Israelite tribal deity, whose domain was a particular territory beyond which he had no jurisdiction and only limited power. Even in his own domain he usually had to share power with other regional deities, such as *Baal* and the *Ashera* (*Ashtoreth* – Astarte, also called the Queen of Heaven; see Jeremiah 7 and 44). When one of his prophets brought off a miracle – e.g., revived a dead child or cured a king of leprosy – Jehovah's standing and that of his followers was enhanced, but it was never exclusive. In the reign of King Ahab, one of Jehovah's best agents, the prophet Elijah, had to outdo a whole school of the prophets of Baal in spectacular fireworks before the king would listen to him. Jehovah was worshipped in much the same way as other gods of the age. Every divinity had his or her own sacred objects and sites, elaborate rites, favourite sacrificial animals, taboos and precepts. The Israelites had brought from Egypt a ban on pigs and the custom of male circumcision. They shared some festivals with other Canaanite peoples, distinguishing their own version by minor particulars. For example, the ban on "seething a kid in its mother's milk" (upon which the Jews later built an immense edifice of dietary rules, separating all dairy products from all meats, or even poultry) was meant to distinguish the Israelite harvest festival from that of the Canaanites, at which that dish was ceremoniously eaten.

We know that there were images in David's house, as there probably were in all the Judean-Israelite houses. When he was fleeing from his father-in-law, King Saul, his wife Michal tricked his pursuers by placing an image – i.e., a life-size idol – in David's bed, covering it with a sheepskin and saying that he was ill (1 Samuel 19: 13–16). Later, we see that David carried off the Philistine idols, which had been left on the battlefield (11 Samuel 5:21), just as the Philistines had earlier captured Jehovah's Ark. The altars of Jehovah were horned, like those of other Semitic gods, and anyone grasping the horns was – at least in theory – secure from assassination. As for the Ark of the Lord, no one knows what was in it, but there are indications that it was a dangerous object. Many people, from the time of Moses until the arrival of the Ark in Jerusalem, died or were injured through coming into contact with it. When the Philistines kept it they were smitten with bubonic plague. Indeed, it was so dangerous that David hesitated to bring it into his city, and tried it out first on one of his vassals (11 Samuel 6:9–12).

King David lived in the 10th century B.C., some three hundred years after the Pharaoh Tutankhamen. At that time, the great pyramid and the Sphinx were already 1500 years old. Babylon had been conquered by the Assyrians, and Crete had already succumbed to the Doric invasion, its marvellous city of Knossos a heap of charred ruins. Athens was still a village and Homer as yet unborn. In India, the Buddha was five centuries in the future. Men, having discovered that they had a share in the begetting of children, had everywhere seized power, not merely on earth but in the heavens. For the past millennium goddesses had been systematically demoted while male gods, proud of their fertilizing ability, were promoting new macho cosmogonies. But in David's time the goddesses were still powerful, and traces of their worship can be discerned in the Bible, even through the editorial fog and traditional interpretations. But because the Bible is seen as holy scripture, rather than as ancient literature, even important archaeological discoveries associated with it are treated with circumspection. For example, some years ago an engraving was found on a rock in the Negev, depicting two human-oid figures, clearly male and female, beneath which is inscribed in ancient Hebrew: "ʏʜwʜ Shomron and His Ashera". Though this is the only known family portrait of the Israelite Jehovah and his wife, the discovery was met with a deafening silence. When it comes to the monotheistic religions – Judaism, Christianity and Islam – even the tabloid press treads carefully. (You can hardly imagine a scream-ing headline, *"Portrait of God and His Wife Discovered in Desert!"*)

The Hebrew Bible is a very ancient text, a collection of many sources, spanning several hundred years, containing disparate mythologies, historical narratives, genealogical lists, wisdom literature, dynastic apologetics, ritual and social laws, religious and warrior verse, and erotic poetry. It has more in common with other ancient epics, such as the *Mahabharata* or the works of Homer, than with the pious religious texts of later ages. For most of its history it was copied by hand, and it is marred by lacunae and errors and some crude edi-torial meddling. (For example, the suffix *-baal at* the end of many Israelite names was later changed by the Hebrew editor to *-bosheth,* "shame", to extirpate the traces of Baal worship. Fortunately, the edi-tor did not have a word-processor and so failed to weed out every case, leaving us with plenty of clues.) Sometimes the text was altered, or a passage inserted, to satisfy later traditions. That is why we shall never know who really killed Goliath, or why Solomon succeeded his father as king of Israel.

The story of Avishag is a window upon the world of David and his kingdom. I tried to avoid seeing it from the vantage point of our time, in any political, social or religious sense. There is a terrific story here, enjoyable for its own sake. Biblical research and archaeology have shown that Jerusalem in the 10ᵗʰ century B.C. was quite unlike its traditional depiction, Jewish or Christian. Fortunately, the Book of Kings contains some vivid descriptions of the polytheistic culture that flourished there before the Babylonian exile – they were meant to illustrate the sinful practices of the Judean kings. (II Kings 23 is especially graphic.) I say fortunately, because it's much more interesting than the censored version.

About the author

Yael Lotan
Photo by Ephrat Beloosesky

Yael Lotan was born in Tel Aviv, and has lived in Jamaica, England and the United States. She is the author of *The Other I*, *Mangrove Town*, *Phaedra* and a biography, *The Life and Death of Amos Orion*. In addition to her writing, Lotan is a literary critic, translator and journalist.

The fonts used in the book are from the
Garamond and Meta families